BAIN

PITTSBURGH TITANS

By
SAWYER BENNETT

Find Sawyer on the web!
sawyerbennett.com
www.twitter.com/bennettbooks
www.facebook.com/bennettbooks

Table of Contents

CHAPTER 1	1
CHAPTER 2	12
CHAPTER 3	23
CHAPTER 4	34
CHAPTER 5	49
CHAPTER 6	61
CHAPTER 7	75
CHAPTER 8	84
CHAPTER 9	94
CHAPTER 10	105
CHAPTER 11	119
CHAPTER 12	129
CHAPTER 13	139
CHAPTER 14	147
CHAPTER 15	154
CHAPTER 16	164
CHAPTER 17	175
CHAPTER 18	183
CHAPTER 19	192
CHAPTER 20	205
CHAPTER 21	217
CHAPTER 22	225
CHAPTER 23	235
CHAPTER 24	248
CHAPTER 25	260

CHAPTER 26   270

CHAPTER 27   280

CHAPTER 28   286

CHAPTER 29   293

CHAPTER 30   301

CHAPTER 31   311

CHAPTER 32   320

CHAPTER 33   329

CHAPTER 34   337

Connect with Sawyer online   351

About the Author   353

Dear Reader,

As I sometimes like to do, you'll note that this story runs concurrently with another. If you've read *Camden* already, you'll see the storylines parallel, intersect, then diverge again. I love doing this so you can see some scenes played out from another perspective.

If you haven't read *Camden*, no worries. You will not be lost because all my books can be read as true standalones.

Happy reading!

Xoxo,
Sawyer

CHAPTER 1

Bain

PARKING MY CAR a few blocks down, I walk through the posh neighborhood toward Brienne Norcross's mansion for the team Christmas party. Although I've been with the Pittsburgh Titans for a month and a half, I'm still getting my social bearings. On the ice, I've seamlessly integrated as a defenseman onto the first line, replacing Nolan Carrier in a trade that took me from the two-time champions, the Arizona Vengeance.

The trade was a lucrative deal for me. On a personal level, I'm still not sure. My time with the Vengeance was more than meaningful as we were a patched-together expansion team thrust into a competitive league. We defied all odds and won back-to-back Cups, and within those two years, our team bonded like no other.

It was painful to leave.

But trades happen all the time and in this business you can never really set down solid roots. Your fate is mostly in others' hands.

As I approach Brienne's house—aglow with thousands of festive lights on the outside that give me a tingly feeling because I fucking love Christmas—I take a moment to consider the similarities between her and the Vengeance owner, Dominik Carlson.

Both owners take a very personal interest in their players. They're hands-on in their concern for our welfare but otherwise trust the general manager and coaches to make us good. While they're both incredibly wealthy, they're also down-to-earth and approachable. Hell, Brienne Norcross is dating our goalie, Drake McGinn. She's a multibillionaire CEO of an empire and while he's important to our team, he's just a regular guy compared to her level of success.

As I trot up the front steps to the massive double doors, I hear music and laughter from within, telling me this is going to be a fun party.

I expected no less because Brienne is just good people.

It's three days before Christmas and I've been hyped up for the holiday for a while now. I decided on renting a downtown condo until I can figure out the city. Plus, my parents are coming in for a visit and to catch a game. I've already got my tree up and all the necessary ingredients for my mom to make her decorated sugar cookies that will ensure I have to do double duty at the gym.

I don't bother knocking on the door but enter a

cacophony of raucous laughter and a group of people singing Christmas carols from somewhere in the house. It's hard for me to focus on anyone in particular because I'm momentarily stunned by the grandeur of Brienne's home. I understand it was her family home, but it doesn't fit the sleek, modern woman who is the Titans' owner. It's opulent in an old-fashioned way. It reminds me a bit of the Biltmore Estate I visited one summer. Dark-paneled walls and elaborate embellishments grace the ceiling, showcasing intricate designs of flowers, leaves and vines. The floor is marble, the tiles creating a round pattern in the foyer. A chandelier the size of a car and covered in thousands of shimmering crystals hangs above the sweeping main staircase. The furniture looks like the type not meant for sitting and the massive oil paintings look like they should be in a museum.

All in all, it's far too formal for my taste but that doesn't make it any less beautiful.

I'm nearly bowled over when three little boys whiz by, chasing each other with empty wrapping paper tubes. I grin as Drake's kids hurtle past a round table holding a translucent vase, nearly hitting it with one of the tubes. My grin goes wider as Drake appears from nowhere and snatches two of the kids by their shirt collars and calls a halt to the other. They all three sheepishly hand over the tubes to their dad whose glare isn't intimidating at all. I met the little rug rats last week when Drake brought them by the arena.

"Bain," someone calls out, and I turn to see Stevie with Hendrix holding her hand.

I walk over to them, standing just inside what looks to be a formal parlor. I get a bro hug from Hendrix and a real hug from Stevie. I've gotten to know her well this past month, especially since we've been hanging at her bar quite a bit in our off time. I admire the spitfire of a woman who isn't afraid to break up a brawl in her establishment.

And well, Hendrix… he's fucking over the moon about this woman. I think his days as a single guy are truly over.

"Some house, huh?" I say, glancing around.

Stevie leans into me and whispers, "I feel like I'm in a museum."

"Exactly my thought." I glance around, then back to Hendrix and, in particular, the drink in his hand. "Where're the libations?"

He points across the foyer to another large room that houses more expensive-looking furniture. "There's an open bar. All top-shelf liquor." He then points past the staircase. "Dining room is laid out with a buffet. Try the tenderloin. You will not be disappointed."

"And the shrimp," Stevie chimes in.

"I'll hit the bar first. Catch you two later."

I meander into the other room, stopping to talk to

some players. I've been able to meet a lot of the significant others since I've been here, but not all of them. At the bar, I order Blanton's neat and tip the bartender a twenty. She hands over my drink and I turn slightly, lifting the glass to my lips.

A thrilling zing of excitement sizzles through me as a woman walks into the room from another entrance that looks to lead from a music room. She's tall but curvy, her body accentuated by a pair of well-fitting dark jeans tucked into black boots that come up over her knees. The heels are thin pegs of four-inch sexiness. Her cranberry sweater is one of those fuzzy ones that you know would feel like heaven against your skin, and I'm a fucking lecherous dude so I can't help but notice how nice her breasts look in it.

Dark blue eyes scan the room casually, not as if she's looking for anyone in particular but just checking out the scene. I'm a sucker for blonds and her long hair, ribboned with highlights, falls over her shoulders.

As much as blonds do it for me, her mouth is catching my attention more than anything. Full lips shiny with gloss, and as she smiles at someone who walks by, I see her teeth are perfectly straight and gleaming white. She could definitely pass for a supermodel and I can only assume she's a girlfriend of one of the guys... or a puck bunny.

In either case, that would make her off-limits to me,

but until such time as I confirm she belongs to someone else, I can't help but be drawn toward her.

Winding my way through the crowd, her gaze turns to me as I approach. And she doesn't just meet my eyes but rather checks me out. I'm talking about full-blown, slow visual roam over my face, down my chest, past my hips to my legs and then a leisurely climb back up so that by the time we're staring at each other, she has me feeling a bit hot under the collar.

And fuck me to high heaven, she bites her lower lip just briefly, as if she's considering something about me.

I need to know what it is.

When I come toe to toe with her, I can see she's even taller than I first thought, although those boots have something to do with it. Regardless, I like that she doesn't have to break her neck to look up at me as I top out at six foot seven. She has to be at least five ten herself.

Pointing upward, I say, "It must be fate."

She appears confused as her eyes lift to the spray of holly leaves, cranberries and tucked inside... mistletoe. It's hanging on the archway that opens between the two rooms.

The woman tilts her head, brows furrowed. "Fate?"

"That's mistletoe." I point upward again. "It's good luck to kiss under it."

Her eyes move around the room briefly before coming back to me, her expression amused. "Now how do you know that's mistletoe?"

I take a step closer. "My older brother told me about it. Said it was guaranteed to get a girl to kiss you."

She laughs, tipping her head back, and fuck me... those dimples. When she looks at me again, I extend my hand and she takes it. "Bain."

"Kiera," she replies and neither of us pulls away, and she asks, "So I'm just supposed to kiss a complete stranger."

"We're not strangers," I reply, looking pointedly at our palms still pressed together. Her grip is strong, but her skin is soft. Her nails are unpainted and short but well-manicured. "You're Kiera, I'm Bain. And now we know each other."

With an almost reluctant sigh, she tugs her hand from mine. "While the idea has merit, I'm not sure it would go over well."

"Are you here with someone?" I ask.

"You mean, am I here with another man?"

I just stare at her, because that's exactly what I'm asking. I need to know whether to move on. She shakes her head with a wry laugh. "No way. Happily single."

"You say that like it's a creed or something," I observe with a knowing smirk.

"Oh, it is."

"Commitment averse?" I guess.

She nods quickly. "No one depending on me."

"Totally get that. Able to come and go as you please."

"Taking what I want, when I want it."

I grin. "We're like two peas in a pod. Relationships give me the wiggins. But speaking of taking what you want, when you want it… if you want that kiss, I'm more than happy to find a private area."

Kiera appraises me for a long, silent moment. Then she surprises me by taking my glass from my hand, lifting it to her lips and sipping. She holds the liquid in her mouth, savoring the taste before swallowing. She licks her lower lip and hums with appreciation.

Christ, that's sexy as fuck.

Handing it back to me, she says, "I'm going to have to decline."

I never actually expected her to run off with a stranger for a kiss, but I'm curious about her reasoning. "I promise I'm safe."

"Yeah… I can actually tell you're a big ol' teddy bear." She's not wrong about that. Despite being a defenseman and participating in my share of brawls, I'm quite the pacifist. Kiera gives me a sly smile, lowering her voice as she leans into me. "But in this instance, I can tell that if you and I engaged in a kiss, it would never be enough. We'd surely find ourselves naked and sweaty in some closet in Brienne's house."

Shouldn't have chosen that moment to take a sip of my bourbon because I almost choke on it. As it is, I'm able to keep my surprise to a gasping cough. She stares back at me, blue eyes sparkling with humor, but I can tell… she's not joking.

"At the risk of sounding too forward—but somehow thinking I'm safe in saying it—I'm more than willing to leave this party right now if you want to go somewhere and have a drink. Get to know each other."

"And have sex?" she asks, one eyebrow arching high, but I can hear the teasing in her tone.

"Mind-blowing sex," I correct her. "But whatever you want to call it."

She laughs again, taking my glass from me. Her fingers caress mine as she pulls it free and takes another delicate sip before turning it back over. "It's a shame I have another commitment or I'd take you up on that offer."

Okay, shocked once again and where I thought I was on equal footing with this woman, I'm clearly not. "Are you serious or joking?"

"Serious as a heart attack." She inclines her head, her expression genuinely regretful. "It was nice to meet you."

I'm the guy who's always the quick-witted flirt, but she's reduced me to muteness. It's only when she starts to walk away that I jolt out of it. I take her wrist. "Wait." She smiles at me with raised eyebrows. "Let me have your number."

"Want to sext?"

My jaw drops but I recover, offering a sly grin. "I'm really good at it. But I was thinking we'd start with dinner."

"Kiera," someone calls out, and we both glance to the foyer to see Brienne standing there with Drake's kids. Brienne waves her over.

"Sorry," she says, tugging her wrist free. "Duty calls."

"Duty?" I ask with confusion.

"Got to get my nephews to bed. I promised Brienne I'd help since she's the hostess of this party."

Nephews?

Fuck... this is Drake's sister.

"Thanks for the banter," she says. "A shame we're not able to scratch each other's itch."

And once again shocked silent, I can only watch her walk away. When she reaches Brienne and the boys, the ladies exchange words and then Kiera ushers the boys upstairs. I'm assuming to put them to bed.

Something bumps my shoulder and I see Coen standing there.

"What's up?" I say, my eyes still on the staircase, even though Kiera is gone.

"Don't go there, dude."

I turn to face him. "Go where?"

"Anywhere near Drake's sister," he says. "He made it

Highsmith late in the third period wasn't enough to win the game.

Now all three boys are tired and pissy that Daddy lost.

I put my hands to Colby's and Tanner's backs, leading them across the family lounge to a grouping of chairs and couches. "Sit here. Your dad won't be long."

Once the boys are situated, I unlock my phone and hand it over to Jake. He takes it without hesitation and expertly navigates to the Disney+ app that I keep downloaded with some movies for them to watch. I'm not sure how parents or caretakers of children ever survived without something like this to keep them occupied.

"Do you guys want anything to eat or drink?" I ask. The Titans keep the family lounge stocked with fresh buffet foods and an arrangement of drinks for both before and after the game. This is usually where the players will come to meet spouses and kids or visiting family members. Brienne often comes in before the game, walking around and introducing herself to every single person she doesn't know.

On days like today, when the boys are here, I expect her to arrive any moment for the handoff. She'll keep an eye on them until Drake showers and changes, but she's probably giving a quick postgame interview.

"Cookies," Colby says with bright, hopeful eyes.

"Carrot sticks," I reply, and he wrinkles his nose.

"I'll get you a plate you can share," I promise.

I know Drake and Brienne are going to take the boys out to dinner, so I put some veggies on a plate along with ranch dip, which will induce them to eat it. I grab water bottles and set them down on the coffee table. They're all three hovered over my phone, watching *Toy Story* and ignoring the food.

My stomach rumbles since I haven't eaten since lunch and I'm not going out with the gang for dinner. Brienne invited me, but I declined, more so just to give them time together as a family. I'm around them so much by virtue of being the boys' secondary caretaker that I try to give them as much family bonding time as they can get. It's only been a few weeks since they all moved in with Brienne and I want them to solidify. The boys need to feel stable and settled, especially given the upheaval their mom has caused over the last few years. It appears she's gone for good since none of us have heard from her in months.

I also declined the invitation to dinner as I'm looking forward to having the evening to myself. The workweek starts early tomorrow, back to my day job and picking the boys up after school and caring for them until Brienne or Drake are home.

Best of all, because there's food here, I won't have to cook.

I head back to the buffet line and see a couple checking out the offerings… a man and a woman who appear to be in their late fifties. I haven't seen them here before, but they have the look of someone's parents.

"Hi," I say brightly as I grab a plate from the end.

They both smile at me and the man nods at the silver chafing dishes over Sterno warmers. "This is a nice touch. They did something similar to this in Arizona."

"Ahh," I say with a knowing look. "You must be Bain's parents."

The super-hot hockey player that I had a very interesting exchange with a few days ago at the Titans' Christmas party.

"Yes," his dad says and holds out a hand, his smile popping. "I'm Dave Hillridge and this is my wife, Sheila."

I shake their hands. "Kiera McGinn. Drake is my brother."

Dave grimaces slightly. "He had a rough game."

That he did, facing a whopping thirty-eight shots on goal while we only managed to get off thirty against our opponent. "It's part of the business, right? But Drake can be pretty circumspect."

"Not our Bain," Sheila says, moving in closer to whisper. "He takes it all very personally."

Interesting. I got a very laid-back vibe from him when we met. Not that you can be mellow after a loss.

The spirit of competition runs hot with these guys, but in just those few minutes of conversation, I could tell that Bain is confident and well balanced. I suppose he could still let the weight of defeat rest on his shoulders. He's a defenseman and his job is to help protect against the shots.

And then it hits me... I could be seeing him again.

Any moment, really, and a thrum of excitement swims through me. I had imagined we'd cross paths again at some point but didn't think it would be this soon. I rarely go to the games, usually the one watching the boys in the evenings since Brienne has to be here too.

"Have you met him yet?" Sheila asks, and I blink a moment, realizing I'd zoned out.

I manage a quick smile. "Yes, actually. At the Christmas party but only for a few moments."

"He's single, you know," she says slyly, and her husband rolls his eyes, muttering under his breath.

I see Brienne and Drake walking through the lounge door and I set the plate down on a table. "I'm sorry... but my brother just walked in and I need to hand over his kids. It was really lovely meeting you."

"We hope to see you again," Sheila says. "We live in Virginia, so we plan to come to as many games as we can. We're so happy to have Bain back on the East Coast."

"I look forward to seeing you both again."

I gracefully step away, my heart racing a bit that Bain's mom would just come right out with the matchmaking. I have no desire for that and what little I've come to know about her son, he's not into that either.

I smile internally as I head over toward the boys to round them up, remembering the conversation with Bain. He and I seemed very much alike, neither of us interested in anything serious. I've had amazingly bad luck finding someone to have a fling with since moving here… maybe he's the one.

Granted, I've been incredibly busy between work and the kids, but now that Drake's seeing Brienne, the boys are with her on the nights he travels to away games. I meet my brother at the couch and step into him for a hug in commiseration. "Sorry about the loss, bro."

He squeezes me. "Thanks."

My eyes go to Brienne and I share my empathy with her as well. It's her team, so the loss stings just as much. She smiles wanly, her hand reaching out absently to tousle Colby's hair. He tips his head back and smiles at her. My heart does a flippity-flop because Brienne used to be terrified of kids. Now those boys adore her and she's going to make a wonderful mom to them. There's no doubt in my mind that Drake will be proposing. There was a time when I never thought he would marry again because of how bad his first marriage had become.

But Brienne is a one-in-a-million woman and I know he's never going to let her get away.

"You sure you don't want to come to dinner with us?" Brienne asks.

"Yeah… come eat," Drake says.

I shake my head. "No offense to you or the rug rats, but I want some 'me' time. I'm going to hit that buffet, fill my belly, then go home and binge-watch some TV while drinking wine."

"That does sound nice." Brienne sighs.

There are more hugs, mainly extra squeezes from me to my nephews who are by far the most important things in my life. I promise we'll go to the indoor trampoline park when I pick them up from school tomorrow, which, for the moment, makes me their favorite aunt.

Well, I'm their only aunt, but if I had rivals, I'd be the best.

By the time they're walking out the door and I'm back at the buffet table, I see that Bain's parents are gone. Disappointment settles in as I'd looked forward to at least laying eyes on him. Maybe slipping a saucy wink his way.

The room is mostly cleared out. Kirill's family is visiting and they're all eating at one of the tables on the other side of the room. Waitstaff hustle around, cleaning up empty plates and glasses. They're starting to close down the food stations.

I quickly walk through, grabbing grilled pork chops, mixed vegetables and my weakness... fresh rolls with whipped butter. I settle down at the nearest table and scroll through my phone while I eat.

I tear off a piece of crusty bread and don't even bother to use the knife. I drag it through the soft butter on my plate and pop it into my mouth just as a shadow falls across my table.

I lift my head, eyes widening to see Bain standing over me. He's freshly showered and wearing a dark navy suit.

Jesus... he's tall. He towered over me the night of the Christmas party and I had on some major kick-ass heels to add to my height.

My mouth is stuffed full of butter and bread, but I manage to mumble a quick *hey* before frantically chewing.

He smirks and pulls out a chair. I swallow my food as he plops down next to me. Before I can bring my napkin to my mouth, Bain's finger touches the corner of my lips. I don't need a mirror to know there's butter there.

I almost pass out when he glides the pad over my lower lip and then pushes it into my mouth. I react on instinct, sucking gently on the tip of his finger, and my breath stutters when I see his eyes darken with desire.

He pulls away. "Are you going to slap me if I tell you the image of my finger in your mouth inspires a million dirty fantasies?"

I look around wildly. "Where are your parents?"

Bain throws a thumb over his shoulder. "Out in the hallway. I told them I wanted to say hello to you. My mom mentioned on no fewer than three occasions in twenty seconds how pretty you were and that I should ask you out."

I'm barely able to follow his train of thought. I'm still lost in how turned on I was when he put his finger in my mouth. We've barely spoken a total of five minutes and I'm ready to crawl onto his lap and do dirty things.

"So, what do you think?" he asks.

"What?" My mind is muddled, my tongue thick.

He smirks, knowing he's discombobulated me. "A date."

I need to get some semblance of control. I take my napkin, dab at my lips to give myself a second to think. "I don't think that's a good idea."

Bain's eyes flash with mischief. "Because your brother would kill me? I was already warned off by Coen at the Christmas party when he saw me staring after you."

Something warm unfurls in my chest. The fact that Coen could parcel out that Bain was attracted to me just by the way he stared tells me that his look was hot and covetous.

"My brother has nothing to do with it," I manage to

say.

"Then why not go out with me? I can guarantee a good time."

"I bet you could," I murmur. "But the truth is… you couldn't handle someone like me."

"Oh, baby… I could handle you with one hand tied behind my back. Actually, both my hands tied behind my back. I'd only need my mouth."

I suppress a groan at the fantasies he's just inspired. "I don't date."

"Funny," he muses, rising from his chair. "Neither do I. But I'd make an exception for you."

I want to say yes, but I sense that this man is trouble with a capital T. He's the type of man I could get addicted to and I'm just not willing to let myself fall like that.

At least I think I'm not.

He could be worth a taste.

"Are you going to the New Year's Eve party at Stevie's bar?" I ask.

Bain grins, his dimples popping. "I was considering it, but it's a definite if you're going."

"I'm considering it."

"Okay, then," he says, taking a few steps backward, once again thumbing at the door. "Got my parents waiting and have to go. Maybe I'll see you New Year's Eve."

"Maybe."

He stops, gives me a wicked smile. "You know there's a tradition when the clock strikes twelve, right?"

"I've heard mention of it."

Bain doesn't respond, just points at me. "I'll tell you more about it on New Year's Eve."

"If I go."

"Yeah… you know… if I go too. Still not sure."

"It's definitely a maybe," I say, suppressing a laugh.

He winks at me, his grin absolutely charming, and pivots away, walking out of the lounge.

I stare after him, maybe the same way he did after me at the party. One thing I know for sure—both of us are showing up at that party.

CHAPTER 3

Bain

I HAD TOLD Kiera that I might come to the New Year's Eve party at Stevie's bar, but there was no maybe about it. I was already committed, having been part of a plot to get Hendrix to pull his head out of his ass, which, fortunately, he did.

The question remains, will Kiera show up? Our banter was fun, the teasing and flirting ranging from mischievous to point-blank acknowledgment of mutual attraction. I walked away from her pretty sure we were destined for a hookup but as I sip my beer and watch the clock tick away the minutes, I'm not so sure anymore.

"You seem distracted," Hendrix says.

"You don't," I reply, taking in my friend. Just two days ago, he was a fucking mess, having parted ways with Stevie over a massive misunderstanding. I'm talking about betrayal, drama and intrigue, but Hendrix was being too stubborn to see past what he thought had happened. Coen, Stone and I took it upon ourselves to make him see the truth—that Stevie did not betray him—and the only way to do that was to goad him into it. We had a very loud discussion about spending New Year's Eve in Stevie's bar, which made him go berserk.

He called her a traitor.

We assured him she was not, finally forcing him to be curious enough to learn the truth of what happened. And now here we are, nearly the entire team hanging out to ring in the new year.

Hendrix's gaze sweeps the bar, landing on Stevie. She's not working tonight, but every once in a while, she steps back there if the bartenders get a little too busy. She can't serve alcohol while she's drinking, but she helps by cleaning glassware and cashing out customer tabs.

"It looks like you two are back on track," I observe.

"Thank fuck she's a forgiving soul," Hendrix says dryly. "I was such a dick to her that a part of me still isn't quite sure if I really have her."

I note that Stevie has her eyes on Hendrix as she rings in a drink, offering him a soft smile. I clap him on the shoulder. "Oh, you have her all right."

Hendrix's expression becomes dopey as he smiles back in her direction and I roll my eyes. Never did quite understand a man getting so caught up in a woman like that, but what do I know? I'm young and still playing the field. My facial expressions range from amusement to twisted pleasure, but never that lovesick, besotted visage.

"Maybe I should make a bigger overture?" he muses.

"Bigger than getting her diary back from that douchebag reporter?"

Without taking his eyes off Stevie, he asks, "You think that was enough?"

I don't answer him, though, because my attention is caught on something far more important.

Kiera just walked in.

Leaving Hendrix's question unanswered, I step away, winding through the crowd toward her.

Only to veer hard left to the bar when her fucking brother walks in behind her, holding hands with Brienne.

Well, shit… that puts a crimp in my plans, which were to flirt with and seduce Kiera so we could go home together tonight. Having her brother here will make that difficult but not insurmountable.

At the bar, I order a beer and once it's in hand, I walk over to the pool tables. Two of them have doubles games going on, but on the third, some of the guys are playing individually. I set my beer on a high-top table and watch Camden and Boone play nine-ball. Foster and Kirill join us and for the next hour, we take turns going up against each other. It's a fun night, using this time to bond with my new teammates. We single guys are definitely congregated together with a few of them scoping out the women in the bar.

I keep half an eye on Kiera as she moves around,

talking to different people. She's clearly comfortable among the players and I wonder if she's dated any of them. I know Drake just came to the team this season, so it stands to reason Kiera's been here no longer than that. Truth is, I don't know much about her other than I'm extremely attracted to her.

Attraction shouldn't be the only thing that has me scoping her out and it's not. Just the small verbal exchanges we've had have been fun, quick-witted and flirty with an underlying crackle of sexual tension. I'm fucking drawn to her beyond anything I've felt before and I've had my share of beautiful women.

Maybe it's that she's unattainable because she's not falling all over me and because her brother is a road-block. Maybe I just need to fuck her once and get it out of my system. While we teased about a date, I don't want that, and according to her, she doesn't want that either. I think we're both on the same page.

Now I just need an opportunity to spend some time with her tonight.

♦

I'M WATCHING AS Foster and Kirill play a game of pool. Camden and I are chatting at the high top and fortuitously, Kiera is playing doubles with Stevie on the next table over as they take on Drake and Hendrix.

Unfortuitously, with Drake standing right here I

can't so much as start a conversation with Kiera, so I've got to be content with watching her.

Lusting after her, really.

She's sexy as fuck tonight in a pair of jeans with rips in the thighs and knees and a pair of brown winter boots. She's wearing a loose white button-up blouse that's tucked in and capped off with a brown leather belt. All that glorious blond hair hangs over her shoulders and spills down her back, but my favorite part of her ensemble is that her top three buttons are undone. Every time she's at the far end of her pool table and bends over to take a shot, I get a nice peek at the swell of her breasts.

Of course, everyone has the same view as I do, but when I glance around, no one is looking the way I am. I'm assuming that's because her brother is looming beside us, or maybe I'm just a fucking pervert but this woman is driving me crazy.

And if I didn't know any better, I'd think she's intentionally giving me a show because every once in a while, her gaze will cut to me as if she's making sure I'm watching.

"Your shot," Kiera says as she hands Stevie her pool stick.

The match-up is interesting. I know for a fact that Stevie is an incredible player and sadly, Kiera is not. Their pairing does stand up well against Drake and Hendrix, who are both decent.

"I'm going to get us another round," Drake says to his sister.

When he walks off, my heart pounds as Kiera meanders over to me. With Camden on the other side of the table, and Hendrix and Stevie in the vicinity, I cannot enact any hard-core flirting, but I do manage to stake my claim. "Glad to see you here tonight."

"Goes both ways," she says, her eyes pinned on Stevie as she goes on a run.

She cleanly sinks the five and engages in her own flirting with Hendrix. I don't begrudge them because I want to do the same.

Laughing, Stevie moves to Hendrix and fists his shirt. She pulls him in close for a swift kiss, but he doesn't let her pull away. I can't quite hear the words, but I can see his mouth moving against hers and I can read his lips.

I love you.

"Disgusting display, isn't it?" Kiera murmurs as she leans my way.

"I can barely stand to look," I quip, and we grin at each other. She thinks Hendrix and Stevie are cute, same as me, but the PDA isn't something either of us particularly like. That's the way of it for those of us committed to the single life.

Hendrix releases Stevie and says, "Put us out of our misery."

And she does.

Just as Drake returns with beers, Stevie runs the table and cleanly sinks the eight ball. "Damn," he mutters, handing over drinks. He then pulls out his wallet and hands Kiera a twenty.

"You thought I'd be a liability to Stevie, didn't you?" she says, then kisses the bill.

Drake snorts. "I thought Hendrix and I would at least have a fighting chance with you as Stevie's partner."

"Want to go double or nothing?" Kiera asks her brother, and there's no mistaking the taunt. I can tell these two are close, but there's also rivalry.

"No fucking way," Drake says, his gaze moving to Brienne playing pool on the next table over with some of Stevie's regular customers. "Going to go watch my girl play."

Kiera turns back my way, her eyes flashing victoriously as they briefly go to Camden, but then come to rest on me. "Come on... who wants to play?"

The question was addressed to both of us, but I'm faster on the draw. "I'm in."

As I'm fishing money from my pocket to pay, Drake gives me a frigid glare of warning.

I try to keep my smirk on a low boil. "Relax, dude. It's a game of pool."

"Don't pay him any attention," Kiera drawls with a grin. "He's mad he just lost twenty dollars to me."

"You in?" I ask Hendrix but he shakes his head,

pulling Stevie to him.

I move around the table, squatting to put four quarters into the slot to release the balls.

Kiera comes to stand at my side. "Looks like it's just you and me."

"What I've been angling for all night."

She hunkers down, making a show of helping me put the money in. "I like the way you watched me."

Christ. Those whispered words pack a fucking punch and I have to stand up to move away from her because if she keeps talking that way, I'm going to have to drag her into the bathroom and I'm sure her brother would not like it.

I move to the high top and watch as Kiera racks the balls. Camden's gone and Hendrix and Stevie are wrapped up in each other.

Kiera's eyes lift to mine as she hovers over the table, knowing her shirt is open and I can see straight down it. I don't avert my gaze but take what she's offering.

When she's done, I grab my pool stick and line up the cue ball. Kiera comes close and I twist my neck to talk to her. "Do you mind?"

She gives me an innocent look.

"I can't concentrate when you're that close," I grumble.

"Why ever not?"

"You know why," I say and attempt to ignore her as I

bend at the waist to break the rack.

Kiera moves even closer, resting her hip on the table. My eyes cut over to her brother, but Drake is fully involved with Brienne and not watching.

My gaze goes to Kiera. "You like distracting me."

"Turnabout's fair play. You putting your finger in my mouth kind of threw me off stride."

I can't help but laugh and it breaks some of the sexual tension. I pull back the stick, slam it forward with surety and the cue ball decimates her rack. Two solids and a stripe sink into the pockets.

It's still my shot, but I take the opportunity to address the elephant in the room between us. "You going to let me come home with you tonight?"

"I am," she says, and tension I'd been carrying all night seeps out through my pores, leaving me languid and mellow.

"Good," I reply and turn for the table, but another thought strikes. I again glance over at Drake, satisfied his attention is still focused on Brienne. When my eyes are back on Kiera, I say, "I know we've been doing a lot of flirting and teasing, but I'm really not looking for a relationship. Whatever this is between us... it's just casual, right?"

Kiera scrunches up her face. "Please... the thought of a relationship makes me slightly nauseated. This is nothing more than getting our rocks off. Then we're going our own way."

Hmmm... not sure how I feel about this being a onetime-only thing, but I'll worry about that later. "Sounds like we're on the same page, then."

Suddenly, the jukebox is turned off and someone calls out, "It's almost time."

Stevie has televisions all around the bar and the volume is turned up. There's one right across from us on a wall-mounted bracket broadcasting a show in Times Square to watch the ball drop. The timer on the top left of the screen shows about thirty seconds until midnight.

Pity that I can't kiss Kiera as the New Year rings in. This thing with us has to be on the down low. Couples pair off, moving toward the TVs with their arms around each other. I ignore it all and walk around the table for my next shot, which I miss.

I hand the stick to Kiera and enjoy watching her instead of the countdown. She's a horrible player, but my eyes would rather be on her than anywhere.

Everyone in the bar chants the numbers. "*Ten... nine... eight...*"

She misses and by the time she's handing me the stick, it's New Year's and everyone is cheering, blowing toy horns and kissing.

I accept the pool cue from her, my hand closing over hers and not letting go for several long moments as we stare at each other. I hope she sees in my eyes that I'll make up for it later… this inability to claim her mouth as the new year rolls in.

We can't kiss but we're touching, and for some weird reason, I can't remember another New Year's Eve party I've been to. I also intrinsically know I'll never forget this moment because it's the lightest of foreplay before I delve into something that's going to be combustible later on.

CHAPTER 4

Kiera

BAIN AND I are slightly drunk when we get into the Uber. My urge is to climb right onto Bain's lap and kiss him, but I don't want to cause an accident if the driver is watching. As it stands, Bain is holding my hand—he took it the minute we slid into the back seat—and has it perched on his thigh with my palm resting against the denim.

I can't stop thinking about what's resting a few inches higher. Would he get hard if I stroked him with my thumb, the only part of my hand that's mobile? Would he think that too forward? What would happen if I kissed him?

"... for a living?"

"What?" I ask, bringing my gaze from our clasped hands to Bain's face. It's shadowed with temporary flickers of light across it as we meet oncoming cars.

He knows I'm distracted and it amuses him. His mouth curves, and now I can only think about kissing it. "I asked what you did for a living?"

For a living?

What do I do?

"Oh," I exclaim, as if I just got the answer to final *Jeopardy*. I do indeed know what I do for a living. "I'm an oncology nurse."

"Whoa," he murmurs, his hand squeezing mine a bit. "That's got to be a tough gig."

"It can be. But I'm not actively in the office practicing. I'm actually working remotely for the clinic I worked for back home in Minnesota. I'm a patient liaison so I help cancer patients coordinate other services, like psychological counseling or arranging transportation for treatment. I help them navigate insurance and find discount medications. Stuff like that. It's mostly phone work, talking to patients and holding their hands virtually."

"Impressive. Did you ever do actual patient care?"

"Yeah... I only moved into this position about a year and a half ago."

"Do you miss the hands-on patient time?"

I'm surprised by his question. Not one person has ever asked me that. "I do. I talk on the phone with my patients a lot, but it's not the same as being there and being hands-on with them."

Bain shifts to face me and it causes my hand to slide higher up his thigh, but he doesn't seem to notice. "Could you potentially look for a job here that lets you get back to active care?"

"It's not a good time. My other job is helping Drake care for the boys. I mean… it's not like a paying job, although I am living in his house rent-free. It's why I moved here—as you can imagine with the travel, being a single dad to three boys is incredibly hard."

"I saw you for only a few moments when you took the boys to bed at the Christmas party. You can tell they adore you and vice versa."

"They're a big part of my heart. They've had it rough. Drake's ex-wife isn't a good mother and has been absent for a huge chunk of their lives. I stepped in to help and well… they're just an integral part of my life and who I am."

"I can see that," he says and then lifts our hands to kiss the inside of my wrist. It feels like my pulse is going to jump right out of my skin. When he drops our hands, they rest even higher on his leg. I can't tell in the gloom of the back seat, but I think his dick is hard. If I could just move my hand a few inches—"Maybe you could find something part time in a clinic."

My eyes snap to his. "Do you really want to talk about jobs?"

"We could talk about all the ways I'm going to make you come tonight, but I thought that might embarrass you in front of our driver."

Oh yeah… my face flames hot that he called me out

like that and I hear the driver make a choking sound. But I'm not about to let Bain control the narrative. I slide my hand over his crotch, immediately noticing he is indeed somewhat hard. I squeeze him, watching his face carefully as he inhales, nostrils flaring wide. "Maybe we should just ride in silence," I suggest.

I slide my palm over his erection, careful not to press down too hard where the zipper is. I stroke back and forth, feeling him grow under my touch.

God, I want to undo the button and zipper, take him in my hand so I can feel the heat of his skin against mine. Bain doesn't make any move to stop me, but he seems to not be able to talk with my current ministrations. He even shifts his hips slightly and widens his legs to give me better access. He sucks in a quiet breath and I watch as he lets it out slowly.

"Here we are," our driver says, almost as if he's in a panic and cannot wait for us to get out of his car.

I look out the window to see we've indeed pulled into the driveway of Drake's house—or rather, my house since I'm living here now.

Bain takes my hand off his cock and threads his fingers through mine, pulling me out of the car. As we rush toward the front porch, he asks, "Your brother's not here, right?"

Laughing, I shake my head and tug my hand away so I can grab my keys out of my purse. "No. He's fully moved in over at Brienne's house. We kept the boys' rooms the same so they could stay here when he's out of town, but he already had me installed in the master bedroom."

Slipping the key in the lock, I go still when Bain steps into me from behind, both of his arms coming around me. Not in a hug or gentle embrace, but in a fiery grasp of possession. One hand goes to my breast to squeeze and the other straight down between my legs to cup me.

Groaning, my head falls back against his shoulder.

"Better open that door or I'm going to fuck you out here on the porch."

I snicker and shrug his arms away, managing to turn the key. I open the door and we practically burst inside, his hands on my hips to steady me. I manage to just input the code on the alarm panel before Bain seizes me. He slings me around to face him and his mouth slams onto mine, instantly devouring me with an insatiable hunger I've never felt from another man. His tongue probes my mouth and our teeth clash. My head spins in wonder at how his lips can be so soft and fierce at the same time.

Tearing his mouth away, Bain looks wildly around my living room. His sense of urgency provokes a rise of lust within me and I'm kind of hoping we go at it on the floor.

Instead, he grabs my arm, walks me around to my couch and pushes me down. Bain wastes no time tearing off my clothes. He does it roughly—boots, jeans, sweater—and I have to wiggle to assist him as he peels my panties and bra off with shaking hands.

"Your turn," I rasp as I push up from the couch and give him a rough shove backward. His eyes glimmer in challenge, but he does me a solid and tugs his sweater over his head.

God, he's a beautiful specimen of a man. His chest is broad and sculpted, cutting down over a ridged abdomen and narrow waist. Now that I'm out of my boots, Bain is a giant before me. His arms are powerful, threaded with thick muscle and golden skin. He's so big everywhere and it makes me wonder just how far that extends. That brief touch I had in the car wasn't enough and I'm dying to get my hands on him.

He watches me in the glow of the single table lamp. It casts enough light that there's no mistaking the desire and hunger I see in his eyes as they roam over my body. I know he's trying to decide just what to do to me, but I'm not one to wait around.

I step into him, my lips pressing to the center of his chest as my hands go to the button on his jeans. It pops open with no effort and I slide the zipper all the way down.

Tipping my head back, I look up to see Bain staring

at me with what seems to be a million emotions flickering over his face. Mostly it's the way his jaw is locked that tells me he's wound tight, so I don't think to make him suffer.

Pushing at the denim and his boxer briefs underneath, I manage to get his cock out and just... oh damn. It's as big as the rest of him and my body shudders at the thought of that thing driving in between my legs.

Or sliding against my tongue.

My mouth waters and without any real thought or plan, I sink onto my knees before him. Bain sucks in a breath as I stroke his length only once before bringing the tip to my mouth. He's so tall, he has to bend his knees to accommodate my need.

If I thought I was in control, I'd be wrong. His hands grasp my head like an iron vise and guide me onto his erection. Bain utters a guttural snarl as my mouth envelops the head of his cock and his fingers tangle in my hair. My tongue laves and I suck at him hard, drawing a deep moan. I bob on his dick, drawing him in deeper until he's knocking against the back of my throat. Hands to his ass, I pull him roughly into me and when he mutters "F-u-u-c-k" in a deep rumble of need, the ache between my legs becomes almost unbearable.

Bain's hips start to thrust and I glance up to see his eyes glazed with pleasure. I move faster on him, needing him to come in my mouth. I want to be the one to conquer him, but suddenly, Bain pushes me off.

I think something might be wrong, but he hauls me up his body and kisses me roughly. "Christ, you're driving me crazy."

"Good," I taunt. "Put me back down on my knees and let me send you over the edge."

"Another time," he growls, and then I find myself on the couch again. This time on my knees with my torso resting across the back.

Bain pushes my legs wide apart and I cry out from pleasure when I feel his mouth on me from behind. His breath is hot as his tongue plunges and laps, and it takes no time at all before I feel an orgasm brewing.

My head hangs low, my eyes squeeze tight and when Bain slips two fingers into me, I'm obliterated with a hoarse scream of release. My entire body seems to have blown apart and yet I still need more.

"You better be about to fuck me," I say as I look over my shoulder. Bain drags a hand over his wet mouth, our eyes locking for a moment before his gaze drops to my ass.

His hands go to my hips as he steps close to me and I feel the head of his cock nudging at my entrance.

Yes, this is exactly what I want.

No, I need it.

I circle my hips, managing to draw him in a bit and Bain hisses through his teeth, "Fuck. You're so wet and hot. I am so going to make you come again."

I feel so empty and embarrassingly needy, the first orgasm having waned, but the feel of his cock just breaching me is making me delirious. I crane my neck, look at him over my shoulder. "Will you hurry up and fuck me?"

Bain takes in a breath and I can see he's trying to steady himself. I don't give him the opportunity. I push back, trying to force myself onto his cock. I taunt him. "Come on, Bain. What are you—"

He slams into me, and while I'm indeed wet and lax from that first orgasm, his size stretches me uncomfortably. His pelvis presses into my ass and one arm comes around my stomach. Bain grabs my face with his other hand, forcing it around so I meet his gaze. "You good?"

"God, yes," I wheeze. "Just… move, okay?"

Leaning forward, he presses a hard kiss to my mouth and then his hips start to hammer at me. He's so long and thick, every thrust is an erotic adventure. My body melds around him and I grip hard to the back of the couch, hanging on for what I know is going to be the ride of my life.

Bain fucks me like I've never been fucked before. He's hitting something deep inside me that must have had his name on it because he drives me closer and closer to another release. It's so close and I need it.

My hand drops between my legs, my fingers barely

sliding against my clit when Bain grabs my wrist. "Oh, no you don't. You're going to come again only by my doing."

God help me, but those words almost knock the orgasm loose. It's so primal and controlling and as Bain slams into me over and over again, I know without a doubt I'm about to be destroyed.

Bain lifts my hips so I can take his cock deeper. His breathing is harsh, ragged, and under his breath, he mutters filthy curses. The pleasure he produces is so overwhelming, tears form from the beauty of it.

Ultimately, it's his words that tip me over. "Love this pussy, Kiera. It was made for my cock."

The growl, the need, the frenzy he's unleashing upon my body. It all culminates until I'm once again shredded with pleasure. I cry out, my back arching downward. Bain grunts, lifts my hips even higher so he can drive at a deeper angle. Another electric pulse explodes down low in my belly and tears leak from my eyes.

"Gonna come," he says.

No... it's a promise.

Blindly, I reach back with my hand, for what I'm not sure. I manage to cover one of his hands on my hip and I can do nothing but squeeze his fingers. Bain slams hard into me, forcing me across the back of the couch as he roars out his release. His hips rotate and grind, his body jerking as he empties himself into me.

Into. My. Body.

Shit. We didn't use protection.

As much as that thought alarms me, it's quickly doused when Bain wraps his arms around my stomach and pulls me upright. I'm on my knees on the couch and he's standing behind me.

His embrace is all-encompassing, warm and sensual. His cock is still thick inside me and I have a crazy urge to demand he go again.

Bain rests his chin on my shoulder. His voice is gruff, sated. "That was a little crazy."

I tell him the truth. "I'm wrecked."

He chuckles and squeezes me.

"We didn't use protection," I murmur.

His entire body tenses against me and his breath rushes out in a curse. "Fuck. I didn't even think about it."

"I didn't either. We were drinking—"

"We're not that drunk."

No, we're really not. We should have stopped that frenzy. We should have slowed down and made sure we were safe.

Bain huffs out a frustrated breath. "Christ... I'm sorry, Kiera."

"It's not on you. I forgot too. Or maybe I didn't forget. Maybe I just wanted it to happen so bad, I didn't care."

Another squeeze and his lips press against my temple. "For what it's worth, I've always used protection. I'm positive you don't have anything to worry about from me, but you also don't know me. I'll get a test, though."

"I will too," I rush to assure him. "Same as you... I've always practiced safe sex. But just to ease our minds."

It's silent a moment, then he hesitantly asks, "And birth control?"

"I'm good," I assure him, my arms coming up over his for my own squeeze of reassurance. "I'm on the pill."

His exhale is lusty with relief. "Thank fuck."

The tension leaves my body and I lean back into him for a moment. "Thank fuck is right."

We stay that way, silent as we contemplate what just happened. And then it becomes awkward so I wiggle a bit to dislodge his arms from me and he steps back from the couch.

I feel the rush of his semen run down the insides of my thighs. "I'll be back," I say, pausing to scoop up my bra and panties before heading into the guest bathroom.

After I clean up, I slip into those bare essentials and return to the living room. To my relief, Bain is almost fully dressed, not that he had to do much other than zip up his pants and put his sweater back on.

I had thought he might want to stay the night and that's a hard pass for me. I've found over the last few years that if you remove that intimacy—of actually sharing a bed to sleep—you avoid the rapport that develops through conversation the next morning. I wasn't kidding when I told him I don't do relationships, and apparently, he doesn't either. I'm grateful for it.

Bain smiles and throws a thumb at the door. "I called an Uber. There's one close by that'll be here in a few minutes."

"Probably the same one that dropped us off." I bend to nab my jeans and sweater but don't bother putting them on. I'm going straight to bed after Bain leaves.

"We weren't that fast. I know that seemed like a whirlwind, but we both had some staying power."

"Yeah," I reply softly, almost dreamily. That was some amazing sex.

More than amazing. I connected with Bain in a way that's unknown to me and I can't figure out why. I hardly know anything about him, other than he's cute and charming.

Maybe it's just that he's a sexual powerhouse. I usually hate men trying to control me or thinking I can't fend for myself or make my own decisions, but tonight I very much enjoyed how Bain decided this would go down once we crossed the threshold.

Interesting.

"Penny for your thoughts," Bain says as he glances at his phone, presumably the Uber app to check on his driver.

I'm jolted from my introspection, my eyes going to his. I shake my head as if it wasn't important but then figure he can handle my truth because I think it's his as well. "I was thinking that sex with you was kind of fantastic and also that I'm relieved you're not staying."

Bain laughs and moves to me. His hand goes around the back of my neck and he kisses me on the top of my head. "I had a great time too. Maybe we can do it again sometime."

"Yeah… maybe," I concede, although if he grabbed me right now and threw me back down on the couch for another round, I wouldn't object.

"Let me get your number," Bain says as he taps his phone screen.

"Why?" I ask, my tone defensive.

"Relax," he croons with a chastising look. "I want to text you the test results."

Embarrassment hits hard and I flush. "Oh, sorry."

I give him my number and he enters it into his phone. His gaze lifts and he smiles mischievously. "I promise I won't call just to talk or check in."

I give a mock shudder. "Thank God."

"Most definitely won't use it to ask you out or any-thing."

My face scrunches up with exaggeration. "I certainly hope not."

"In fact," he says dramatically, walking backward to my door, "I'll just text a single word to you… positive or negative."

"If it's positive, I'm going to be pissed," I warn, following him to the door so I can lock up behind him.

Chuckling, he once again pulls me to him with his big hand behind my neck and this time, his kiss is on my lips. A soft brush of farewell. "You have nothing to worry about, just as I know I have nothing to worry about."

When he pulls away, I ignore the forlorn feeling that he's leaving. "I'll text you back my results."

Bain winks and walks out the door. There isn't a backward glance and I don't linger to watch him. I close the door, lock it and set my security code.

CHAPTER 5

Bain

G LANCING AT MY watch, I sigh with frustration as I slump further down onto my couch. Only five minutes since I last checked, making it close to nine p.m. My eyes are glued to the television as I watch a much-anticipated game between the Carolina Cold Fury and my former team, the Arizona Vengeance.

"It's been an intense matchup so far," one of the sports announcers says.

"No shit," I mutter to the TV. Two prior Cup champions battling it out.

The second announcer's voice has a nasal tone I can't stand. "That's right, Bob. The Cold Fury's goaltender, Max Fournier, has been on a roll tonight. He's made some incredible saves, denying the Vengeance any chance of scoring."

The frustration is clear on my former teammates' faces as the end of the second period winds down. I glance at my watch again, my left leg bobbing nervously.

"Oh and look at that. Nadeau's stick caught Cold

Fury winger Garrett Samuelson up high. The referee wasted no time in raising his arm to call that penalty."

I sit up a little straighter, waiting for the replay. "Come on, Riggs. That was stupid."

He knows it too. I can see the lines of anger etched on his face as the camera follows him into the penalty box.

"It's a tough break for the Vengeance. Let's take a closer look at the replay here."

I wince as Samuelson's head snaps back, Riggs's stick catching him just under the tip of his visor. It wasn't intentional, but it's still not allowed and will be called ten times out of ten.

"The Cold Fury's first line has been lethal through-out the season on the penalty play. I expect we'll see—"

I point the remote at the TV and mute the sound. I can't stand that one fucker's tone but more than anything, I'm having a hard time concentrating on the game. My brain is spending far too much time thinking about Kiera.

Or more specifically, about the mind-blowing sex we had on her living room couch three nights ago. She's absolutely ruined me. I went out last night with some of the single guys on the team and we had women swarm-ing all over us. I had my pick of the ladies to take home and yet I left alone. I didn't want any of them.

Only Kiera.

Leaning forward, I rest my elbows on my knees, lost in a mental tug-of-war. Move the fuck on or try to see her again?

I understand the dangers of getting too attached or rather, too addicted. Going back for more of Kiera is only going to fuel my need. I know I'm also treading into forbidden territory with Kiera being Drake's sister. I'm not sure how much a complication that is, but I have to keep it in mind.

My head lifts and I stare at the TV.

Unmute it or throw caution to the wind?

"Fuck it," I mutter, rising from the couch and heading for the door.

I'm taking a huge fucking risk, but the allure of Kiera is just too damned tempting to resist. One more night is all I need. Get her out of my system and then I can move on.

♦

NO PART OF me is ashamed I'm ringing Kiera's doorbell at nine thirty and I make no apologies for not calling ahead. I'm an impulsive guy and I do what pleases me.

Also, I didn't want to take the risk she'd shoot me down. If she does it face to face, I have a better chance of talking her into letting me come in.

The front doors are two-thirds glass with dark-stained wood bottoms. I can see Kiera as she walks into the living room from the side hall, wrapping a robe around herself. She doesn't seem surprised, so I'm guessing she checked me out on her security app when I first rang the bell.

She doesn't look irritated to see me, which is good, but I can't read much on that exquisite face of hers.

"What are you doing here?" she asks after opening the door.

I know one of the things that had Kiera interested in me originally was my boyish charm and confident, flirty nature. I turn that up high, giving her a rakish smile. "Just out and about… thought I'd stop by."

She arches one eyebrow, crossing her arms over her chest. It plumps her breasts and I can't help the quick ogle. Her stubborn refusal to be charmed has me pulling out my phone. I tap the screen a few times, scroll and then hold it up for her to see. "I tested negative. Just wanted you to know."

"You could have texted," she says. "I would have told you mine was negative too."

"I could have texted," I murmur in agreement as I take a step closer. She stands her ground at the threshold, but that's fine by me. I slip my fingers under the belt of her robe and give a playful tug. "But then I wouldn't have had the opportunity to see you wearing this sexy thing. What do you have under it?"

Her lips twitch and that's indeed a good sign. She

knows exactly what I'm here for and she's not pushing me away. But there's uncertainty in her eyes.

"Come on, Kiera," I murmur with gentle persuasion. "Let's indulge in one more night of hot-as-hell sex. One more night… no strings attached."

Her gaze locks on mine, but there's way too much hesitation in it. I imagine she's facing the same internal battle I went through not long ago. It seems she needs convincing.

Closing the distance between us, I lightly graze my fingers along her jawline. Her breath hitches at the touch, lips parting slightly. My other hand deftly pulls the loose half knot from her robe belt and I slip my hand in to rest on her waist. Whatever she's wearing is soft and silky but I don't dare look away. I need to convince her to let me in.

"Don't tell me you haven't thought about our night together," I say, dipping my head down to peer at her. "In fact, I bet you've even pleasured yourself to the memories of the way I fucked you."

Air gusts out of her mouth, but she remains silent.

"Tell me some of the dirty things you've done to yourself while you thought of me. I'm hard right now just thinking about it."

I'm almost knocked backward as Kiera crashes into me. Climbs right up my body, arms around my neck and legs around my waist as her mouth melds to mine. I groan at the sensory onslaught—her smell, her taste, the way my palms cup her ass—and manage to carry her inside and shut the door without breaking my neck.

No clue where her bedroom is, but I'm sure it's too far away. I swing right and press Kiera into the wall, pinning her with my hips and the thick erection I'm now sporting.

With one hand still under her ass to hold her up, I dive the other into her hair where I grip it hard. Tugging gently, I expose her neck and scrape my teeth along the tender skin. Kiera moans and bucks against me.

"Wait a minute," she gasps, and I rebel against the idea she's putting on the brakes. But when a woman says stop, you stop.

I lift my head, staring down at her.

"This is it… just one more time, right?" she asks.

Even though my brain is nodding furiously in agreement, something in my stomach pitches at the thought of this being truly the last time. Still, I assure her. "One more time, then we go our separate ways. No other expectations, no attachments."

"Good," is all she says before her palms come to my cheeks so she can kiss me. Her tongue tangles with mine and I let myself fall back into the swirling lust.

I'm able to determine through roaming hands that she's got on a silky nightshirt and what feels like a G-string. While I'd love to watch her strut around in it, I'm loath to put her down.

We kiss like we're starved, every luscious pass of her mouth over mine making me crazy with need. I think I'll go berserk if I can't fuck her and we've barely touched each other.

Wrenching her mouth from mine, she jerks her head to the right. "Bedroom's back that way."

"Why would we do that when we light your living room on fire?" I whisper. With Kiera still pinned to the wall, mostly held in place by my hips and her legs around my waist, I lean back to see what I'm working with. Her pink robe is parted and the silk nightie is the same blush shade. I keep one hand firmly under her ass and with the other, I lift the edge, bunching the material around her waist so I can see.

Fuck yes... a translucent slip of material covers her pussy, held together with mere strings. Despite the fact it looks like tissue paper, I'm smart enough to know that shit doesn't shred.

But it does stretch. I pull at one edge, tugging it out of the way and exposing what I really want to see.

Kiera's forehead touches mine and I realize she's watching what I'm doing.

My hands are occupied, one under her ass and the other pulling her panties aside. "Touch yourself," I order, my words sounding harsh and thick with lust. "Tell me how wet you are."

Kiera curses something under her breath but she doesn't hesitate. Her fingers slip in between us and I watch mesmerized as she circles her clit. I glance up only to see her eyes hazy and her bottom lip held between her teeth. When I glance back down, she sinks a finger inside her pussy and when she drags it out, it's shiny.

We lift our heads, eyes locked to each other, our chests heaving. She traces that wet finger on my lower lip.

Christ, I'm going to die.

"Hold this," I order, giving her panties another hard tug that I know bites into her skin. Kiera moans and that tells me she's not averse to a little sting of pain. Her hand replaces mine, holding the material so her pussy remains exposed.

I use sheer determination and dexterous fingers to work my jeans open, hefting her up with my other arm to give me the room needed. My cock springs free and I fist it tightly. Somehow, my mouth is back on hers but I can't maintain the kiss because I'm too desperate to get inside her. I adjust my position, find the perfect angle and with short punches of my hips, I work my way inside.

Kiera's warm, willing and taut, and it takes only a few thrusts before I'm bottomed out in fucking heaven. Kiera shudders, her head lolling on the wall and her eyes delirious with the need to come. I can see the desperation swirling in those deep ocean depths.

She fits me like a glove and I have to choke back the need to let loose on her. My head swims as I try to get some semblance of control. "You feel amazing," I admit through gritted teeth. My face burrows into her neck, taking in the scent of her flowery shampoo and the intoxicating aroma of her arousal.

My fingers dig hard into her ass as I move my hips. Testing the waters, I rotate my hips against her and the wave of ecstasy that washes over me from just that small motion causes my legs to shake.

Fuck, I'm coming apart.

"I'm not going to last long. This feels too good." Another shift of my hips, another bolt of pleasure.

"I suggest you let go," she murmurs in my ear, her words giving me the freedom to succumb to my primal instinct. I lean back, search her eyes and I see within her expression an equal need to take the jump with me.

I groan, kiss her hard and then bite her lower lip. "Going to fuck you so hard." I thrust into her again, her back colliding with the wall. A gasp of pleasure escapes her as her eyes flutter shut. I claim her lips, my tongue exploring the sweetness of her mouth as my hips drive rhythmically against her.

Kiera claws at my shoulders, hands going into my hair to jerk at it. She writhes in my arms, panting and begging for more.

I'm practically seeing stars from the overwhelming pleasure and I'm afraid I might leave her behind. But then Kiera's body stiffens and I lift my head. Her eyes lock onto mine and I feel her pussy ripple around my cock as she starts to orgasm. Her nails dig down into my scalp and I ignore the sting, instead leveraging my body to unleash everything I have. I slam into her over and over again, grunting with each tunneling thrust, and it only takes a handful of them before I'm coming so hard, I can't even make a sound. My teeth clench tight as the power of the orgasm tears through me, and for a moment, I have the insane thought that maybe I'm going to die because nothing should ever feel this good and I'm not deserving of it.

My hips continue to rotate and grind against Kiera as she shakes in my hold. The pace slows until I'm lodged deep inside her, both my hands squeezing her butt as I try to settle my heart rate.

Kiera's head falls to my shoulder as she gasps for air. I can still feel tiny tremors of her flesh against mine and my cock jumps in reaction to it.

Finally, I lift my head and Kiera does the same. Her face is flushed, eyes still bleary. She looks sleepy and sated and I have a deep need to take care of her.

Trusting my legs to hold me up, I stand straight and readjust her weight against me. My cock remains lodged deep as I carry her to the bathroom where she cleaned up the other night.

It's a full bath with a large vanity and I sit her down on it. My cock slides free and I can't help the groan that rumbles out of me at that last feeling of flesh against flesh.

I take the hand towel, run it in the cool water and as Kiera watches me silently, I push her legs open further so I can clean her up. Her hips jerk as I rub the soft cloth against her and I imagine she's still sensitive. I know if she put her mouth on my dick right now, I'd have no problem getting it back up.

But that wasn't our agreement.

Setting the towel down next to the sink, I pull my pants up and refasten them. I put my palms on the granite on either side of her hips and stare at her a moment, wondering what she's thinking. She's not said much, not that I needed words with what we just did. Her body told me all I needed to know... I rocked her world the way she rocked mine.

I look deep into her eyes, willing her to say something. I'm not sure what I want to hear, but she merely smiles before gently kissing my lips.

When I pull back, I'm the one who speaks. "I better get going."

"Yup," she says with a nod.

I step back from the sink and Kiera hops down and readjusts her panties. She makes no effort to close her robe and I take one long, last look.

Her hair is a mess, lips swollen and nipples hard against the thin material. She's the absolute most beautiful thing I've ever seen and if we do grace each other's presence in the future, it will only be in passing.

Nothing to stop me from walking out without a single word, but before I do, I place a kiss on top of her head. Her hand comes to my chest as my mouth lingers there, and it feels like a final goodbye.

I turn away but take no more than one step before her hand is on my wrist. I look back, eager to see what she might finally say.

It does nothing but confuse me more because she doesn't say anything. Simply shakes her head to note she's changed her mind about speaking and her hand falls away.

I offer a small smile and nod. "See you around."

"Yeah… sure."

Just like the other night, she walks me to the door, and when I'm on the front step, I hear the snick of the lock. I don't turn around to watch her through the glass but trot down the steps and to my car.

That should have done it. She should be out of my system now.

As I open my car door, I do take one peek at her house and find her at the door watching me.

Yeah… no. She's not fucking out of my system but not a damn thing I can do about it. We both agreed that this was it.

CHAPTER 6

Kiera

I T'S WEIRD, HANGING out at Brienne's house to watch the boys. Drake and his sons haven't been living here long, but Jake, Colby and Tanner have acclimated well. Not just because they're getting used to their dad being in love with Brienne and her becoming a mother figure, but because they just did a huge move from Minnesota to Pennsylvania at the start of the season and had just gotten used to that house.

Brienne's home is so big, I've gotten lost in it once—and that's no joke. But it's beautiful, and her legacy, and I'm happy this will be the boys' forever home.

Yeah... I said it. This is it for Drake. There's no doubt in my mind he's going to marry Brienne and they'll live here forever.

I stand in the massive family room, surrounded by the comforting chaos of three wound-up hellions. The sound of their laughter echoes through the space, filling the tasteful and expensively decorated area with warmth and love. Currently, all three are chasing one another around in a mad game of tag that doesn't seem to have any rules.

Their energy is without limit. They've already had dinner and baths, and I allowed them to watch one period of their dad's game tonight against the Florida Spartans. I've got the game still on the TV, but it's muted for the time being.

"All right... McGinn monsters," I call out to get their attention. "Let's assemble for bed."

As rambunctious as they are, they're the sweetest kids and they obediently line up before me. As their unofficial mom, I relish these moments, cherishing the bond we've formed as I care for them when Drake is on the ice.

"It's time to clean up and get to bed." I help them pick up their toys, coaxing them with banter and playful tickles, making cleanup time as fun as playtime.

While Brienne's house is big enough each kid can have his own room, they wanted to stay together. Drake had a three-tiered bunk bed for them at the other house and simply bought another one for here. I expect they'll want separate rooms at some point, but for now, they're thick as thieves, even in slumber.

"Who wants a story tonight?"

Their eyes light up and they clamor for their favorite books. We settle on the couch along one wall in their massive room, their small bodies pressed against mine. I read to them about adventures in far-off lands. Jake, being the curious and thoughtful one, interrupts the story with a question that has been on his mind.

"Aunt Kiera," he asks, looking up at me with wide, innocent eyes. "Do you think Daddy will marry Brienne?"

The zing of shock over the unexpected question renders me momentarily speechless. I know Drake has talked with the kiddos about his feelings for Brienne and there was even a conversation with Brienne included before they moved in about them being a family. But marriage was never discussed, as far as I know.

While I believe Drake will make it official, it's not my place to tell them that. I pause for a moment, carefully considering my response. This is a delicate topic, one that holds a mix of hope and uncertainty. I smile and gently stroke his hair before answering.

"You know your daddy and Brienne love each other very much, right?" All three boys solemnly nod. "Marriage is a big decision, and I think they're taking their time to make sure they're ready."

Colby, always eager to contribute, chimes in, "Will Brienne be our new mommy then?"

I glance at Tanner, who looks up at me with a mix of curiosity and concern. It seems this is a question they've all been wondering about, and I need to address their feelings with care.

"Brienne loves all three of you as much as she loves

your dad," I say, emphasizing my words. "She's like a mom to you already, right?"

"Just like you are," Jake points out.

"You are the luckiest kids in the world. You have lots of people who care about you and want the best for you."

Tanner's face scrunches up. "What if our real mommy comes back?"

I take a deep breath, realizing the complexity of their young minds trying to make sense of the world. Their birth mom is a drug addict who hasn't had much to do with them in a very long time. She showed up a few months ago and scared the crap out of them because she was high. Drake has since started proceedings to terminate her rights, but the legal system moves at the speed of molasses.

I gather them closer, wrapping my arms around their small frames.

"If your mommy comes back, it will be something your daddy and Brienne will handle," I say gently. "You guys haven't said much about your mom lately. Do you want her to come back?"

"I don't," Jake says, no hesitation at all. "She doesn't love us and she's so weird."

"I think your mom has issues that you can't understand, but deep down, she loves you." No matter how fucked up Crystal is, I know she loves the boys. I think the drugs make it impossible for her children to be her priority.

The boys exchange glances, absorbing my words. I see the wheels turning in their heads as they process the information.

"I think this is something we should all talk to Daddy and Brienne about. These are all wonderful questions you have."

Colby and Tanner nod in agreement, their little faces filled with a mixture of innocence and acceptance. Jake looks far too wise to be seven as he says, "I know Daddy will always take care of us."

As I continue with the bedtime routine, the boys' questions and curiosities fade into the background, replaced by the comfort of routine and the promise of sweet dreams. I get them all into their respective bunks, using the ladder to pepper kisses on Jake's and Colby's cheeks. When I get to the bottom, I tuck Tanner in snugly and boop him on the nose, relishing in the sounds of their giggles.

Best of all are the three little voices calling "I love you" as I walk out the door.

Sighing, I make my way to the kitchen to clean up from dinner. There's a TV in there so I turn on the game. While I tell myself I'm watching first and foremost because my brother is the goalie, and secondly, because I'm a Titans fan, I find myself mostly looking for Bain. He was traded from the Vengeance, a sought-after first-line defenseman. He's quickly become the team's enforcer, doling out punishment with hard hits into the boards and a drop of the gloves for a fight if necessary to protect the forwards.

I hate that I'm compelled to watch him because he should be no more important than any other member of the team. He means nothing to me other than being a man who's made me see stars twice now. Despite the undeniable chemistry and desire between us, nothing can come of it.

I know this and he knows this, so we're moving on.

It's only after I realize I've stood at the counter for almost ten minutes without cleaning up because I'm staring at the television to catch a glimpse of Bain that I curse at myself and turn it off. I've got to get him out of my head.

♦

"KIERA," I HEAR from what I think is a faraway place, then someone is shaking my shoulder. I open my eyes to see Brienne hovering over me. "We're home."

"Oh… good," I mumble as I sit up on the couch and rub my eyes.

"Why don't you go on up to one of the guest rooms? Stay the night." Brienne heads into the kitchen and I follow her, yawning big. I don't even remember falling asleep.

"Any problem with the boys getting to bed?" Drake

asks. He's at the refrigerator, pulling out a bottle of beer.

I smile empathetically because I know that's not a victory beer. I did manage to watch the entire game. "Yeah… they went down fine. I'm sorry about the loss."

Drake shrugs, but he's by no means making light of it. He's always bothered by a loss but he never wants to talk about it, so I leave it be. Besides, comforting him is more Brienne's job than mine these days.

She does it at this moment, moving to his side and sliding an arm around his waist. She doesn't tell him he did good, or he'll do better next time, or even shit happens. Merely gives him a squeeze and that's all he needs. She knows him probably better than I do—she's perfect for my brother.

"I'm going to head up to bed," Brienne says, and Drake bends to kiss her. "Don't you dare fall asleep. I've got things planned for you."

I dip my head and smirk. Brienne doesn't even blush, nor should she. She's a powerful, independent and confident woman. "Damn right, you do," she quips, then her gaze comes to me. "You'll stay, right?"

"I think I'm going to head home but thank you." I know I'm always welcome to stay, but this has become their home and Drake's former home has become mine. While I love my brother, his girlfriend and the boys, I enjoy my space.

Brienne moves to me, giving me a hug. "Want to

have lunch this week? Or a drink?"

"Absolutely," I exclaim, always happy to hang out with her.

"I'm not going to the away game on Wednesday."

"Drinks and dinner?" I suggest.

"I'll text you details and we'll get Chrissy to watch the boys."

Chrissy lives next door, or rather on the next estate over. Her parents are plastic surgeons and she's a great babysitter in a pinch.

"I'll walk you out," Drake says, moving to my side and slinging an arm over my shoulders. We head toward the front door.

Drake hugs me and then opens it, but before I can step onto the porch, he says in a low voice filled with secrecy, "Listen… need your help."

"Sure," I reply.

"I want to propose to Brienne—"

I yip with excitement and Drake places his huge hand over my mouth, glaring at me. "Sorry," I mumble against it and it falls away.

Dropping his voice to a whisper, he says, "Got some time in the next week or so you can come look at rings with me?"

I must look like I'm about to squeal with excitement as his hand claps back over my mouth, which irritates me, so I lick his palm. He jerks away, rubbing his hand on his pants. "That's so gross."

"Keep your hand off my face," I snipe, but then I let the excitement take over. Making sure I'm as quiet as can be, I say, "Yes... I am here for ring shopping."

Drake grins. "Excellent. And we can talk about ideas."

"Listen," I say as I fish my keys from my purse, "this is good timing as the boys were asking me about you and Brienne tonight."

It's not worry in his eyes but deep interest with a resolution to fixing something if need be. "What about?"

"Nothing bad. Just wondering if you two were getting married, if Brienne would be their mom. Stuff like that. But I think they're also wondering what will happen if Crystal comes back."

Drake nods. "Yeah... okay. I'll talk to them, but only in general terms about asking Brienne to marry me. They'll never keep that secret."

I laugh and reach for another hug. "Smart man."

"Good night, sis. Drive safe."

"I will."

"Love you," he says as I step onto the porch.

"Love you more," I say. I catch one more smile, then he shuts and locks the door. He has Brienne upstairs waiting for him.

I'm wide awake now. The exciting news that Drake is going to propose to Brienne has me practically bouncing as I walk to my car.

Only I come to a dead halt as I see a figure leaning against it. I don't even startle over a stranger lurking there because I immediately recognize Bain in the glow from Brienne's house, still decorated with Christmas lights.

"You're a stalker," I say as I stop before him.

Bain pushes off the car, flashing a disarming grin as he stares down at me. "Maybe so, but give me the truth… you've been thinking about me as much as I've been thinking about you, so you're not exactly disappointed I'm stalking you."

I don't reply because I'm not going to admit to anything.

"Stubborn girl," he murmurs as his hands go to my hips and he gives a hard tug so I fall into him. I balance myself against his chest, but before I can even get my bearings, his mouth is on mine. His kiss is electrifying, searing to a crisp all of my common sense. When his tongue touches mine, I can't help the tiny moan as I melt into his body.

Emboldened, Bain slides a hand down my ass, cups it from behind and squeezes hard. His mouth lifting slightly, he says, "I'm not averse to bending you over the hood of your car right now."

"That would be great. My brother would look out, see you banging his baby sister and there would be hell to pay." I manage to extricate myself from his embrace and take a step back.

"I think you're making too much about your brother being upset," Bain says.

"He'd kill you," I retort.

"I've got several inches and a good thirty pounds on him. Not worried about it."

I'm not worried either because while Drake blusters a lot about his teammates staying away from me, he's not that domineering. He's putting on the front of protective big brother and I let him have his fun with it, but he doesn't control me.

No one does.

"But really," I say, crossing my arms over my chest. I disregard the way my heart is still thumping from that kiss or the ache between my legs at the thought of him bending me over my car. "What are you doing here?"

"Well, I knew you were here because you told me you watched the boys on home game nights."

"And?"

"And I thought maybe I could talk you into letting me come home with you tonight," he replies, his eyebrows arching with hope.

"But we said we weren't going to see each other again. Remember? It was a one-night stand."

"We were together two nights, so we can't say that anymore."

"Whatever. The point is, neither one of us want commitment or monogamy. We both like to play the field."

"All true," he concedes and then surprises me with an incredibly gentle move. He steps in close, tucks my hair behind my ear and studies my face a moment. "But you have to admit, the sex is out of this fucking world and I was thinking, since neither of us is sleeping with anyone else at the moment—"

"Who says I'm not sleeping with anyone else?" I ask.

Gone is the easygoing, charming man as his eyes ice over. "Are you?"

"No," I mutter. "But maybe I'll want to."

"Little liar," he says, his words rumbling with censure.

"I'm going home," I say and start to turn away, but he has my arm in his hand.

Reeling me into him, he brings his other hand to hold me behind my neck. I'm almost paralyzed with tension, wondering if he'll devour me right here.

Instead, I get more words. An argument, really. "Look... there's no way we can't not see each other. There will be parties, games, team events. It's going to be difficult for either of us to pretend antipathy, especially when we both know how combustible we are together. So I have a suggestion."

I'm hypnotized by his words, how good he smells

and the sexual energy vibing between our bodies. "What's that?"

"We go full-on friends with benefits. We can be friends at all these social events where we'll see each other, and on the down low, we'll fuck like wild animals. It's a perfect situation."

Hmm… the concept of friends with benefits has always held allure to me, although I've never really tried it. Since my last serious relationship, which ended in absolute disaster, it's been one-night stands and never with anyone I liked well enough to be friends.

But Bain is so charming and fun. He'd make a great buddy. "But we'd just be friends. Nothing more than that," I press.

"Right. Just friends." He grins at me, hand squeezing the back of my neck. "Who fuck like wild animals."

"Are we agreeing to monogamy?" I ask carefully, because that's a tricky line to cross. It sounds an awful lot like commitment, which I'm firmly against. I don't want to be at his behest or beck and call. I want to be my own person who can just have great sex when we can fit it into the schedule.

"I've given that some thought and I'll give you my two cents. We've both had unprotected sex and then we took tests. Right now, with you on birth control, we don't have to use condoms. And I'm sure you'll agree, it's better without. So I'm willing to stay monogamous if you are." He leans in, puts his lips near my ear. "Nothing better than fucking you bare."

A shiver hits me hard, standing my hair on edge. Bain is such an easygoing guy so when he talks dirty, it's like a triple punch of lust-inducing magic. He's not wrong about how good that feels.

Conflicting emotions battle within, as I weigh the risks against the undeniable pull Bain has on me. It's tempting, an opportunity to satiate the desires we both share, without needing to commit to him completely.

Only my body, but never my heart.

After a moment of contemplation, I meet his gaze. "Okay, then... friends with benefits. We have monogamous sex but past that, we owe each other nothing. There are no expectations other than if we want to break the monogamy agreement, we just let the other person know."

Triumph flashes in his eyes but I don't mind it. I know he thinks he won something, but hell, so have I.

"Can I come home with you tonight?" he asks.

Memories of our two prior times together, both so frantic we didn't even get past my living room, surge through me. "Yeah," I murmur, lifting to my tiptoes to press my lips to his neck. "Let's try to make it to a bed, though, okay?"

CHAPTER 7

Bain

THE VISITING TEAM'S locker room in Ottawa emanates an aura of fierce competition. The walls are adorned with motivational quotes and pictures of their past victories, a definite rubbing of our noses. I sit on the bench in front of my cubby and put on my skates. My teammates are all getting their gear on as we prepare for this crucial game against the Cougars. The air is charged with anticipation as each player mentally prepares for the challenge that lies ahead.

Despite the loss the night before last, we're closing the gap against Ottawa who stands at the top of the division. Only one point separates us and a win here tonight will propel us into first.

I take a moment to survey the room, my eyes flicking over the faces of my teammates. Some are deep in their pregame rituals, tapping their sticks against the floor or meditatively visualizing their plays. Others engage in light banter, trying to ease the tension that invariably accompanies such a high-stakes matchup.

I've got my own ritual. A routine I've been doing since I was a teenager. I have no clue if it puts me in a better place, but I'm afraid to not do the ritual at this point. I take my time lacing up my skates, meticulously pulling one string at a time to tighten them. With every tug, I imagine a skill that's necessary to be at the top of my game and I visualize the perfection with which I must operate.

Tug. I must be agile and fast.

Tug. My defensive positioning must be fluid.

Tug. I must do everything in my power to disrupt my opponent's play.

Tug. I must be accurate in my outlet passing.

Tug. I must be willing to sacrifice my body.

I don't say the same things every time as there are hundreds of micro-skills I have to be perfect at. But the repeated affirmations of my job duties help to get my head in the right space. It helps me clear everything away that is not hockey.

Case in point would be Kiera McGinn. She's been on my mind pretty much continuously since I first met her, but it's become almost obsessive since she and I entered into this friends-with-benefits relationship. The last two nights I've been to her house and I wouldn't be surprised if the neighbors heard us. We're insatiable around each other and some furniture might have gotten broken. We go at it, once, twice, sometimes three times in an evening. But when we're done, she says she needs to get to sleep because she has a lot of work to do, and I graciously make my exit since I have practice the next day. There's no falling asleep in each other's arms or cuddling. We fuck, we get off and then I get gone.

Exactly like we want it.

And now I'm irritated with myself that I let my brain lose focus. I banish thoughts of Kiera as I jerk my laces loose so I can start again.

Tug, tug, tug. I repeat my affirmations as I tighten my skates and when they're double-knotted, I'm clear.

Coach West strides into the locker room, his presence commanding the attention of every player. His young face and affable smile belie the coaching genius that he is. His passion for the game is intense, but he's so caring about his players and has forged deep bonds with all of us. I've only been with the Titans for two months, but I know I could go to him with any problem in the world and he'd help me figure it out.

"All right, listen up!" Coach West's voice booms, instantly quieting the room. "This is a pivotal game for us. I don't need to tell you what's at stake, so I won't bore you with statistics we all know. Ottawa is formidable, there's no denying it," Coach West continues, his voice laced with conviction. "But we've trained for this. We've poured sweat and blood on that ice to get to where we are today. This team has overcome all the odds to have a real shot at the championship. Now is not the time to rest on our laurels. We can't assume our winning streak will continue and we need to lay our souls down on that ice every goddamn game."

A roar of approval reverberates through the locker room, my teammates yelling affirmations of Coach's words.

"Fucking right," I yell, pounding my fist into the side of my thigh.

"We stick to our game plan, execute with precision and leave nothing to chance," Coach West emphasizes, his eyes scanning the room, making sure his words reach every player. "This is our moment. Let's seize it."

The locker room erupts with a chorus of approval and hands slapping against cubbies. The collective energy surges, entering my body and lighting a fire within me. Every other player in here feels the same.

As Coach West steps out, leaving us to our final moments of preparation, my focus sharpens. I close my eyes, visualizing the plays, the precise movements I need to execute. The adrenaline courses through my veins, heightening my senses, and yet, there's a moment of stillness reserved within that is my bridge to the passion I have for the game. I was born to do this and nothing makes me happier or more fulfilled than being part of a team and coming together for a common goal to win a game.

With my mind sharpened and my spirit ablaze, I open my eyes, ready to step onto the ice and face the Ottawa Cougars. This game is not just about going to the top of the division standings—it's a chance to prove our resilience, our determination and our unwavering belief in one another. We step onto that ice as warriors, united in our quest for victory.

♦

THE GAME IS in full swing, the intensity on the ice palpable. We're five minutes into the first period and I take the ice with my line. Ottawa's veteran defenseman, Frederik Lyon, has been taking potshots at Coen during our first few shifts and I give back a little of what he's been doling out. The puck gets jammed up on the boards and I push Lyon hard in the back with my stick.

He tries to throw an elbow back but misses. The puck squirts free and I give it a push toward Stone, who sets us up for a new play.

With Kirill and I creating a distraction in front of the Cougar goalie, Stone, Coen and Boone execute passes until Boone takes a slap shot. It whizzes by my shoulder, straight for the net. It bounces off the goalie's pads and a scrabble starts in front of the net but Coen hangs back, ready to initiate the start of another play if we can pop it out to him.

All eyes are on the pileup in front of the net and

that's the perfect opportunity. Lyon goes crashing into Coen, hitting him from behind and knocking him to the ice. The Ottawa crowd erupts in cheers as Coen scrambles to his feet, but the puck is covered up by the goalie and the play is stopped.

I skate over to Coen. "You all right?"

"Yeah... fucker is a dirty player," he grumbles.

"Oh, he's going to get his," I promise, the desire to retaliate and defend my teammate burning hot. As the team's enforcer, it's up to me to carry the message that shit won't be tolerated.

The face-off occurs in the defensive zone and I line up to Lyon's right. "Going to kick your ass for that bitch move," I tell him.

"Fuck off, Hillridge," he says.

The ref drops the puck and Ottawa wins the face-off. I don't pay a lick of attention, instead turning my stick parallel to the ice and shoving it into Lyon's chest. Not enough to knock him down or even really hurt, but just enough to piss him off.

He curses and glares.

I drop my gloves, the sound of them hitting the ice like a war drum as I make my challenge. "Come on, asshole."

Lyon doesn't hesitate, agitated enough he slings off his gloves. My fists clench, ready to brawl, and Lyon pulls up his sweater sleeves.

With an explosive burst of energy, we fly at each other, our bodies colliding with bone-jarring force. The crowd erupts into a cacophony of cheers, the Ottawa fans drowning out those Titans fans in small pockets around the arena. Everyone loves a good fight and it can energize a team.

I manage to get a handful of Lyon's sweater in my left fist, twisting the material to strengthen my hold. My right hand draws back and I land a hard jab to his jaw. His head rocks so hard his helmet comes off. This guy hasn't affronted me personally, but he did make the mistake of going after one of my mates and that has to be punished. My fist connects again, this time a hook to his temple. I can tell it staggers him as both his hands try to hold on to me for leverage. The fucker manages to tie up my right arm.

With a heave, I jerk it free, ready to throw one more punch, but his legs go out from under him and he drags me down. I land on top of him hard and his hold on me is broken. I'm able to draw back, ready to let my fist fly, but the refs and linesmen crash in on us and I'm pulled off the asshole.

The crowd goes eerily silent, embarrassed and cowed that Lyon just got his ass kicked. Five-minute major penalties are called on both of us and we're sent off to our respective boxes. I flop down on the bench as the door closes and grab the water bottle there. The Ottawa crowd sitting behind and to the left of the box bangs on the glass, yelling obscenities at me. I ignore them in favor of watching the slo-mo replay on the jumbo screen above.

I smile.

That was a good fight. Short, but a definitive win for me.

As I sit in the penalty box, adrenaline still raging through my body, I feel strong and triumphant.

Sort of how I felt when Kiera agreed to our new relationship. It gnaws at me, the need to understand her reservations, to unravel the mystery behind her fears. And I'm not sure why. I should be rejoicing I've found a passionate, sexy woman who wants to have lots of sex and no commitment. Instead, I find myself fascinated by Kiera and I want to know what makes her tick.

A surge of anger hits me that I'm in the middle of a fucking hockey game and I'm thinking about what makes this woman tick.

This is no good. I have never let another person distract me from the game and I'll be damned if I'll let it happen now. It was probably a bad idea to ever start something with her. I'm supposed to go to her place tonight when the team plane lands. We made plans, but I think I need some distance from her. Cool things off just a bit.

And with that decision made, I focus on the game.

The Ottawa fans are knocked silent as they show my fist connecting with Lyon on the replay. My teammates all grin and laugh as they watch. They're energized.

A new face-off drops in the neutral zone and I laser my focus there. The battle rages on and I'm here for it.

CHAPTER 8

Kiera

I ARRIVE AT Primanti's fifteen minutes before my scheduled time to meet Danica for lunch. We've eaten here a handful of times since Brienne introduced us a couple of months ago, so I order for both of us.

We've become close pretty fast. I'm new to Pittsburgh and Danica was the first female friend I made. Sure, I've got nice relationships with a few players' girlfriends and wives, but we don't hang out often. Danica, however, I talk to almost every day either via text or call, and we get together at least once a week for lunch, drinks or dinner. The beautiful widow of one of the players who died in the crash, Danica is so easy to talk to and laugh with, and we have the same irreverent humor.

I'm just settling at a corner table when I see Danica walk in. I wave to get her attention and she lifts her chin as she winds through the tables while unbuttoning her coat. I've got my sandwich unwrapped and to my mouth when she reaches me. I try to mumble a hello, but she's not paying attention. Lured by the smell of fresh pastrami, she tears at the wrapping.

Studying Danica, I realize she cut her hair. I swallow my food, rub a napkin over my lips and take a quick sip of water before exclaiming, "I love what you did with your hair."

Danica blushes and ducks her head slightly as she tugs on a lock. "It doesn't look stupid?"

I send a massive eye roll her way. "Not even going to justify that with an answer. Someone as obnoxiously beautiful as you has no right to be asking such stupid questions."

She waves a french fry at me like it's a sword. "Easy for you to say, Miss You Should Have Been a Supermodel."

I snicker. "Okay, okay... I get it. We're both stunningly beautiful. Which also makes me wonder why we're both depressingly single."

But I'm not depressingly single. In fact, I'm quite happily single now that I've got this friends-with-benefits relationship going with Bain. Although, I'm not sure I do have anything worth buzzing about.

Bain had a there-and-back trip to Ottawa last night and he was supposed to come over when the plane landed. He never showed so I went to bed. I got a text this morning with a quick apology saying they landed too late and he had an early-morning team meeting. He then asked to get together today but I had work and plans with Danica for lunch. I suppose I could have invited him over tonight, but I didn't. Maybe I was a bit miffed he didn't come over as we last planned. Plus I needed to show him I have my own life too.

Bain's got a game tomorrow and plans with the guys after. In comparing calendars for the weekend, he said he had loose plans but would see if he could squeak in some time. I didn't have any plans but didn't want to sound like a loser, so I told him I was busy. Tuesday of next week, the team leaves on an extended road trip with games in San Francisco, Anchorage, Edmonton and Calgary.

So yeah… this has probably fizzled already.

"I don't have time to date," Danica says, and I jolt out of my thoughts. "What's your excuse?"

"Oh, I don't know. How about the fact I have a full-time job and look after three nephews?" That clearly leaves little time for dating. Hell, it's apparently not even enough time to sneak in a quickie with Bain this week.

Danica grins. "Oh yeah. I guess we're in the same boat."

Part of me wants to blab all to Danica right this minute and get her thoughts on Bain, but I'm hesitant. We've gotten close but we've never discussed our sex lives. Danica was widowed ten months ago and sex isn't something she's ever brought up. I don't advertise my carefree, bang 'em and leave 'em ways because she might not understand.

Still, I should test the waters. My sandwich hovering before my mouth, I ask, "It doesn't mean we can't have booty calls, though. A little wham-bam-thank-you-ma'am is truly all we need."

Danica starts choking and the fact I shocked her tells me what I need to know. "Booty calls? Seriously... who even says that?"

But I do know Danica is neither a prude nor judgmental, so I own it. "Me. I think booty call is a fabulous term."

"Well, that's not exactly something I would understand. Mitch was my one and only."

A stab of pain hits my heart for her. "That's right. He was your first boyfriend so that makes him your first..."

"Yep. I have never been with another man other than Mitch. Thus I've never had a booty call."

I decide to poke at her, because Danica is most definitely not conservative or without confidence, so I would think she probably had a healthy sex life with him. "Did Mitch, like, ever come home from the arena for a quickie?"

"Yeah." Her eyes go dreamy as if she's recalling just such an occasion. "He did."

I grin at her. "Then that was technically a booty call.

A monogamous one, mind you, but a booty call all the same."

Danica laughs as she sets down her sandwich and pulls a fry from under the bread. "I feel so progressive."

"Well… I have perfected the art of non-monogamous booty calls so if you ever want advice, let me know."

Although apparently I'm willing to give monogamous ones a try. At least I willingly went into that agreement with Bain, all because we made a mistake and had unprotected sex. While that ultimately turned out fine and opened the door for us to ditch the condoms, I do wonder if maybe the monogamy aspect has made this a little similar to a committed relationship and that's why Bain and I haven't been trying overly hard to make plans to get together.

Or, that little prick of my conscience says, *You're afraid it could turn into something more so you're sabotaging this before it gets going.*

"Have you had booty calls since coming to Pittsburgh?" Danica asks.

Heat prickles on the back of my neck thinking about my last one with Bain. Let's just say he takes sixty-nine to a whole new level. "Yes, I have and it was fabulous."

"I want to be like you when I grow up." Danica sighs, but I'm not so sure I'm all that grown up. I avoid commitment like it's a scaly disease and part of that is my inability to see past my own limited experiences. Not very mature, I know, but I'm comfortable with my decisions.

For the next half hour, I manage to put Bain out of my mind and instead slip into the ease of pure friendship I have with Danica. I tell her about Drake's proposal to Brienne on the horizon and we bat around ideas to make it special.

"He should take out a front page ad in the *Pittsburgh Times* and ask her that way," Danica says with a laugh.

It's a running joke in this city that Drake has had a tumultuous relationship with the press. They dogged him relentlessly when Crystal made up false allegations about him betting on hockey and then he turned around and announced right on national TV that he was in love with Brienne Norcross—his boss.

"Oh God, that would be funny." I laugh. "I'm going to suggest it to him."

Danica shakes her head. "It really should be done privately. I can see Drake doing it at a family dinner with the boys. I know that's more Brienne's style and he's going to make it perfect for her."

"Nailed it," I exclaim, because as powerful, wealthy and somewhat famous as Brienne is, she'd prefer to be at home with Drake and the kids rather than have some razzle-dazzle.

Danica puts her sandwich down and wipes her fingers on a napkin. Eyes laced with concern, she asks, "How's your work going?"

I sigh, my shoulders slumping ever so slightly. "It's good."

Danica looks at me pointedly, not willing to accept that.

"Fine," I say with a laugh, holding out my hands in surrender. "Work is fine."

"But," she prods.

"But I want to go back to school to become a nurse practitioner. I'm not cut out to work from home long term and want to get back to patient care."

Danica nods empathetically, her brows furrowing with understanding. She knows I've been antsy, not finding as much fulfillment in a remote position. "Why can't you enroll in school?"

I shake my head in resignation. "It's not a good time. Drake depends on me so much with the boys that I need to be flexible."

As soft as Danica's expression is, I also see something a little steely within. "You're such a caring sister, Kiera. It's admirable how you prioritize your family, especially your nephews. But Drake is more than capable of finding help with the boys, especially now that he has Brienne in his life."

I'm startled by her suggestion. "Oh, no. I couldn't do that to Drake or the boys. They depend on me."

Danica nods. "I get it. I really do. But you can't do that forever and I seriously doubt that Drake expects that of you. You came here to help him get settled and provide stability for the boys with the move. Well, they're all settled. Sure, you can babysit and watch the boys on occasion, but Drake and Brienne have the resources to lessen that burden on you, so maybe you can get back on track with what you want to do with your life."

It has never once crossed my mind to move away from my responsibilities and the support I promised Drake. But she's absolutely right. When he asked me to move to Pittsburgh, he told me it was just to help him and the boys get settled. I don't think it was ever supposed to be permanent. I sort of believed I'd move back home to Minnesota when he was stable, but I'm finding I like Pittsburgh a lot.

I push it aside because Drake and Brienne are so damn busy and have so much going on, it's not a good time to think of such things.

Lunch is over far too fast and I never feel like I get enough time with Danica. Walking out of Primanti's and button our coats against the cold.

We step into a quick hug. "Let's get the boys together soon. Maybe Travis can do an overnight."

While he's a few years older than Jake, all four kids play well together. We've done a few outings as a group.

"He'd love that." Danica checks her watch and frowns. "I've got to get going to make the carpool line. He'll be furious if I'm late since he's going skating this afternoon with Camden."

My eyebrows jet upward. "Really?

It's not so much that Camden is helping Travis, but it's the tone of Danica's voice. Sort of breathy.

Her look is chastising. "He's just a friend. I've known him a long time and Travis knows him. He offered to help him out since Travis is starting youth hockey next week."

Hmm… maybe I didn't hear what I wanted to hear. Maybe I want everyone to hook up and have great sex like Bain and me. Or rather, we were having it. Not sure if we will again.

I tease her a bit. "That's awesome. I have noticed that Camden is unbelievably handsome."

A myriad of emotions cross Danica's features. First a cute smile, a silent agreement that she does indeed think Camden's a hottie, followed by guilt.

My hand wraps around her arm and I give her a gentle squeeze. "There's absolutely nothing wrong with you admiring a man for his looks."

And I know something about this. I've taken my fill of Bain in full naked glory and stared unabashedly at him every single time. He's so damn gorgeous, he constantly has me tingling with desire for him.

Ugh… stop thinking about him.

I'm pulled back into our conversation when Danica says, "I know. And I love you to death for trying to normalize those things for me. Not one other person in my life has ever broached the idea that there could be something for me after Mitch. And I'm not saying that's Camden… just thank you for reiterating there's nothing wrong with moving on."

"There's not," I say gently, my smile hopefully giving further validation. "Besides, you're not really moving away from Mitch. He'll always be a part of your life. Maybe just consider it, like, you're opening the door to add to your current life."

Danica shakes her head slightly. "I'm not ready for that just yet."

"But there will be a time when you are."

She inclines her head. "How do I know when it's appropriate?"

All I have is a helpless shrug. "I expect you'll just know in your heart."

Kind of like the way I know that I'll never be ready for something like that.

CHAPTER 9

Bain

SATURDAY MORNING ARRIVES with a cloud of frustration hanging over me. Lying in my bed, I stare at the ceiling and assess how I'm feeling. Last night's game was a success—we won against the Minnesota Raiders—but I didn't feel the normal high I get after a victory. I went out with Camden and Boone to celebrate but my mind kept drifting to Kiera. My vow to push her out of my thoughts by cooling things off isn't going as planned.

It's perplexing how we've reached this point, but I suspect some dumbassery on my part. We agreed to keep things casual, just friends with benefits. I mean, who the fuck doesn't love that?

But we're not exactly taking advantage of it.

I didn't see her after the Ottawa game three nights ago because I was feeling hemmed in and then she claimed she had plans the next day. I said I had plans the next night and everything just shifted out of whack.

Instead of feeling more grounded and in control by

pulling back, it feels like everything is spinning wildly. The biggest spiral I have going on right this very moment as I lie in this bed staring at my ceiling is a very fucking inconvenient need to see Kiera and ask her what in the hell has happened to us. Maybe she'll have some clarity.

I glance at my phone, hoping for a message from her, but there's nothing. She said she had plans today, although she didn't give me a single detail. What we do outside the bedroom is irrelevant, right? We're fuck buddies and we don't share those types of things with one another.

Christ… I really want to know what she's doing today because I would like to see her. To do what, I don't know. Ideally, it would be to fuck, but things are weird now, so I'm thinking we might need to talk.

Against my better judgment, I make a spontaneous decision. I'm going to her place, uninvited, hoping she's there. It's still early—only half past eight—and hopefully her plans for the day haven't taken her from her house yet.

I roll out of bed, slam a cup of coffee and take a quick shower. I bundle up extra warm because it's supposed to snow. The heavy precipitation won't roll in until tonight, but I'm ready in my thick coat, gloves and knit hat if it starts now.

I arrive at Kiera's doorstep, feeling a mix of nervousness and anticipation. Before things got so off-kilter, I'd normally show up at her door and she'd welcome me with open arms and open legs. I'd whisk her off to bed.

Or a couch.

Or bend her over a counter.

It was all raging hormones and blistering sex, both of us nearly going up in flames every time we were together. It was the perfect relationship, really, and now it's all messed up.

I ring the doorbell, wondering how Kiera will respond to me if I just haul her in for a deep kiss. Unfortunately, my confidence and swagger—born of the truth that I know how to make her scream—seems to have taken a hit.

Christ… what am I doing? This is all wrong.

I just about resolve to leave when she opens the door, surprise etched across her face. "What are you doing here?"

Before I answer, I take a good, long look at Kiera. It's been four days since I've seen her and I'm not sure how it's possible—maybe four days of absence and yearning—but she looks a million times more beautiful.

Her blond hair is in a messy bun on top of her head and her face is free of makeup. She's wearing worn jeans, a long-sleeve Henley and fuzzy socks. In one hand, she holds a red velvet bow.

My eyes move to lock on hers and I try to be as honest as I can. "I have no clue why I'm here. I just wanted to see you."

Confusion radiates from her gaze, a reflection of my tangled thoughts. Our relationship has been confined to mutual physical attraction and pleasure. While we've labeled ourselves friends, we've never acted the part before. Now everything has become inscrutably more complex and I feel like I'm on uneven ground. I think she's feeling the same if her expression is any indication.

"Oh," she murmurs, looking more unsure of herself than I feel on the inside. She steps back and motions with her arm. "Want to come in?"

Yes, I do. I want to grab her, kiss her, strip her naked and worship her body. But again... things are a bit off.

"Sure," I say and cross her threshold. I wasn't invited to stay, but I take off my coat, gloves and hat, tossing them on the back of her couch. I glance down at the bow in her hand. "I don't think that will look good with your outfit."

Kiera's dimples pop and some tension releases from my shoulders because I'm still able to charm her, even if just a little. "I'm packing up my Christmas decorations. I have an insane amount of red velvet bows all over the house."

These are her plans for the day? To put away decorations?

On impulse, I blurt, "Can I help?"

She laughs, her disbelief evident. "You want to help?"

"Yeah... why not?" I challenge. I don't have a good answer to why I'm here, asking to spend some non-sexual time with her, but I can't deny the desire to be in her presence if that's all I can have at this moment.

She opens her mouth, I'm confident to rebuke me with the fact that we're just fuck buddies, but then snaps it shut just as quickly.

Kiera's eyes cut over to her Christmas tree—sadly, something I had not noticed on the few times I've been here—then back to me. "I have a ton of stuff to do today as it's the first free day I've had in ages. I've got to get all the decorations put away, clean the house, do laundry and go to the grocery store. So I don't have time to fuck around."

"Fuck around as in amazing sex or fuck around in like goofing off?" I ask for clarification.

"They're both one and the same. I don't have time, so if that's what you want, I'm going to have to pass."

I'm not dissuaded or turned off by that proclamation. Surprisingly, my offer to help is genuine, but it doesn't mean I won't try to seduce her later. "Let me help," I say, giving her my most earnest Boy Scout smile.

She lets out a sigh of resignation. "Um... yeah, sure. Why not? I could use an extra pair of hands."

I glance around and notice for the first time the actual décor. The walls are a cream color and the massive sectional sofa I fucked her on is gray leather. It sits in the middle of the room and faces a large-screen TV hanging over the fireplace, sleek glass end tables with chrome detailing at each end. Abstract art hangs on the walls. If I had to guess, this is all Drake's style and not Kiera's and I wonder if she'll redecorate.

There's a huge tree in the corner that I truly never even noticed on my other visits because my focus was on sex and as anyone can attest, that will often blind you to other things. There's a large box beside it, which I'm assuming is to pack away lights and ornaments. There are wreaths, candles, figurines and all sorts of other holiday decorations all over the place, on tables, on the mantel and bookshelves, all of it a reminder of the festive season that has now passed. I took down my stuff last weekend.

"How about you strip the tree and I'll start packing up all the figurines and such?" Kiera says. She gives me a quick course on how to wrap the glass ornaments to prevent breakage and we get to work.

For a solid half hour, it's silent between us. Not a word of conversation, although Kiera actually hums Christmas tunes while she wraps various breakables. There are a million things I want to ask her and I did come over to talk, but her voice is beautiful and it lets a little of the holiday spirit linger.

I finish the tree first and help her tape up the boxes she's already packed. Under her guidance, I insist on carrying all of it out to the garage where I stack them on custom-built shelving on one side.

Back in the house, I point to the tree. "Hold on to it so I can loosen the screws at the base. Are they still doing curbside pickup?"

"Fortunately, yes."

That's all I need to know. "Hold the top," I repeat and she steps in. I drop down to the floor where I lie on my side to unwind the screws free of the tree trunk. "Got it secure?"

"Yeah... I'm good."

I slip out from under the tree and nudge Kiera out of the way. Reaching in through the prickly branches, I lift the tree from the base and manage to wrangle it outside with help from Kiera guiding me out the front door. As soon as I step onto the driveway, a few snowflakes dust my face and I take in the change in the weather. The sky is filled with gray clouds and the wind is stirring. It's fucking cold as hell since I didn't bother with my coat, so I double-time it to the curb where I deposit the remnants of Christmas.

As I turn, I see Kiera on the porch watching me, her arms wrapped around herself to ward off the cold. The wind blows strands of hair around her face and I can see she's freezing as she waits for me to return.

When I reach the top step, without hesitation and operating only on instinct, I wrap my arms around her and pull her close. She comes willingly, and for the moment, all the weirdness is gone, even though it's slightly odd for me to be touching her in a non-sexual way.

Rubbing my hands briskly over her back, I ask, "Any reason you're out here without a coat?"

She burrows into me. "You don't have one."

"Ahh," I say with a chuckle. "But I have shoes on and you only have socks." I release her, turn her toward the door and swat her on the ass playfully. "Get inside."

She gives a return glare over her shoulder but before she turns her back on me, I see the glint of amusement in her eyes. I follow her in and she heads to the kitchen. "Want something to drink?"

"Coffee?" I ask.

"I got you covered."

Kiera makes us each a cup in a very fancy machine that grinds the beans for you. We stand at the counter, sipping our drinks. "Thank you for helping. That was sweet."

"So, what's next? Clean the house, grocery shopping or laundry?"

She glances around and shrugs. "Not sure yet. I'll figure it out after you leave."

Bringing the mug of fragrant coffee to my lips, I stare at her over the edge before actually taking a sip. "Oh, I'm not leaving."

Kiera's eyebrows shoot up.

"I'm helping you today," I clarify.

"But why?" she asks suspiciously.

"Why not?"

She's totally annoyed with me now. "Because we're just fuck buddies, Bain. We fuck and that's it."

"No, that's not quite true."

Pursing her lips, she puts a hand on her hip. "You've got to explain that one to me."

"We're friends with benefits," I explain. "That isn't the same as fuck buddies. There's a friend element that, granted, we haven't quite exercised yet, but it's there. So I'm here *as a friend* to help you out."

Kiera's brow furrows slightly, her eyes narrowing. "You want to be friends?"

"Why not?"

"Because it's not what we're supposed to be doing." Setting her cup down, she turns away with an exasperated gush of air.

She moves to the sink, looking at the gray-tinged landscape outside. I set my cup down and move behind her.

I speak in the language of control and touch, one hand gripping her hip and the other wrapping around her chest. I step in close, trapping her against the counter. The minute our bodies touch, she instantly relaxes. She sinks into me and for all her bluster that she doesn't have time for such things today, she's capitulated and I could fuck her if I wanted.

I do something far more important, though. Putting my mouth near her ear, I murmur, "What you and I have is not easily defined. It's a first for me. I'm starting to understand you might be out of your element too."

"But neither of us wants a commitment," she says.

"You're right. We don't owe each other anything, and yet here I am… having a not-so-bad time helping you out today. What do you know? I tried something different and I liked it. You liked having me here too."

She doesn't reply and I expect that's because she's afraid to voice the truth. It's more than confirmed when she turns, draping her arms over my shoulders. Her voice is husky, provocative. "How about I blow everything off and we just go to my room and break the bed?"

Instantly, my cock agrees, jumping in my pants. "I am never going to say no to you if you want to have sex. So let's do it." Triumph gleams in Kiera's eyes and she grabs my hand to lead me to her room. I hold my ground, though, and she looks back at me curiously. "After we're done fucking, though, we'll go to the grocery store and do your shopping. Then we'll come back and I can help you clean, do laundry. We'll cook dinner together and—"

More confusion flickers in her eyes. "That sounds like a date."

"No," I growl, pulling on her hand and jerking her to me. I nuzzle into her neck. "That's friends with benefits. We'll do the benefits part right now, then friends later, okay?"

"But—"

My mouth moves to hers, capturing her lips in a cock-hardening kiss. Lifting her in my arms, Kiera's legs go around my waist. I turn for the bedroom, unrelenting in my assault because if I do, she might get back in her head again.

I don't know why I'm pushing this friends-with-benefits thing—and exercising the friends part of it—since all I've done the last few days is try to get her out of my mind. All I know is that at this moment, and whatever led me to be where I am right now, it feels right.

CHAPTER 10

Kiera

I FIGHT AGAINST the drooping of my eyes and the pull of slumber. Bain is deep under and I've been listening to his heartbeat as my head rests on his chest. The rise and fall tells me he's sound asleep.

Ordinarily, after an enthusiastic, raucous round of sex, Bain leaves. But this time is different.

Everything about today is different, from the moment he showed up on my doorstep to his proclamation that we needed to exercise the friends part of our relationship. Not sure I believed that, but since he wanted to knock some of our benefits out of the way, I was all for it. I fully expected him to roll out of bed and proclaim he had stuff of his own to do. I certainly don't expect him to help me with cleaning the house, laundry or grocery shopping.

But he didn't leave.

He stayed in bed and pulled my sweaty, naked and exhausted body half on top of him. His hand stroked my lower back as we both floated down to earth, but within a few minutes, he had fallen asleep.

I lift my head and stare at his peaceful expression. Bain is one of those guys who's always smiling and has a perpetually mischievous look on his face. All of that is smoothed out now as he sleeps, and I resist the urge to brush aside a lock of his dark hair that's fallen over his forehead.

I could wake him up and kick him out. What we do best is already done, but instead, I slowly push myself off him and slide out of bed without waking him. A quick trip to the restroom to clean up, because this whole sex without a condom thing—while hot as hell—is messy. After I nab the T-shirt he'd been wearing under his Titans sweatshirt, I slither into it. It swallows me up, coming just below mid-thigh, but it smells so damn good.

Grabbing my laundry basket as quietly as I can, I slip out of the bedroom, pulling the door shut behind me.

The first thing I do is start a load of clothes before considering what part of the house to clean first. The living room needs a good vacuuming from all the dead pine needles. But that will create noise and for some reason, I feel proprietary of Bain's sleep. Well, I know the reason... he made me come three times before finally letting himself go so he deserves a nap.

Smiling to myself, I put my earbuds in, crank up some Lizzo and start on the kitchen. I unload the dishwasher and reload it with a sink full of dishes I'd let accumulate. I shimmy, bop and gyrate to "Juice," and by the time I'm scrubbing a pan that I made a casserole in a few days ago, I'm extolling right along with Lizzo about how much I love "Boys."

I do a running-man shuffle from the sink to the cabinet to return the casserole dish and after closing the door, I prepare to shuffle to the laundry room.

I screech as I see Bain standing there, leaning against the wall with his arms crossed over his chest. Wearing nothing but his briefs, he's grinning at me as one of my hands goes to my heart, which nearly leapt out of my chest. I remove one earbud.

"Jesus, you scared the crap out of me," I gasp.

"Did anyone ever tell you that you got some serious fucking moves?" he asks, eyes dancing with amusement.

"A time or two," I reply dryly. "I was a dancer long before I became a nurse."

"Really?" He pushes off the wall and walks toward me. Bain takes me by the hips but doesn't pull me in, merely stares down at me with interest. "What type of dancing?"

"A bit of everything from ballet to jazz to tap. I really got into hip-hop in high school and was on a dance team in college."

"It's sexy as fuck," he says, leaning back to take me in. "Especially in my T-shirt."

"Maybe I'll twerk for you sometime," I tease.

Bain releases me, his hands clasped over his chest. "Please, please don't let that be a joke."

Snickering, I lay my earbuds on the counter. "I've got to switch the laundry."

"How come you didn't wake me up?" he asks as he follows.

"You deserved it after the orgasms you gave me."

"Got more where those came from," he says, his tone suggestive enough that I know he'd dole them out right now. But before I can discern if I want to blow off more work to jump back into bed, he says, "Where's your vacuum? I'll start on the living room."

For the next two hours, Bain helps me clean the house. There's not much to it since I mainly only use the living room, kitchen and my bedroom, but things accumulate since I'm so busy. He even helps me fold my laundry, insisting on handling my panties and bras so he can check them out.

We talk amiably as we work at the dining room table where I dumped all the clothes fresh out of the dryer.

"What was your Christmas like this year?" I ask curiously. "You said you already put your decorations away."

Bain's inspecting a black thong as he answers, "My parents came to visit."

"Are you close to them?"

"Very. Also to my older brother, Carson, but he

jetted off to Cabo with his girlfriend. What about your parents?"

"My dad bolted when I was little. I don't really remember him so it's just been me, Drake and my mom."

"And she's back in Minnesota?" he asks, his eyes flicking to me before going back to fold a pair of lime-green panties.

"Yeah… she's got a huge group of friends there and is active in the church."

"That's cool." Bain holds up a lacy black bra. "You were wearing this Tuesday night."

Laughing, I shake my head. "Good memory."

"Hard to forget you in black lace," he mutters, and my tummy flutters over the awe in his voice. He folds it and sets it on the pile. "When are we going grocery shopping? And what are we making for dinner?"

I pause folding a pair of jeans, tipping my head slightly. "Is this becoming an all-day thing?"

"And an all-night thing," he clarifies. "Maybe we should have pasta tonight so we can get good carb energy."

I choke I laugh so hard, shaking my head. "Wow, things changed fast."

"But we're not dating," he reminds me in a stern voice.

"No, of course not," I mimic very seriously. "Not dating at all."

Bain's hand shoots out and grabs my wrist. He tugs me to him and drops his other hand to my ass, which is still very bare under his T-shirt. His fingers lightly stroke one cheek. "We don't have practice tomorrow since we're getting ready to go on a seven-day road trip. What do you think of me hanging with you since it's the weekend?"

"I thought you hockey pros either practiced, worked out or played a game seven days a week."

"I mean… a typical week is three to four games, one to two practices and then off-ice training, so yeah… we're pretty hard-core. But tomorrow we get recuperation time, and with the extended road trip, we're all taking it easy."

This I knew because Drake had told me he and Brienne were going to chill out with the kids. That left me two days to clean the house, read books and do whatever I wanted.

But now it seems I might get to have sex all weekend.

"We would need lots of carbs," I muse, tapping my finger on my chin.

"And water," Bain says with a grin. "We need to stay hydrated."

"So if I'm hearing you correctly, we'll stay here and have sex for the next two solid days?"

"I mean… I've heard of crazier things."

I pretend to mull it over, eyes lifting to the ceiling as

I hum low in my throat. When I bring my gaze back to his face, I shrug. "I suppose I've got nothing better to do."

Bain moves so fast, I give a startled yip, but he has me in his arms and spins me around a few times. I'm dizzy as he lets me slide down his body, so very slowly. The friction as parts of me rub against parts of him is tantalizing, and when my feet hit the floor, something rumbles from Bain's chest. A deep growl of need.

Suddenly, his T-shirt is gone and he has me spun around, facing the dining table. "Hands behind your back," he orders as he snatches the black lace bra he'd been fingering a bit ago.

I comply and he uses it to bind me.

Chills break out all over my body because I have no clue what he's going to do with me.

I can't say it's a disappointment when he turns me around and one large hand threads through my long hair. He grips tight at the back of my head. "Get on your knees for me, Kiera."

I let him push me down, no fight or hesitation from me. My knees gently come to rest on the plush rug under the dining table and Bain frees his burgeoning erection from his briefs.

Tipping my head back, I look up at him. Naked desire flushes his face, but I also see something in his eyes that's close to wonder as he watches my mouth open for

111

him. I give him a long lick and he hisses. "Christ…
you're going to be the death of me."

A slip of a smile breaks free but then is replaced by
his cock in my mouth. Bain's eyes close, his head lolls
back and he groans as I suck him in deep.

♦

FINGERS BRUSH ALONG my neck and my eyes pop open.

"You're starting to drift off," Bain says. "Want to go
to bed?"

"Not really," I say as I push onto my elbow. I'd been
lying on the couch, my head on Bain's thigh as we
watched a movie.

Today has been a nonstop whirlwind of discovery
with this man. From us barely speaking this week to him
hanging with me all day and wanting to stay the rest of
the weekend. Rousing sex, good conversation, excellent
food. The only downside is the movie we chose is so
boring, I can barely keep my eyes open.

"What do you want to do?" he asks as I twist my
neck to look at him. He holds one hand out as if to ward
me off. "But don't say sex. I've had far too much today."

I grin at him. "People like you and me… we can
never have too much."

He nods with a grave expression. "So true."

I have an idea. I pop up and move to the other end
of the couch, the armrest supporting my back, my legs

crossed in front of me. "Let's just talk."

Bain gives a dramatic groan, letting his head flop against the couch. "Ugh... women... always wanting to talk."

I kick his thigh. He laughs, latching onto my leg and dragging me across the couch. I'm powerless to stop him and next thing I know, I'm straddling his lap.

But he doesn't touch me in any way other than to rest his hands on my thighs. "Okay... what do you want to talk about?"

"Well, you're the one who opened the door to this whole friends thing. But it got me thinking... why are we the way we are? Let's be honest... you and I were both cooling things off the last few days and we were doing it intentionally."

Bain stares at me, almost as if he's perplexed by my straightforward observation. His hands squeeze my legs. "Yeah... I was backing away."

"And I wasn't exactly scrambling to make time for you," I say.

"And yet here we are, spending the weekend together as friends."

"There was sex involved, though, and that was by far the better part of the day. No offense to either of us as friends."

"No offense taken." He laughs. "But yeah... why are we the way we are? I guess I'm just young and don't want to settle down. My parents were a bit older before they got married and they always preached to me and my brother to live our lives to the fullest before we got married and had kids."

"That's fair. And probably good advice."

Bain's hands move to my hips. "What about you? Still sowing your wild oats?"

I snort. "You make it sound like I'm fucking half of Pittsburgh."

"I wouldn't judge if you were," he says.

"No, you wouldn't." Bain is as progressive as they come and has never once made me feel bad for having a healthy sexual appetite. And I've made no apologies for it.

Bain stares at me for a long moment and I can tell he's sizing up something. "Bad relationship," he says with confidence and a smug smile.

Two words and he has me pegged.

"Yeah," I admit with a dry, humorless laugh. "Really bad relationship."

"Want to talk about it?" he asks, and I'm surprised that his question sounds genuine.

And yet... no, I'm not all that surprised. Despite us having a rocky patch where both of us floundered a little trying to figure out what we were to each other, I know Bain's a good guy.

"It's not that interesting of a story," I admit. "His

name is Peter and we were college sweethearts. He seemed perfect until he wasn't."

"Like how?"

"He became really controlling."

Bain's hands squeeze reflexively as his face darkens. "Abusive?"

"Not physically but mentally, verbally. He became obsessive and tried to cut me off from friends. If I went out, he'd accuse me of cheating on him and then call me names and scream obscenities. Always apologetic, but that was part of the cycle. His behavior got scarier and I finally broke up with him. He didn't take kindly to it, so there was a bit of stalking after."

"What did he do?"

My stomach pitches thinking about it. It was a terrifying time in my life. "It started as more annoying than anything. Calling and breathing into the phone. Then it was nasty letters, which turned into nasty phone calls until I changed my number."

"How come I feel like that was the easy stuff?" Bain asks hesitantly.

"It got worse. My tires were slashed and there was a dead cat left on my doorstep."

"What the fuck?" Bain snarls, sitting up straighter.

"He'd sit outside my house all night in his car."

"Please tell me you called the cops."

"Yeah… they don't hand out restraining orders easily, but I eventually got one. I guess that scared him because he moved back home to Indiana."

"Jesus," he murmurs. "How long ago was this?"

"I ended things about four years ago. It's all fine now. Haven't heard from him in a long time. But it sort of put me off serious relationships."

"It scared you," he surmises.

I smile at him because he understands far better than I would've imagined. "Yeah. A lot. I know it's not fair for me to think all relationships will be that way, but I can't help it. The minute love came into the picture, things went downhill fast."

"Sounds like he was mentally unbalanced," Bain ponders.

I shrug. "It's in the past and I don't dwell on it."

"I have a question." Bain throws his head in the direction of the kitchen. "I saw an admissions packet for the University of Pittsburgh on your counter."

"Nosy," I chide teasingly.

He looks in no way abashed. "You thinking of going back to school?"

My gaze drops as I rest my hands on his. "Nah... not really."

"Then why do you have an admissions packet?"

Pursing my lips, I shrug. "I don't know. It's what I wanted to do before Drake got the offer with the Titans, but once I committed to come here and help watch the kids, it sort of got put on the back burner. I guess I was curious about the curriculum so I ordered the packet."

Bain's eyes bore into mine. "I don't buy that for a second. It's not just curiosity. You want to go but you can't figure out how to balance it all."

"Okay, fine… I want to go, but it's not about figuring out the balance. I simply can't. I have to watch the boys when Drake travels."

"But do you really?" he asks with enough sarcasm the answer must be evident to him already. "I mean, Drake and Brienne have resources for the kids. There's a whole community of players with wives who will help. You could still chip in, and I know damn well that Brienne is sometimes staying home from away games to watch the kids."

"Yeah, but—"

Bain's fingers cover my lips. "No buts. If you want it, do it."

It's the same advice Danica gave me so maybe there's something to this. Maybe it is possible for me to start back on achieving my own goals. But now's not the time to broach it with Drake. He's focused on proposing to Brienne and with that comes a whole host of issues with the boys. I know he wants to make sure they're okay with it.

"Just fill in the application. What does it hurt?" he asks.

I hedge a little, my tone uncertain. "It doesn't. Not really."

"Then do it."

Up until this point, I've enjoyed the friends aspect we explored today, but it's been all light and fun. Now Bain is hitting on something I have deep feelings about, and while I know his heart is in a good place—and he's encouraging me—I feel uncomfortable. It crosses over from this being sort of fun and casual. He's giving me strong advice and while it touches me he would care enough to give it, it blurs the lines again.

I must distract. I take Bain's hands in mine and raise them from my thighs, putting them over my breasts. I'm wearing his T-shirt again with only panties underneath—we showered together before dinner—and he wastes no time taking my cue.

His hands contract and squeeze before pinching my nipples. His eyes burn with lust as he stares at me. "You're good at distracting."

So he has me a little figured out.

I've got him figured out too.

Lifting the bottom of the T-shirt, I pull it over my head. My hands lace around the back of his neck and I pull him forward. Bain hums just as his mouth latches on to one of my nipples and liquid heat pools between my legs. I gasp as he uses his teeth, and that's enough for Bain to surge off the couch and carry me to my bedroom.

CHAPTER 11

Bain

DESPITE THE LATE hour, I'm exhilarated as I board the team plane headed to Anchorage where we'll take on the Blizzard. We're leaving the beautiful city of San Francisco after thoroughly trouncing the Bay Brawlers in a 5–0 shutout. This game was especially significant as they were at the top of their division and every time we can take down a top-tier team, it lets the world know that these wins aren't flukes.

We have a team worthy of a championship.

Of course, I'm not going to get ahead of myself. We're only halfway through the regular season. But it cannot be denied that Callum Derringer managed to put together a team that has clicked in all ways. He mined the raw and sometimes unnoticed talent, turning it over to Cannon West to shine up. The two men were featured in a national sports magazine week before last, dubbed the Dynamic Duo. And they are quite a pair, except... it's not really a pair who's responsible for this. The players were up in arms that Brienne Norcross wasn't

SAWYER BENNETT

included in the formula for our success, but Drake assured us she wanted no credit. And given that the Titans' operations have been running so smoothly, she's going to be pulling back to manage her billion-dollar empire that is separate from hockey.

There's no one person and no single reason for our success this year but rather a lot of good decisions made along the way. I'm hoping I'm one of those good decisions. I feel positive about my time here in Pittsburgh. It's been two months and I've meshed incredibly well on the first line. I've formed solid friendships along the way, although no doubt I miss my buds in Phoenix.

Probably best of all has been reuniting with Baden, who was my teammate on the Vengeance. When he was injured the summer before last, it pulled that team together, bonds forming unlike any I've had before in my life. When Baden decided to move into coaching and left us for Pittsburgh, it put holes in everyone's hearts. Being here with him on a team that's bouncing back from tragedy and watching him own his new role has been the most unexpected pleasurable side effect of my transition here.

I don't make it but five rows into the plane before I see an empty seat next to Camden. He and Hendrix are the two I've hung out with the most. That started as three single guys around the same age and years of play in the league who liked to go out and have fun. Hendrix has Stevie now, so I'm not sure how much he'll be coming out with us, but really… Stevie owns a bar. We'll probably all just hang out there.

Slumping down into the seat with my backpack on my lap, I unzip a side pocket and pull out my earbuds. I give Camden a quick glance. "You were on fire tonight, dude."

He lifts his chin. "Thanks. Now I just got to keep it up to that level."

You'd think this might be an awkward conversation because Camden and I play the same position. The only thing separating us is that we play on different lines. I'm on the first, he's on the second. When Nolan Carrier was traded for me, I went right onto the first line as my stats were better than Camden's. It's never something he begrudged me, though, and that's because he's a great guy. He is, however, making it known via his spectacular game play that he'll never stop gunning for my spot.

And good for him. That's what makes our team better. Because I know he's coming for me, I'll bust my ass to stay ahead of him.

"Everything else good?" I ask, placing my backpack on the floor and pushing it under the seat before me. All the seats are wide with plenty of legroom to accommodate hockey players. I'm the tallest on the team and my knees don't even come close to bumping the seat in front of me.

"It's all copacetic," Camden says, and that's all I think needs to be said. He missed practice last week, freaking everyone out. Coach went to his house, probably expecting the worst that he'd somehow died, but Coach was relieved—and pissed—that Camden had merely overslept.

Camden filled me in on the aftermath, which included Coach West insisting he go to a meeting of the support group that formed after the crash. I can only assume something is going on with Camden and he's still suffering the trauma from being a survivor—guilt and all—but we didn't specifically discuss that.

A flight attendant brings Camden a drink and he lowers his tray. She passes the glass across me and I smell bourbon. I should order a drink, but I'm not feeling it tonight. Instead, I ask her for a mint tea.

"Lame ass," Camden teases before taking a sip from the highball glass.

"Fuck off." I put my earbuds in so I can't hear any reply but I do see the smirk on his face. Flipping through my music library, I choose the *White Album*, set it to shuffle and bop along to "Blackbird." I lower my tray and move over to my text messages.

Glancing around, I see Camden's engrossed in his own phone but other players are brushing by me, so I'm careful when I pull up the string I have going with Kiera. Within the various messages we've sent each other since I left on this extended road trip yesterday are a few sexy pictures. She's fucking brilliant at sexting and never sends me anything outwardly obscene, plus she never shows her face. It might be just her breasts, plumped up in a sexy bra. She sent me one last night of her lying back on her bed, feet on the floor. She had on a tank top and I could just see the swell of her breasts and the skin of her lower belly, but that wasn't the focus of the picture. Kiera had propped her phone against something on her bedside table so most of the view was of her hand down the front of her panties. Her legs were slightly spread and I couldn't see anything explicit, but it was the message that came with it.

Thinking of you while I do this.

You can be damn sure I jerked off in the shower this morning to the image saved in my head.

What has me going to the text thread is not to look at her pictures but to reread the messages. Short little conversations, out-of-the-blue funny statements and memes. The last one came in as I was getting ready for the game tonight. It was short and sweet and dirty.

Good luck. Help my brother get a shutout and I'll give you a blow job that will have your eyes crossing.

I grin as I reread that, especially since Drake got the shutout. Of course, the woman already has my eyes crossing every time she touches me, so it's not like she's promising something new. It's more of a good reminder to both of us that while we've leaned into the friendship a bit, it's still all about the benefits with us.

I didn't respond to that message because I didn't have time. We were getting ready to head onto the ice for warm-ups before the game and I'd only done a quick check of my phone.

Admittedly, I was checking to see if she'd texted, but I truly didn't have time to respond.

I do so now, knowing she won't see it until morning. She's in deep slumber on the East Coast. *As requested, I helped your brother get a shutout. Can't wait to collect.*

Grinning, I scroll backward through the string, unable to stop smiling at some of the silly conversations we've had.

Kiera: *I was wondering, and since you're a friend, I'm sure you can fill me in... what's up with dudes and the chin lift when you see each other?*

Me: *Aah... the chin lift. That's some deep stuff you're asking about.*

Kiera: *I thought it was just a greeting.*

Me: *I'm not sure your female brain can comprehend the way our male brains work. We are all about simplifying things and we can carry on entire conversations between chin lifts and head nods.*

Kiera: *Wow... I never realized the male species was so brilliant.*

Me: *Honestly... we're not. You know how you'll be talking to us, then you ask a question, and we respond with "Huh?"*

Kiera: *Yeah. You weren't really listening.*

Me: *Wrong. We heard you, we're just buffering so that the answer we ultimately give is what you want to hear.*

Kiera: *I can't with you.*

She added a string of laughing emojis and I'd rather not dwell on how much it pleased me that I made her laugh, even if only digitally.

All of it... the conversations via text, the ones at her house the two nights I spent with her this weekend... all silly, light and without much depth.

In other words, it was safe.

And yet, I find myself missing her. Mostly, I'm missing the sex, which has easily become an addiction. Kiera is wild and uninhibited. There's not a shy bone in her body and nothing she's not willing to try. She's every man's fantasy.

But I also miss being with her because she's comfortable to be around. No strong expectations, she's funny as hell and I feel good in my soul when I'm near her. If I were so inclined to settle down, Kiera would be the type I'd consider. Maybe.

Christ, it's going to be a long week. After we play the Blizzard, we'll head to Edmonton and then Calgary. We don't get back to Pittsburgh for another week, and I know the first thing I want to do is see Kiera.

We had not made plans so I shoot her another text.

Got plans on the 19th?

I send it off and don't offer any more. I hope she responds that she's free—then I'll make the move to ask her to do something, which will most likely be me asking if I can come over to her place to fuck her. Maybe dinner before if she wants.

My fingers itch to say more, but I can't. It means she would be more than what was agreed and we have to watch that boundary. I know Kiera would agree with me on that.

It doesn't stop me from looking at my calendar the rest of that week, though, plotting through some other potential times we could hook up.

And there you go. Camden's birthday.

"We're still good to celebrate your birthday next Friday?" I ask him.

He doesn't answer and my head turns his way. I see he's got his earbuds in as he scrolls through his text messages.

Pressing pause on my music, I nudge Camden's shoulder.

"What?" he asks, pulling out one bud.

"I asked if you're still cool with us doing a little birthday celebration for you next week?"

Camden scowls. "What were you thinking?"

"Nothing fancy. Maybe we all go hang out at Stevie's bar. We've got almost a week off so why not party one night, and your birthday is a great excuse."

One of the best things about coming off this very long and exhausting road trip is that we've miraculously got several days off where we'll be able to rest and recuperate, although there will be some practices and team meetings I'm sure.

"As long as there aren't balloons and cake, and I'll kill anyone who sings me happy birthday."

I frown at him. "Are you serious?"

"As a heart attack," he replies. "I don't like that shit, but I'm down to hang out. Who all would be there?"

"Whoever you want, dude. It's your birthday."

"Just invite the team and SOs."

Significant others. Is that what Kiera is to me? Because I'm damn well inviting her. Of course, I'll invite her brother, too, so that might mean I have to keep my distance but at least I can look at her. As long as she comes home with me after, I'll be satisfied.

"Coaches?" I ask Camden. That's always a weird line when we party.

"Yeah, man. That's cool."

I punch him lightly on the shoulder. "Consider me your party coordinator. Any other requests other than no balloons, no cake and no singing?"

"Yeah, no puck bunnies."

My eyes flare because this is a prime opportunity to get laid. I mean, I don't need willing women there as I have Kiera and she's more than enough for me, but it's his birthday. I know plenty of women who would like to blow on his candle. "You're kidding, right?"

He shakes his head. "The older I get, the less tolerance I have for that. Plus… they make a fuss and I don't feel like having them hanging all over me."

I have to suppress a laugh. "You are indeed, sincerely… a weird dude. I know no single hockey players who don't love that."

"Now you're just stereotyping," he replies and then puts his earbud back in, effectively ending the conversation.

It's indeed stereotyping, but there is some truth to it. For all professional athletes, I suppose. Fame and money attract beautiful women and it's not hard to get laid.

I think about Kiera. It wasn't hard with her either, but the difference is she doesn't care about my fame or wealth. She knows the hockey world because her brother is in it.

She just wants to feel good, same as me.

In so many ways, she is the perfect woman.

CHAPTER 12

Kiera

D RAKE IS A cautious driver. His massive hands, calloused by countless hockey games, grip the steering wheel. Being the dad of three boys makes him treat those in his vehicle as precious cargo. I tease him often that he drives like a little old lady and then enjoy the way he glares at me.

Despite his colossal build and gruff exterior, there's a softness in his voice as he asks, "How were things while I was gone? You okay?"

Drake got back into Pittsburgh late last night from the long road trip that had the Titans playing games in San Francisco, Anchorage, Calgary and Edmonton. Before he left, he asked me to keep today free as he wanted me to help him shop for an engagement ring for Brienne and I've been so excited to do my sisterly duty.

I laugh, tucking a loose strand of hair behind my ear. "Contrary to popular belief, I can survive without my big brother."

"I know you can." He spares me a glance, then it's

eyes back on the road. "It's just… since I've moved in with Brienne, I worry about you being all alone. Are you sure you don't want to move in with us? God knows Brienne's house is large enough to accommodate and you wouldn't get lonely."

"I'm not lonely," I assure him, and then internally grimace as I think about how much my lifestyle would be cramped by moving in with them. There would be an upside in being able to see my nephews more often, but the downside would be no naked nights with Bain and no way I'm going to give that up.

Another quick look before he prods. "You seeing anyone these days?"

I stifle a laugh, opting instead for a noncommittal shrug. "No. Not seeing anyone." I hope that sounds casual to him and not an out-and-out lie.

I most certainly can't tell him I've been letting Bain fuck me silly when we can arrange the time together. While I, in no way, subscribe to Drake's belief that he can control my life or that he can tell his teammates they can't date me, it's best to keep this secret. Besides, what Bain and I have won't last forever. The shine will wear off and we'll go our separate ways.

I rub at my breastbone because the thought of that doesn't sit well with me.

Unaware of my internal musing, Drake looks over at me and it's long enough to see his expression is serious and thoughtful. It means he's been cooking something up. "You remember Grady from Brienne's executive office, right? Tall guy, brown hair, always dressed in a designer suit and maybe a little too much hair gel?"

I cast him a suspicious glance. "Yeah, I remember him. Why?"

Drake flashes me a smile. "He's asked Brienne if you're dating anyone and we were thinking we could set you two up on a date."

"No thank you," I reply, holding out my hand as if to ward off any future discussion.

Drake isn't quelled. "He's a decent guy. Ivy League educated, successful. You know, not a puckhead like the rest of us."

I snort and roll my eyes at the same time. "And you think I should go on a date with him? Because he's not a puckhead?"

"Because he's a successful guy. Give it a shot," Drake insists as he pulls into the parking garage. He winds up to the third level and his eyes narrow on an empty spot ahead. Drake puts on his left signal and starts to turn, but a sleek BMW cuts him off, whipping into the spot Drake had wanted. The driver hops out—late twenties, wearing a crisp suit and aviator sunglasses, smirking arrogantly at us. The very picture of the man Drake was trying to sell me on moments ago.

The irony is not lost on me.

Drake's face hardens, a low growl rumbling in his chest as he rolls down the window. "Hey, asshole! You saw I was turning into that space."

The suited man doesn't even pause, lifting his hand high and flipping Drake the bird.

"Oh, fuck no, he didn't," Drake snarls as he slams the Tahoe into park. He jumps out and takes off after the guy. I follow at a more sedate pace as I know Drake won't hurt him, but he's going to scare the fuck out of him.

The man hears Drake's thundering footsteps, glances over his shoulder and only sees a hulking figure bearing down on him. I see the panic on his face as he makes a run for the stairwell door, but just as he tries to jerk it open, Drake is there and slams his hand against it so it stays shut.

The man no longer looks so full of himself as he takes in Drake's large frame, the tattoos, the scowl etched on his bearded face. I lean against the passenger door, watching with interest.

"Wait a minute," the man stammers as his eyes go round as saucers. "You're Drake McGinn."

"Or as some like to call me, the man who's going to stomp your ass if you don't move your car from that spot."

I snicker.

"Oh, shit, man, I didn't realize... here, let me move

my car." The dude babbles, practically tripping over his words in his haste to get to his BMW. "I wasn't thinking. I was in a hurry and there were more spots just on the next level—"

"Less talk," Drake growls. "More moving of your car."

It takes only a minute for the BMW to back out and jet out of sight and for Drake to pull in. "You're so badass," I say, a true compliment to my brother.

Drake chuckles. "What a way to start the day, huh?"

"I can't wait to tell Brienne about this," I say, wiping a tear from under my eye because I can't stop laughing.

"Don't you fucking dare," he says as he turns off the ignition.

"Afraid of her?" I taunt.

"No," he growls, nabbing his keys and phone from the center console. "It's just... if you tell her, then she'll ask what we were doing here and I don't want to mess up the surprise."

"Uh-huh," I drawl, knowing that he is indeed worried about how she'd react to him scaring the piss out of that guy.

We exit the parking garage and enter the boutique jewelry shop that I found after some careful research of local jewelers. They're selective and I was able to make a personal appointment so Drake could look in privacy.

Entering through the glass door, we're met by a

beautiful woman with sparkling hazel eyes and an elegant silver chignon. I couldn't even begin to guess her age because although her hair is silver and she's dressed conservatively, her skin is as flawless as porcelain.

"Welcome, Mr. McGinn," she says, offering her hand. "My name is Bella Tisdale." She then turns my way. "And you must be Kiera. It was lovely talking to you the other day while setting up the appointment."

Bella leads us down a hall and into a private room that has a round table made of cherry wood with cream-colored leather chairs. On the table sit several trays of diamond rings nestled in royal blue velvet and in the corner, an armed security guard.

After we enter and sit down, the guard walks out and closes the door.

"This is our premium collection." Bella reaches out, turns the trays and arranges them to face Drake. He studies them as she educates us. "Diamonds are graded on cut, clarity and color. The better the cut, the better the sparkle. The clarity refers to the absence or inclusion of blemishes, and the higher quality diamonds are colorless. You'll note that the rings aren't all necessarily large in carat weight as sometimes the cut, clarity and color can provide all the brilliance you need."

It's silent as Drake peruses the various rings and I find it endearing how serious he's taking this. It's truly a testament to how much he loves Brienne, and I'm not talking about his willingness to buy an expensive ring, but that he wants to learn and make a personal choice that speaks to his heart, knowing it will speak to Brienne's.

Drake points to a ring and Bella plucks it from the cushioned fold. There's a delicate string on the bottom with a tag. She reads it and then hands the ring to Drake. "This is an exquisite choice... a round cut, three-carat diamond ensconced in a halo setting. It's GIA graded D, which is the apex of the scale, and utterly flawless. The price is $98,000."

I make a slight choking noise but Drake doesn't even flinch. He studies the ring and then turns to me. "Give me your hand."

He slips the ring on and then admires it thoughtfully. I'm dazzled by the brilliance and my heart even flutters a little, wondering exactly how Brienne will feel. The romanticism of it all hits me, which is very weird. Romance got obliterated from my vocabulary when I broke up with Peter four years ago. I erected a wall so it never entered my mind again after he left a dead cat on my porch.

"What do you think?" he asks.

My gaze goes from the ring to the tray and then back to the ring. "It's beautiful."

"It's too old-fashioned," Drake muses, nodding to the tray. "Let's try one of those square-shaped diamonds."

Bella's eyes shine with amusement, grabbing two for him to consider. "This one is a princess cut and this one is an Asscher cut."

We spend an hour trying on rings, Drake carefully studying each one on my hand. In the end, he ends up choosing a four-carat, radiant-cut diamond that's dazzling to behold. It's set on the most delicate platinum band with small diamonds crusting it and of course, nothing but the best clarity and color grading. It ended up costing him $132,000 and I was breathless just from the adventure of it.

The jeweler is going to hold the ring until Drake is ready to propose, more for safety reasons, given the cost.

"You have time to grab an early lunch?" Drake asks as we walk back to the parking garage.

I glance at my watch. I took the morning off from work, which isn't a problem. Given my position is remote, I can set my own hours as long as my work gets done. Not only that, I work in the evenings a lot, having a much easier time reaching my patients via phone.

However, I do have plans this evening. Bain and I have kept in contact via text this past week he's been gone. It's been easy conversations and hot sexting. We're able to transition back and forth. No actual phone calls, though. Pretty sure that would proclaim a deepening of the relationship that both of us have sworn not to go near.

At least I think that's how we both feel.

I'm not sure because we haven't talked about it, nor do I think we will.

All I know for sure is that Bain's last text to me was right before Drake picked me up for ring shopping. It was an order, really, but I didn't mind in this instance.

I'll be there at six. I expect you to be naked and ready.

Just thinking of what the evening will hold has my belly fluttering. Equally as exciting as the pleasure I know both of us will dole out tonight, I'm curious to see if our playful conversations continue outside the text realm. While Bain slept over for two nights before this most recent road trip, I have no expectations that will occur tonight. It's just as possible he'll roll straight out of bed after we're done and head home. I'm perfectly fine with either.

"Yeah… I can do lunch," I say to my brother, mentally calculating the work I need to accomplish before Bain comes over. Anything I don't finish this afternoon I can surely do tonight after he's gone.

Or, if there's time, I could cook dinner. That's a friendly thing to do. Doesn't mean anything other than we both need sustenance, right? Of course, that means I really need to get my work done before Bain comes over.

"A short lunch," I amend. "I've got a ton of stuff to do today."

Drake loops his arm around my shoulders and drags

me into him as we traverse the sidewalk. He squeezes hard and presses his lips to my head. "Thanks, sis. For all your help. I love you."

He releases me and I tip my head back. "I love you too."

The smile on his face radiates pure joy and happiness. His future is nothing but sparkling promise and adventure and I'm here to watch it all go down.

CHAPTER 13

Bain

CHRIST... KIERA IS hot as fuck tonight and I'm having a hard time keeping my eyes off her. They say absence makes the heart grow fonder, but I'm sure that logic applies to lust as well. By the end of our seven-day road trip, I was obsessing about Kiera, or more accurately, obsessing about fucking her.

I got back three days ago and I've been with her every night. Our return to Pittsburgh started an almost unheard-of seven-day break in the schedule. While we have some practices to stay sharp, it's an amazing amount of time off for the team. Some of the guys asked me to go out and party with them last night, but I declined. Merely told them I had other plans, which included rolling around with Kiera in her bed until we fell into an exhausted sleep.

Admittedly, it doesn't feel weird at all to stay the night with her. I know it's something more than what we agreed to with our no-strings-attached sex bargain, but this whole friends thing just makes it so easy to hang with her.

Tonight is Camden's birthday party and I have to pretend Kiera is nothing more than a casual friend. I have to treat her like she's Drake's little sister, and while he's not here tonight, it's common knowledge among all the players that she's off-limits. I can't even imagine the level of concern that would result if any of these dudes knew I was banging her. They'd be afraid that Drake would kill me and yeah... he'd be pissed.

But Kiera's her own woman and can do what she wants.

Just like I'm my own man and can do what I want.

The irony isn't lost on me that we're both here at Stevie's bar and can't acknowledge the truth to anyone.

Some say the secret makes it hotter, but right now it just sucks that I can't touch her. Hell, I can barely talk to her without calling attention to myself.

Earlier tonight, I was playing pool and she was talking to Danica. I don't know what Kiera was saying to her, but I knew she was talking about me. I could tell by the appraising look in her eyes when she looked at me and the way their heads were bent close. Her luscious mouth curved appreciatively as I lined up a shot.

A few minutes later, as I moved around the pool table, I had the good fortune of catching Kiera alone. I was able to sneak in a very short conversation.

"What were you and Danica talking about?" I'd

asked as we stood side by side, watching the pool table action and pretending to talk casually.

"Your arms," she said and that caught me by surprise. I turned to look at her. She boldly ran her gaze over my torso. "That black shirt you're wearing fits you like a glove and your arms are pure porn."

I nearly choked—a ruthless combination of laughter and lust. God, I wanted to take her into the storeroom and fuck her in the dark shadows. Or, just as appealing, I wanted to sit with her at the bar and have a beer. Talk about life and make each other laugh.

I'm so fucked when it comes to her.

As the night wears on, I have a choice to make. Kiera is having a blast, which doesn't hurt my feelings. It's a pleasure to watch her be herself with the women of this team. She's partying it up with Stevie and Tillie. At one point, they're doing shots of who knows what and when "Bad Reputation" by Joan Jett is cranked, they all three dance around the bar singing along with the rock queen.

The choice is I decide to stop drinking as I'm going to be the one driving Kiera home. We had planned to meet at her house tonight after the party, but since she's on her way to a good drunk, I'm feeling compelled to stay sober to watch out for her and make sure she gets out of here safely.

Standing at the end of the bar where I can watch Kiera unobtrusively, I see Camden coming back inside the bar. He'd walked Danica out to her car and his face is red from the cold. He moves straight to me and I have a fresh beer waiting for him. He's the birthday boy, after all.

"Thanks, man," he says before taking a sip.

"Danica get out of here okay?"

"Yeah."

Something in his tone has me wondering. It's almost a hint of guilt, but maybe I'm wrong. I lift my eyebrows but Camden shakes his head adamantly. "There's nothing there, dude. I walked her to her car to make sure she was safe."

"Okay," I drawl.

"We're just friends," he says, and I think he's protesting too much.

I keep my tone neutral. "I can see that."

"Then get that look off your face," he growls.

My expression widens with innocence. "What look?"

Camden speaks through gritted teeth, a sure sign I'm way under his skin. "As if you know a secret about me. There's nothing to know."

There's something haunting within his denial and I decide to quit teasing him. Instead, I give him the best piece of advice I can render. "There's no bro code in effect."

Camden frowns at me. "What?"

"Mitch is dead," I say, and he actually flinches. I

ignore it. "She's single. You're single. There is no bro code in effect."

I can see that does not affect Camden. He's not buying that there's a clear path to Danica if he's interested. He's not ready to make that move.

"Whatever," he mutters.

"I'm just saying, if you had an interest—"

"I don't."

If there is something between them, I don't want Camden denying it so hard that he's forced to adhere to a stance. So I poke a little. "Sure looks like you did to me. In fact, I think it's evident you both have a connection. Anyone in this bar could see it tonight."

Camden's eyes dart around us as if he's afraid someone heard me say that, but no one's near us and the music is loud. When his gaze comes back to me, he says, "We're just friends."

He doesn't give me a chance to respond but instead walks away.

Whatever, dude. I can see there's clearly something there.

My eyes seek out Kiera and I see she's playing pool with a big, burly biker who's got his eyes pinned to her ass. Blood boiling and hand clenched way too tightly around my bottle of water, I'm forced to sit back and not do a damn thing about it. That would give us away.

Just like Camden, I can't admit to feeling a fucking

thing for a woman.

♦

I LIKE DRUNK Kiera. She's silly in a way that's not annoying, and I made the very gallant and public offer to "drive Drake's sister home safely" to those stragglers who were left as Camden's birthday party wound down. It was basically Boone, Kirill and Kace, three of the more established playboys, although, without a doubt, Kirill is the biggest man whore among them. He was sitting in a dark corner making out with a woman when I led Kiera from the bar.

She waved and blew kisses to those left behind. When we were on the sidewalk, she looped her arm through mine and laid her head on my shoulder, which I found sweet. Not sloppy drunk, but she's super buzzed.

Sighing, she walks a little unsteadily as I lead her down the block to my car. "When we get to my place," she drawls thickly, "I'm going to do the dirtiest things imaginable to you."

Okay, sweet and completely sexy. I like this combination, too, and that region south of my belt likes her promise.

"Or," she muses, coming to a stop and turning toward me. She tugs playfully on the waistband of my jeans. "We can slip down one of these side alleys and I can give you a quick blow job."

She tips her head back and grins at me. Doesn't matter if she's serious about her offer, that's never going to happen. Dipping my head, I kiss her on the nose. "You're cute, but not about to have you bruise your knees just for me. I can wait for us to get to your place."

Although truthfully, not sure anything's going to happen tonight. My bet is on her being passed out before we get there, and I'll probably just tuck her into bed.

"At least kiss me," she says breathlessly. Her head falls back even more and she looks up into the sky. "It's a beautiful night under the stars, I'm feeling fucking fantastic and I want the hottest guy I've ever known—who gives the best orgasms in the world—to kiss me like I'm the only woman he's ever wanted."

So fucking adorable, but her words move me. I think she's laying feelings out there that otherwise would be stuffed down deep without alcohol.

What's a guy to do? I dip my head and kiss her. My arms tighten around her lower back and her hands slide up so that her fingers can play in my hair.

A coughing sound jolts me back, although Kiera is a little slower to respond. I turn toward the bar and see Boone standing outside the door. He just saw that. By the look on his face, he heard what Kiera said too.

"Um… Kiera forgot her purse," he says, holding out a black clutch with a silver chain strap.

"Oops." Kiera giggles, not in the least bit worried we

got caught.

I'm not worried either. Boone's a good guy and I doubt he'd say anything to Drake. I release my hold on Kiera and give her a command with a pointed look. "Stay right here."

She gives me a snappy salute. "Yes, sir."

Rolling my eyes, I walk to Boone and he hands me the purse. He nods at Kiera. "I hope you know what you're doing."

"It's good," I assure him. "Just casual. Keeping it on the down low because neither of us wants to hear it from Drake. It's just some fun between two consenting adults."

The corner of Boone's mouth twitches as he reaches backward for the door handle. "I don't know... hottest guy and best orgasms. I'd say she's pretty smitten."

I grin as I walk backward, holding my arms out as if to showcase me as the entire package. "Who wouldn't be?"

Boone shakes his head with a smirk and slips back into the bar.

I pivot to face Kiera and she's watching me with a look on her face like she wants to eat me up. If she's still awake by the time we get to her place, I'm going to let her try.

CHAPTER 14

Kiera

THE AX LODGED in my forehead finally wakes me up. I open one eye gingerly and wince that the light increases the pain tenfold. Listening carefully, I can't detect any noise so I have no clue if Bain is here.

At least I'm not so hungover as to forget last night. Granted, some bits and pieces are fuzzy, but I know for sure that I got drunk, Bain brought me home and pretty sure I mauled him sexually.

There's a flutter in my belly as I think about what we did and… a frown comes to my face.

A grimace, actually.

That's not my body reacting to memories of sex but rebelling from copious amounts of alcohol. I burst out of the bed, get tangled up in the sheets and almost break my neck, if not for a pair of strong arms that catch me.

"Whoa there, speedy." Bain's voice is low, soothing. "Got a garbage can right here."

He turns me to the left, points to my tall kitchen container with a fresh bag in it and I manage to bend over just before my heaving starts. Nothing comes out but the lining of my stomach, which makes me gag from how gross it is. Bain's hand rubs my lower back in gentle circles.

I stand up with a groan and find a cold wet cloth at my forehead. Bain takes my arm and leads me back to the edge of the bed where I slump onto the edge. "I'm dying," I say, my voice dry and croaking.

"You're not dying," Bain says, and I take a moment to really look at him. He's wearing the same outfit he had on last night, but I know at one point, we were both naked. "You were pretty sick around four a.m. Pretty sure you filled up a dozen toilet bowls."

I wrinkle my nose, grateful I don't have that exact memory, but then my hand reaches up to feel my hair tied in a knot. I do remember something... Bain holding my hair out of the way so I could throw up. At some point, it got tied out of the way.

"Think you can handle some ginger ale? Crackers?"

I shake my head. "No. Nothing just yet."

Bain takes my chin and levels an expression that looks slightly the way my mom looked at me when she was being extra mom-like. "You need hydration. Water or ginger ale. Take your pick."

"I don't have any ginger ale," I mutter, pressing the cold cloth to my head.

"You do," he says with a wink. "I ran out and got

some a bit ago along with some saltine crackers. Or I can make you toast."

I fall back onto the bed with a moan of pain and nausea. I'm not sure I can handle the combination of feeling this wretched from a hangover and being utterly charmed by Bain's thoughtfulness.

Then something strikes me. I lift my head, look down my body and realize I'm naked.

Bain notices me noticing. "I tried to get you into some pajamas or a T-shirt but you kept taking it off. Insisting you were going to fuck me all night."

My eyes widen. "I did?"

He smirks, nodding. "You were cute. It's an offer I'd like to take you up on sometime when you're feeling better."

I push up to my elbows so I don't strain my neck to look up at him, which I know causes my breasts to jut out. But I'm feeling decidedly unsexy. "I do remember we had sex last night."

"That we did," he says as he bends over me on the bed. His palms go to the mattress and his face hovers before me. Not to kiss me because yuck… I have vomit breath, but to look me in the eye. "I'll make you some toast and bring you two Tylenol. You need to eat and drink. But then I have to get going. I've got some things to do today."

"Okay," I say wanly and flop back down.

"No," Bain says, taking my arm and pulling me up. "Get back in bed under the covers."

I do as he instructs, hating myself for loving his care. I've always been the caretaker and no one has ever done this for me before.

Bain pulls the covers up to my chest and starts to turn away, but I latch onto his wrist. "Was I a horrible turnoff last night when I got sick?"

"So disgusting," he says with an exaggerated shudder. "Not sure I can fuck you again."

"At least not until I brush my teeth," I quip.

He laughs. "That's for damn sure. I'll be right back."

While Bain is in the kitchen rustling up hydration and food, both of which make my stomach pitch, I think back on last night. I remember leaving the bar with him, giving him a teasing hand job on the way to my house—just some rubbing through his denim—and then… yeah, I pretty much attacked him.

I remember the room spinning when I stumbled through the front door. I was laughing, completely intoxicated, and turned to pull Bain into me. He came willingly, so freaking hot and sexy. I kissed him and we somehow fell to the couch.

I straddled him as his hands came to my hips. My smile was dopey. I mean, I could feel the lopsided stretch of it and yet I felt the joy in my bones. "I'm glad we're friends, Bain."

"I'm glad too." His eyes danced with amusement over my antics.

"I'm even gladder—is that a word—that we're fucking."

I remember Bain laughed so hard and with a hand on the back of my head he pulled me into him for a quick kiss before saying, "Come on… let's get you to bed."

"No thank you." I pulled my shirt over my head, undid my bra and tossed it over the top of the lamp. "We'll have sex right here."

"We're not having sex." Bain laughed. "You're too drunk."

"Not," I insisted. "I know exactly what I'm doing and we've done this many times already."

Bain was reluctant, I remember that much. But after stripping naked and falling to my knees before him, he merely looked dubious.

By the time I had his cock out and in my mouth, he was on board.

Everything else was a whirlwind. Fragments of the evening spin before me, each one flashing with a brightness that imprints in my memory. I started playing with myself while I sucked Bain down deep. It drove him crazy and he pulled me off. There was a violent kiss where our teeth knocked together, then he pulled me up his body. He put me right back over his lap, legs straddled wide and I sunk down on him. It felt so good as I started to move on him, controlling the pace and watching his pleasure take hold. His mouth found my nipples as I bounced up and down on his lap. Bain grunted in pleasure and my entire body felt like it was going up in flames.

I came first, the orgasm crashing into me from out of nowhere. It was so forceful I could do nothing but shudder my way through it. Bain wasn't there yet so he flipped me over on the couch, raised my legs and in a handful of hard thrusts, he was jerking his release inside me.

What I remember the most... so very clearly, was Bain burying his face in my neck as we were still connected. "I'll never get enough of you."

I didn't give the words back, but I felt them.

And after that, things got a little fuzzy. I assume there was vomiting, hair holding and general nastiness that Bain truly didn't have to stay for. I have no clue why he did, but I'm grateful.

"Just what the doctor ordered," he says as he walks into the room with a plate in one hand and an insulated tumbler with a straw that I'm assuming contains ginger ale. He places both on the table and left in his hand is a bottle of Tylenol. He shakes out two and insists I take them with a few sips of the soda.

It tastes wonderful and at the same time, my stomach rolls. I hope it stays down.

Bain sits on the side of the bed, leans over and rests his hand on my hip. "Can I come back tonight?"

Reaching out, I give a playful tug on his shirt. "If you want… and you are under no obligation, you're welcome here every night that you're on your break."

I put an end date so he doesn't read anything more into it, even though I'm happy to have him here every night.

Bain's smile is huge. "All right… I'll be back tonight. I'll call first to see if you can stomach some food. Anything else you need before I leave?"

I bat my eyelashes at him. "A big, deep, wet kiss?"

Bain grimaces. "No way, vomit breath." But he leans forward and presses his lips to my forehead and for some reason, that's even better.

CHAPTER 15

Bain

THERE'S A ROAR as Boone and I walk into Mario's. We just defeated the Cold Fury 4–2 and the Titans fans can taste a playoff run. We're the Cinderella team, the underdogs gone wild.

It's become a regular occurrence for many of us to come here for beers to celebrate a win and mostly it's a laid-back atmosphere. The fans have learned to let us have some time to ourselves as teammates, but they also know we'll eventually indulge in photo ops and autographs. We had a spot just like this back in Phoenix when I played for the Vengeance—the Sneaky Saguaro. I loved that the players meshed with the fans and I was glad to see something similar here.

The vibe is different tonight. The energy is palpable and it's standing room only. Defeating one of the hottest teams in the league has created an adrenaline surge in the fans, the players... hell, the city itself.

What's weird is that I didn't want to come out tonight. Normally, this would be my jam. I'd hang out with my new teammates, we'd bond over beers and relive the best plays of the night. We'd boast and our stories would get more exaggerated. We'd get drunk and then find hot women to fuck.

There's a part of me that mourns the loss of my desire to do that, but a bigger part of me is irritated I can't just go home to Kiera.

And it irritates me even further that I used the words "home" and "Kiera" in the same thought.

Boone winds his way through the crowd and I follow. We receive back slaps and flirty stares from women. The owners rope off a section in the back for us to hang out in and a good chunk of the team is there already.

Pushing a couple of high tops together, I stand with Boone, Camden, Hendrix, Stevie, Coen and Stone. Harlow's missing as she's in the middle of a big trial, and I can see how proud Stone is when he talks about her. Tillie's back in Coudersport packing up her house as she's making the very big and permanent move here to Pittsburgh.

The one person not here who I wish was is Kiera. I invited her to come to the game and Mario's after. It was a casual request and I made it sound like I was cool if she did and cool if she didn't. It was unspoken, but we'd have to act normal around each other, and by normal, we couldn't be tearing off each other's clothes, talking dirty or eye-fucking each other.

Not that that's all we do.

On the contrary, there's as much friendship as there are benefits lately. It's become clear over this past week, given how much time we've spent together, that there's more to us. Some would say feelings are getting involved.

Maybe.

Maybe it's just that we can't screw and sleep all those hours we're together so we do other things. We talk, watch movies, cook dinner and play board games. Kiera's fun to be around so it's not been a hardship.

I like being around her, so yeah... I wish she were here right now. I have no clue if she'll show. She was supposed to watch Drake's kids. While Brienne often stays home with them when the team travels, as team owner, she's expected to be at the home games. Kiera did say that Drake and Brienne are always happy to hire a babysitter so she can go to some games, but doesn't take them up on it. This I've come to learn over the past week while staying with her. She definitely has a crisis of conscience when it comes to wanting to help her brother versus having some downtime. On top of that, she loves her nephews like they're her own, so she truly loves the time with them. She has a lot to balance and then add in that I'm asking her to come to Mario's after the game, even though we'd have to ignore each other.

It's a bit fucked up.

"You got the invitation for our housewarming,

right?" Coen asks Camden as they stand next to each other at the high top and I focus on their conversation rather than thinking about Kiera. I refuse to text and ask her.

Camden nods. "Yeah, man."

"Well, you haven't RSVP'd yet, asshole. You know we have to know how many are coming so we can prepare."

"All right, dude. Chill out. This is my confirmation… I'm coming. When is it?"

"Next Saturday." Coen turns his gaze to me. "And you're coming?"

"Wouldn't miss it for the world." I don't quite remember getting the invitation, but I do vaguely remember talk of a housewarming party. I make a mental note to look for it and also to get a gift. Maybe Kiera can help me pick something out and I wonder if she's going.

Camden has his phone in hand and says, "I'll be right back."

I give him a chin lift and watch as he meanders through the crowd toward the exit. I almost turn away, but then I see *her* walking in.

Kiera.

The crowd parts, almost as if Moses were lending a hand, and my eyes slide over her. She's wearing a jersey and while I can't see the back, there's no doubt it's her brother's name and number on it. Her hair is in a long, loose braid that hangs over one shoulder with chunky pieces of blond falling around her face.

She's been to Mario's before and she heads right our way, knowing that her hockey family is within the velvet ropes. I'm the only one who sees her coming and her eyes lock right on me.

I can't read a damn thing within them, her expression schooled to keep her feelings a secret.

"... told me that it would be fine and to stop worrying."

"Huh? What?" I turn to Coen who had been speaking to me, breaking the eye contact with Kiera.

"I said Tillie told me to quit worrying about the housewarming party, but I don't want her doing all the work, you know? I know her schedule isn't as hectic as mine…"

I tune Coen out, although I nod every once in a while as I pretend to let my gaze roam around the bar. But I'm really checking on Kiera, getting a little jolt of pleasure every time my eyes pass over her. She moved to Stevie and they have their heads bent in close talking, no doubt about their drunken exploits at Camden's birthday party last week.

Draining the last of my beer, I clap Coen on the shoulder. "I'm going to get another beer. Want one?"

"I'm good," he says. I ask the same question around the table. I look directly at Kiera. "Want anything?"

I'm hoping she reads into the message, which says *come up to the bar with me to order so we can have a few minutes alone*. Instead, she smiles. "Yeah… whatever looks good on tap. Thanks."

Then she turns her attention back to Stevie.

Jesus, fucking kill me now.

I take back all those wishes I threw out a few hours ago asking that Kiera show up at Mario's, now wishing she'd never come. We've both fallen into this polite sort of distant acquaintance with each other, both too fearful we might give ourselves away. It's painful, to say the least.

Eventually, I drift from the table. I can't concentrate on what others are saying because all I can think about is getting Kiera out of here so I can have her to myself. Boone follows me and we circulate around the bar, posing with fans for pictures and signing autographs. For a good fifteen or twenty minutes, I actually get immersed in talking to fans and it's a welcome respite from my obsessive thoughts.

A group congregates around us, a crowd of twenty-somethings, all beautifully dressed as if they're going out clubbing. Both men and women, all wanting to pose for pictures. The men ask questions about hockey and the women flirt.

Some of them in a very handsy way. I'm talking to a curvy brunette who keeps putting her hand on my chest to punctuate her innuendo. I'm polite and don't say anything, knowing that the conversation will soon be over. She asks for a picture. I agree. She moves in so close she's plastered to my side and wraps both her arms around me. My arm goes to her shoulder in a friendly way, but as her friend is taking our picture, her hand drops super low, almost below my belt.

And wouldn't you know it my eyes drift across to the bar area where I see Kiera standing talking to some people and she's staring right at me.

Rather... glaring.

And she looks... hurt?

According to the terms of our agreement, this shouldn't mean anything to Kiera and I should feel no guilt. As long as I'm not fucking the brunette, I'm doing nothing wrong. But fuck if the look Kiera gives me doesn't make me feel like I'm a shit. I do my best to extricate myself from not only the woman but her group of friends.

"Let's get a beer," I say to Boone, but he looks content with his own handsy female.

Fuck it... I'm about ready to leave, anyway.

I search for Kiera, wanting to give her a signal that it's time to go. At first I don't see her, but then the crowd shifts and there she is. Still at the bar, but the reason I didn't see her is that a large guy is talking to her and he's angled in such a way that he blocks most of her from me. He's got his elbow on the bar and whatever he's saying makes Kiera laugh.

He laughs, too, and then reaches out to tug on her braid playfully.

She bats at his chest, grinning and shaking her head, and I'd bet a million dollars he propositioned her but in a charming way. She clearly turned him down, but she makes no move to leave. Instead, she continues to talk with him, and again, they make each other laugh.

My blood pressure spikes so fast, I feel like the top of my head is about to explode. Rage darkens my vision and I move their way. I don't weave delicately through the crowd, instead knocking into people as I barrel toward Kiera.

Just as I reach them, the fucker tugs on her braid again and my hand shoots out to lock onto his wrist. The guy's so surprised, he lets it go and I give him a hard push back.

"Bain," Kiera exclaims, her hand coming to rest on my forearm. I spare her a glance—take in her mortified expression—and then look back to the dude. He's over his shock and now bowing up like he wants to fight. "Keep your motherfucking hands to yourself or I'm going to break them."

"Fuck off, asshole," the guy says, stepping into me. "The lady and I were just talking."

I step right into him and we're toe to toe. Kiera tries

to pull me away, but I ignore her futile tugging on my arm. "I don't give a fuck if you were reading her poetry, you keep your hands to yourself."

"Whoa." Boone is there, stepping in between us. "What's going on here?"

The man points past Boone to me. "Your asshole teammate is trying to pick a fight."

Hmm… so he does know who I am. I have to give him credit because he's got to know I can kick his ass, despite him being a decent-size guy.

Boone turns to me, sparing a quick look at Kiera standing there with her hand on my arm. "What are you doing, man?"

Well, I'm apparently having a full-blown attack of jealousy but that would be stupid, wouldn't it?

There's no hesitation when I play it off as Titans' camaraderie. "He has his hands on Drake's sister. He's not here, so I'm stepping in."

The look on Boone's face tells me he doesn't buy a single bit of my bullshit. He was the one, after all, who caught us outside Stevie's bar last week.

I glance down at Kiera, knowing she'll at least go along with the lie, but she's gone. I glance around wildly and see her heading out the door.

"Fuck," I growl and start after her. But I stop and turn back to Boone. "Not a word about this to anyone."

I get a chin lift in response. The message is, *I got your*

back, brother.

I chase Kiera out of the bar and find her walking through the parking lot. I jog to catch up, taking her arm to stop her. She jerks away and glares at me.

"Why are you pissed at me?" I ask.

"Because you sure looked like you were having a good time with that brunette in there. You didn't even try to stop her from touching you."

That burns me up. "Oh yeah? Well, you were letting that guy touch you." I reach out, pull a few times on her braid and then try to mimic what I can imagine the dude said in a really low voice. "Hey, baby... you're so hot. How about coming home with me tonight and I'll make you scream my name?"

Kiera stares at me, her mouth slightly parted. I brace for her counterattack, but then she snorts followed by peals of laughter. I can't help it... a bark of mirth erupts from my chest and I'm laughing right along with her.

She pats my chest while still chuckling. "What a pair we make."

"Yeah... that we do." I pull her into my arms for a hug, then kiss her temple. "Can we get out of here and go to your house?"

"Yes, we can," she says.

CHAPTER 16

Kiera

I STAND AT the entrance of the grand ballroom, scanning the crowd. I'm first and foremost looking for a glimpse of Bain, although I'm keeping an eye out for anyone I know. For the most part, I love being my own person and embracing the single life, but I'm not going to lie. It would have been nice to come with a date to this event.

Not just any date.

It would've been nice if Bain and I could've come together, but there are too many obstacles. The most obvious… we're not dating. Just fuck friends, and we're doing that in the shadows so we don't offend Drake's tender sensibilities.

A drink is what I need, so I make my way to one of the bars set up with only the best liquor and wines. I order a Shiraz and move to the edge of the crowd. The event isn't going to start for another twenty minutes and I like to people watch.

Handsome men in black tie, women in beautiful

gowns and jewels. Tonight Brienne will be asking for big money for the start of her new charity foundation named after her brother, Adam, who died in the crash.

My eyes catch on Drake and Brienne, both circulating separately. I'll catch up with them later.

Something touches my elbow and I turn to see Bain standing there. How he made it past me without my notice is beyond me, but it's an effort not to let my tongue hang out of my mouth. Casual Bain with his floppy hair and boyish grin is one level of hot. Put the man in hockey gear and I drool—but Bain in a tuxedo?

"My panties just got wet," I tell him truthfully, turning my head back out to the crowd so it appears we're making casual conversation.

"Jesus, Kiera." He shifts awkwardly. "You can't say things like that while wearing a dress that I'm pretty sure is illegal in this state."

My head drops and I smile to myself in triumph. It is sexy as hell. The strapless top plunges down into a sharp V between my breasts and the entire gown fits like a second skin.

"I'm going to have to sit at my table all night as I'll have a hard-on just looking at you," he grumbles but he's totally teasing.

I see Danica and Brienne near the stage and I want to wish them good luck since they're both speaking. Sparing Bain a quick glance, I give him a sympathetic smile. "Don't look at me, then."

"Impossible," he mutters.

I wink at him before walking away and I can feel the heavy weight of his stare on my backside. I give it a little extra sashay for his benefit alone.

When I reach Danica, I take her wrist, forcing her to turn my way. Brienne's talking to an assistant and doesn't pay me any attention.

Danica's eyes light up and she leans in so we can hug. When I pull back, I give her a once-over, admiring her black silk gown. "You look fabulous."

Her eyes peruse me critically. "Pot calling the kettle black. I can only imagine what Drake is going to say when he sees you in that outfit."

I level a dramatic eye roll at Danica, causing her to giggle. "One day my brother will learn that he's not the boss of me." I wave my hand to punctuate that he's of no consequence to this discussion and ask, "Are you ready for the big speech?"

Danica gives a tiny shake of her head. "In a million years, I will never be ready for this speech."

I grasp her hand and squeeze it. "Speak from the heart. It's what you do best and you're going to be fine."

As Brienne's assistant climbs the steps onto the stage and moves to the podium to test the microphone, Brienne turns to me and eyeballs the gown. "That dress is amazing. Please tell me I can borrow it sometime."

Laughing, I touch her arm. "I love the irony of this. Drake will hate it when he sees it on me, but he's going to love it when it's on you."

"That's because he knows no one would dare leer at me when he's by my side, but he can't keep his eyes on you twenty-four seven."

God, if Drake ever found out about the things that happen when his eye isn't on me, he'd have a heart attack. "What my brother doesn't know won't hurt him."

Brienne winks at me. "That will be our secret."

"I'll hold you to that if the need ever arises," I say and then turn to Danica. I give her another hug. "I better go find my table. You've got this. I'll be silently cheering you on."

I move through the ballroom and one of the attendants directs me to my table. I'm actually relieved to see Bain's table is on the other side of the room. I don't want to be distracted by him and if he's within ten feet of me, I won't be able to concentrate on what anyone else is saying.

I am seated between two couples who are exceptionally outgoing and sweet. They're obviously impressed I'm Drake McGinn's sister and we spend time talking about how he outed his relationship with Brienne to the press. I love how people have embraced my brother and Brienne's unconventional partnership and it makes me even more excited for when he pops the question.

Dinner is spectacular and I eat far too much. My favorite, of course, is dessert, a chocolate mousse cake because chocolate is only the best thing in the world. As we're eating, various speakers take the podium. Danica as the director of the foundation leads, followed by Brienne and then a host of other people who have compelling stories about how this new foundation will help those in need.

After dinner, the lights are set to a warm glow and a DJ spins tunes before a parquet dance floor. Bidding farewell to my dinner companions, I swipe a signature champagne drink from a passing waiter. It has elderflower liqueur and fresh strawberries in it and it's light and refreshing. Just what I need after that incredibly filling dinner that I'm quite sure is causing my tummy to pooch out a bit.

Oh, well… worth it.

I mingle, talking to various players, wives and girlfriends I've come to know. Drake finds me, and Brienne will be happy to know he doesn't say one thing about my dress. Probably because he knows I'd kick him in the balls if he did.

He takes me by the elbow and leads me away from a group I'd been conversing with. "Valentine's Day," he says in a low voice.

"What about it?" I ask.

He rolls his eyes. "When I'm going to propose."

"Oooh," I exclaim and then clap my hand over my mouth so I don't squeal. "What are you going to do?"

"No idea," he says with an easy wave of his hand. "I'll think of something good. But I'll need your help with the boys."

"Got it," I say with a firm nod. Valentine's Day is a completely overrated holiday in my opinion and I won't mind spending it with my three favorite boys.

Drake leans down and plants a kiss on top of my head. "Going to find my girl for a dance."

I watch him walk off and then my gaze slides over the dance floor. I see Camden and Danica dancing, and it's sweet they've reconnected after all these months following the crash.

Finishing my champagne, I look around for an empty tray to place it on and my eyes lock on Bain standing at the double doors of the ballroom. He's staring at me with a mischievous smirk. He gives a jerk of his head for me to come his way, then turns and walks out.

Okay, my curiosity is piqued. I hand my empty flute to a passing waiter and walk toward the ballroom exit. I'm trying not to rush as I don't want to call attention, but I'm far too eager to see what Bain is up to.

I turn left out of the double doors and spy him walking down the hall. He doesn't look back at me but strolls along, nodding to people as we pass. A set of restrooms are at the end of the hall and he turns right down another hall. I follow him, hanging back a bit so no one will guess I'm tracking him.

Just as I make the right turn, I see him down a bit, taking a left. Glancing around, I don't see anyone and break into a delicate trot, even though I am in sky-high sandals. I make the left turn but I don't see Bain. Up ahead is another hall and I walk that way, curious where he's gone.

When I reach the intersection, he steps out and grabs my arm. I'm slightly startled but have no chance to yell as he's pulling me into him for a soul-stirring kiss. My arms wrap around his neck and his hands go to my ass to hold me to him.

Our tongues tangle and a low rumble of need pushes from his chest into mine.

"Christ," Bain mutters as he spins us around and backs me into the wall. "This night is taking fucking forever."

"I know," I gasp as his mouth hits my neck.

"Need to touch you for a bit."

I lift my leg—thank you, long slit in my skirt—and wrap it around the back of his so that I can grind against him. He's thick and hard and I know it has to be uncomfortable. If we weren't in a public hallway—although no one is around at the moment—I'd ease that suffering with my hand or my mouth.

Bain's hand comes under my thigh, lifting it higher until it's at his hip. His other hand grasps my jaw so he can possess my mouth.

Someone gasps… a shocked rasp of air and I know we've been caught.

Weirdly, neither Bain nor I jolt at the intrusion, and it tells me that neither of us cares to explain ourselves. His mouth lifts from mine as we turn our heads toward the sound.

It's Danica and Camden, two people I couldn't care less knowing about me and Bain. I grin at Danica, although I notice Camden looks decidedly uncomfortable.

But then I see that he and Danica are holding hands and my jaw drops slightly.

Danica pulls away from Camden and marches up to me, snagging my wrist. Tugging me from Bain, she says, "Come on."

I don't hesitate to follow. My moment with Bain is over, but he's coming to my place tonight so in a few hours, it will all be good. I glance over my shoulder and blow him a kiss. He smirks back.

Danica holds my hand all the way to the ballroom but drops it just as we walk in. She spins on me, steps in close and whispers harshly, "What in the hell were you doing with Bain?"

"It's obvious what I was doing. What were you and

Camden doing?"

Danica looks off to the side, mulling my question. But she sighs and turns back to lock eyes with me. "We've been seeing each other."

A wide smile breaks free. "That's amazing."

"I know. But we're keeping it on the down low, so you can't tell anyone."

I cock an eyebrow at her. "You realize Bain and I are doing the same thing. Secretly banging each other too."

Danica lets out a nervous laugh and looks around. "I'll call you tomorrow and tell you all about it, okay?"

"Of course." I pull her in for a quick hug and she melts off into the crowd.

I glance down at the slim gold watch Drake got me for Christmas two years ago. I think it would be fine if I left. Bain won't be far behind and we can pick up at my house with that amazing kiss that got interrupted. We have another four days before he leaves for a four-day road trip and we need to make the most of it.

I start to turn, but Brienne is standing before me, her arms crossed over her chest. She looks irritated.

"What's up?" I ask warily.

"What are you up to?" she asks, narrowing her eyes. "And don't you dare lie to me."

Hmm… she knows something, but what.

I tilt my head, my tone evasive. "What do you think I'm up to?"

Brienne rolls her eyes and sweeps a hand toward the door. "You know you were less than obvious when you followed Bain out of the ballroom a few minutes ago. And now you're back and your lipstick's smudged and your cheeks are flushed. And I just saw Danica calling you on the carpet about something, so spill it... Is there something going on between you and Bain?"

I can't lie to Brienne. I'd never think to. "Bain and I are... well, we're having sex. Lots and lots of it."

Brienne's eyebrows shoot up. "Just sex?"

"I mean... we hang out some. He's been staying at my house the last few nights. We're friends, you know."

Shaking her head as if she can't understand, she asks, "Are you two dating?"

"No way," I exclaim, holding out my hands. "Just sex." Brienne looks confounded, so I lean in and add in a low voice, "Really, really good sex. Like, the most amazing sex ever."

"All right, I get it," she mutters and then looks around before bringing her gaze back to me. "You need to tell your brother."

I step back and glare at her. "I most certainly do not. It's not any of his business and I don't feel like him getting all wigged out over this. I certainly don't want him going after Bain. You can't tell him."

Brienne huffs out a breath. "Of course I won't tell him if you ask me not to. But if he finds out, it's going to be worse that you're hiding it."

"You're not telling me anything I don't already know. But honestly… this is just so casual, it's not even worth telling Drake. It will probably fizzle sooner rather than later."

Mouth drawing downward, Brienne's eyes turn soft. "So you two don't have any feelings for each other?"

"Sure," I say breezily, not liking her pitying look. "We're friends. We like to hang. We have a good time."

Her head tilts as if she's confused. "And that's it?"

"Why does it have to be anything more if we both like what we're doing and it makes us happy?"

Brienne blinks a few times, shakes her head and almost sounds apologetic. "You're right… as long as you're both happy, that's all that matters."

I'm glad she sees it our way, but I still get the impression she feels sorry for me. That doesn't sit well because Brienne is one of the smartest, most intuitive people I know. Her having concern for me is a little disconcerting, but I blow it off.

Everything is just perfect the way it is.

CHAPTER 17

Bain

KIERA LEANS ACROSS the console of my car, fists my sweater and pulls me to her for a kiss. It's soft and replete. Probably because we came straight from her house where we had some incredibly hot sex in her outdoor hot tub, which is quite draining when you add the heat of the water and the physical exertion.

Worth it.

We're late to Tillie and Coen's housewarming party and no, we're not here together "as a couple." I intend to go back to her house after the party, so we decided to ride together.

My idea, not hers, but she had no hesitation. We agreed we had to enter separately and I parked down the street so no one would see us. It's stupid, really. I'm leaving tomorrow for back-to-back games in New York, then on to Boston. We'll come back to Pittsburgh for one day, then an out-and-back trip to play the Cold Fury again. It's a solid four days before I'll see Kiera, then another away trip the day after.

I'm already missing her and I'm not even gone yet.

"You good to walk to the house by yourself?" I ask as she pulls away. It's about a block and a half, but still... gentleman and all that, I offer.

"I'm good. See you in there."

And then she's gone, exiting the car, leaving behind a swirl of cold wind and my lips still tingle from her kiss. I contemplate why it unsettles me to let her walk in by herself. Deep down, I know it's because it signifies that I view this as something more and that scares the hell out of me. I never planned on settling down with one woman for the long term. At least, not this early.

In fact, I never saw myself doing it before I retired from hockey. The game is what's most important, and with that, my freedom to do what I want, when I want it. When you commit to someone, you have to put their needs right up there with your own and I'm smart enough to know that. My parents didn't marry until they were in their early thirties and kids came a few years after that.

I don't want to confuse great sex with the need for something more. It's why agreeing to a friendship is a slippery slope because the more time we spend together outside the bedroom only increases the non-sexual bond.

But fuck... the sex. It's the absolute best I've ever had. Just the thought of Kiera gets me excited.

She does a slow strip tease. I get excited.

Bops around the kitchen in sweatpants and a tattered T-shirt. Excited.

Wakes up in the morning with gunk in her eyes. Excited.

Every fucking thing about her pushes every button, even ones I didn't know I had. Making Kiera orgasm has become one of my favorite hobbies. She's an enchanting masterpiece of art when she comes and it's the pinnacle of visual splendor.

But there's always a distance between us that we both work hard to adhere to, based on our no-strings-attached agreement. Kiera plays it cool, just like I do. We keep the bulk of our relationship focused on sex, revealing little of ourselves unless prompted.

Lately, though, there have been prompts. Conversations where we intrude into each other's lives, even if we only ask for a glimpse. Sometimes, Kiera reaches out to touch me in passing or as we're sitting on the couch. A comforting graze that brings a sense of ease. There are times when I catch her staring at me... a dreamy look on her face as if she's pondering what-ifs. And those times when we're seeing each other after an absence. With her megawatt smile, she jumps into my arms to first give me a hard hug before a kiss. The fact that I enjoy the hug as much as the kiss is telling.

All of this mulling and wondering presents one very big question: Could I walk away from her right now?

The answer is a resounding fuck no. She's become an integral part of my life and the thought of losing her opens a pit in the bottom of my stomach.

But do I want more?

Also… fuck no. When it boils down to it, what we have right now is enough. It has to be because I truly don't have any more to give. The only reassuring thing is that Kiera feels the same way.

We talked about it last night after she broached the subject. We were lying in bed, watching the late news. I was propped up on pillows and she nuzzled against my chest.

"Check-in time," she announced.

I looked down but only saw the top of her head. Her tone was precise and straightforward, yet I wasn't sure what she meant. "Check-in time?"

She nodded. "Yeah… just want to make sure this is still working for both of us. I mean, I know the sex part is working, because wow." I couldn't help but laugh. "But we're definitely spending more time together than we anticipated. Is that okay?"

Okay with who? Me? Her? I wasn't sure, so I asked, "What do you think?"

"Asked you first," she replied.

There was a long moment as I pondered, all the same thoughts that run through my mind now as I sit here in the car, waiting to put some time between me and

Kiera's arrival. Are we going too far?

"It's working for me," I finally admitted, because if I said it wasn't, there's a good chance we'd go our separate ways. You can't go backward. Only stay in place or move forward.

So many things were left unsaid, but she said it's working for her, too, and that was that.

I check my watch and decide Kiera's been in there a good ten minutes so I should be fine to enter. I don't bother with my coat, even though it's cold tonight, but I do a fast jog up the block to Coen and Tillie's new house.

As soon as I step inside, I locate Kiera in the kitchen talking to some of the women. I walk through the crowd and meet up with Camden.

"Glad you decided to join the party," he says, a smirk on his face. But he moves past me and out the door, which is weird.

I manage to ignore Kiera in the kitchen as I find a large tin tub full of beers on ice and grab one. I twist off the cap, toss it in the garbage can and walk right back out again. I circulate and congratulate Tillie and Coen. I spend time talking to Coach West and eventually end up gravitating to a group of the single guys, which is where I normally belong.

I walk in on what appears to be a debate between Kirill, Boone and Kace.

SAWYER BENNETT

"Bain... greatest horror movie of all time?" Kace asks.

That's an easy one. Got to go with a classic. "*Psycho*, hands down. It set the bar for psychological horror."

Kirill shakes his head, a sly smile playing on his lips. "I have to go with *The Shining*. Kubrick's mastery of tension and atmosphere is unmatched."

"Chill out, Siskel and Ebert," Boone says with a light punch to Kirill's chest and then looks around our group. "*Ringu* is the best."

"What the hell is *Ringu*?" Kirill asks.

Boone launches into a summary about the Japanese psychological horror film, but I tune him out as I see Kiera move our way. I try not to stare, but she makes it hard not to. She looks radiant, her blond hair cascading down her back. My gaze lingers on her and I feel an overwhelming desire to be by her side. To pull her close and whisper in her ear.

I let my gaze fall away as she steps into our group, standing between Kace and Boone. "What's up?"

"Best horror film?" Kirill demands.

"I don't know about best, but I had nightmares for a week after I watched *Paranormal Activity*." She shudders with a grimace. "I believe in all that supernatural shit."

My eyebrows shoot up in surprise. "Really? I wouldn't have pegged you for someone who scares easily or believes in the paranormal. You're always so practical and level-headed."

Kiera chuckles, her laughter like music to my ears. "There's a lot more to me than meets the eye. Plus, there's something thrilling about the unknown, don't you think?"

I'm enthralled by her words. The blend of fascination and deep curiosity makes me want to ask her about her beliefs in the otherworldly.

Except it immediately hits me that I'm on the verge of outing us. I shouldn't even know her well enough to know she's practical and level-headed. That's only something I learned after spending time with her. I mentally kick myself for crossing that line and quickly change the subject.

My gaze goes to Kirill. "You still seeing that girl Mindy?"

Kirill shakes his head, a mischievous smile dancing on his lips. "Nah, man, I'm not one for settling down. I enjoy the freedom of playing the field too much, just like you."

My laugh is forced as I try to shake off the unease that Kirill just labeled me as a diehard player.

I risk a glance at Kiera and the relief is knee-buckling when I discover a mischievous smile dancing on her lips as she winks at Kirill. "Well, I suppose we're all a bunch of players, aren't we? But who knows, maybe one day we'll grow up."

Kiera leaves our group and I don't want her to walk away. Her words strike a reverberating chord and I can't help but wonder if she's hinting at something deeper. That causes both excitement and apprehension, knowing there's a connection between us that goes beyond our casual encounters.

A hand clamps down on my shoulder and I turn to see Drake standing there. He's a big guy, but I've got him by a an inch or so. At six seven, there's no one as tall as me on this team.

His hand stays there and squeezes. "Stone says you ran off some guy who was bothering Kiera the other night."

I freeze, my mind going blank. All I can think about is the rage that went through me when some other guy touched what was mine.

Drake frowns at me but then Boone jumps in. "Yeah... he was a complete badass. Guy was coming on hard to Kiera and Bain set him straight."

I hadn't realized I was holding my breath, but it comes out in a gush that I turn into words. "No worries, man... if I had a little sister, I'd want others looking out for her as well."

Drake beams at me, gives one more squeeze of his hand and heads off. Boone shoots me a look that leaves no mystery as to what he thinks.

I got your back, buddy, but you better sort this shit out.

CHAPTER 18

Kiera

D ANICA'S TEXT HAS me worried. We haven't spoken since that night at the gala when she busted me and Bain kissing in the hallway, and I busted her holding hands with Camden. We had a very short conversation back in the ballroom. I admitted that Bain and I were casually banging each other. She admitted that things with Camden were complicated and I'm guessing that might be an understatement.

Bain left early this morning to meet the team plane and I was just lazing around when I got her text. *I'm all fucked up in the head and need a sounding board.*

I asked her where and when and she pointed me to this little tea and pastry shop near the arena since I'm familiar with that area of the city.

Danica looks terrible when I spot her at the back of the shop. Dark circles under her eyes and her face is pale. I unwind the scarf from around my neck and remove my coat as I walk toward her. Tossing it on the back of my chair, I look at the cup of tea Danica must have ordered for me. A plate of scones sits between us.

I'm a coffee girl and had my one cup today. The tea and scones look nauseating, but I don't say so. "What's going on?" I ask.

Danica shakes her head, her gaze dropping briefly before meeting mine. "I ended things with Camden last night and I feel awful about it."

"So un-end it." I'm very practical and that's an easy solution.

"I can't go backward," she laments.

I pick up the cup of tea, take a sip and it tastes awful. Grimacing, I push it away and lock my gaze on Danica.

"Start from the beginning. All I know is you like Camden and he likes you, so catch me up."

"It's a bit more than *like*," she murmurs.

"On your part?"

"I think on both our parts. The feelings have gotten strong, but it's complicated, for him more than me."

I pick up a scone. "Let me guess... he feels he's in Mitch's shadow and can't handle that."

She shakes her head. "On the contrary, no. We've had those talks and yes, I think he had some insecurities in the beginning, but he trusts that I don't compare. Camden knows what I had with Mitch was amazing, and what I have with him is amazing."

"Then what's his problem?"

Danica shrugs. "He wants us to see each other secretively. He's not ready for the team to know about us. Thinks it will cause waves and people will judge and not understand."

"So what? I mean... if y'all have feelings for each other and they're genuine and deep... what does it matter what anyone else thinks?"

Even as the words come out, I realize they could apply to me and Bain. We're hiding in the shadows, too, because we don't want Drake to know. He wouldn't understand that we're just fine being casual.

"It doesn't matter to me," Danica says with frustration. "I'm confident that I should be able to move on with my life in any way I see fit. I loved Mitch with all my heart and I love his memory. That will never change. But I'm allowed to be happy again and I will be. I'm just afraid it's not going to be with Camden."

"The whole teammate thing is the complicating factor." Again, that tidbit could apply to me and Bain. "I wonder if he's talked to any of them. I mean, I know for one, Drake would never have a problem with you two dating. I bet most would be fine with it."

"I think you're right, especially since most of Mitch's friends..." Her words fade because she doesn't need to say that most of Mitch's friends died when the plane went down.

I hate this is causing her so much pain. "It's nobody's fucking business who we allow into our hearts, Danica."

"I know. I agree."

My anger isn't only for the situation. It's for the man making it difficult on her. "Camden should know it too."

"He knows it." Her expression morphs into one of pain and heartache. "He knows it and believes it, but he's too afraid to go for it."

"Then fuck him," I growl. "Metaphorically, of course."

Danica leans back in her chair, no anger at all in her demeanor. "I can't be mad, though. I understand why he's nervous about the entire situation. It's a legit worry."

I shake my head, considering the scone still in my hand, and the thought of eating it has no appeal. "Those things are dry as fuck." I toss the biscuit down and wipe my fingers on a napkin. "I'm confused. Are we mad at him or not?"

She's unable to contain her laughter. "I'm not mad. Disappointed. Also understanding. Sad. Worried I made a bad decision in parting ways."

"Now I understand why you said you're fucked in the head."

Danica sips at her tea, but I don't miss the wobble of her lower lip or the sheen in her eyes. "What if... what if the reason he doesn't want anyone to know is that this isn't serious for him? I'm... convenient."

"Do you really believe that?" I ask gently. "Because

you're a good judge of character, Danica. I don't know that you could miss something like that and Camden seems like a nice guy."

"I told him if he changes his mind… he knows where to find me."

"Well, there you go. He'll come around."

"And if he doesn't, then I'll know that it wasn't as special as I thought it was."

"So, what's the plan?" Kiera asks, crossing her arms on the table. "Do we set you up with someone hot and rub it in his face? Drive him wild with jealousy so he knows what he lost?"

Danica snorts so loud, patrons at the next table look at us. "While that does sound fun, you know I'm not the type to do that. I think I'm going to have to move on from the loss, the same way I did after Mitch died. While it's two different circumstances, it still hurts."

I take her hand and squeeze it. "I'm sorry. You don't deserve this and I know you're not, but I'm mad at him for this."

Her fingers reflexively grip mine. "You still casually banging Bain?"

The memories of this morning make my blood flow hot. There was a desperation to our fucking. We're only going to be apart for two days and yet it feels like forever. I grin at her. "Every chance I can."

"Is that going anywhere?"

I wave my hand dismissively. "Nah. We're just having fun and neither of us are interested in commitment."

"Are you both seeing other people too?" Her tone carries a hint of curiosity.

"Who needs other people? Bain is a beast and more than enough for me to handle."

Her jaw drops and I grin at her. I love shocking my sweet friend.

"Does Drake know or have any clue?"

"There's no sense in him knowing since it's not going anywhere. I'm sure we'll fizzle soon."

"Doesn't sound like you'll fizzle the way you called him a beast," she quips.

God, I hope we don't fizzle. I don't ever want to give him up. I nod to her cup. "Finish your tea. Let's go shopping… a little retail therapy."

♦

PUSHING MY CART along the grocery aisle, I think about my day with Danica. Our retail therapy was good for both of us. We both have men who confound us and it was nice to get lost in friendship. We tried on clothes that were far too expensive for either of us to purchase and the sales ladies knew it. There was giggling on the scale of thirteen-year-old girls, but it lightened her heart and that was worth it.

I declined her invitation to lunch as I was feeling a

little off. I chalk it up to the very late night I had with Bain, followed by the very early wake-up he gave me. I'm one of those people who needs eight hours of sleep or I operate at the level of a zombie.

Because Bain has pretty much eaten me out of house and home, I decided to do a quick grocery run to get me through the next few days. Without him to feed, my grocery bill will be significantly less, but in fairness to him, he usually pays for the food. The few times we've gone out for dinner or to a bar for a drink, he's always grabbing the check.

He pays for everything now that I think about it and that feels an awful lot like dating. It's not his fault either. I let him do it.

I meander the aisles, picking up things I normally buy. I'm not an impulse shopper and it's a breezy trip through the market to grab the essentials.

In the personal hygiene section, I grab some deodorant as I'm getting low and snag a box of tampons.

My hand freezes on the box, a cold feeling of dread sweeping through me and coalescing in my stomach where it forms a painful knot. Clarity dawns upon me in an instant.

I didn't get my period.

A quick mental calculation—I'm almost a week late.

"Oh God," I murmur, dropping the tampons in the aisle.

A young girl with bright red hair coming the opposite way carrying a handbasket picks up the box and
hands it to me. "Here you go."

"Thanks," I murmur, accepting the nice deed with a
shaky hand.

She frowns at me. "Are you okay?"

"Um… yeah." The quavering voice says I'm lying,
but I manage a smile. "Thanks."

"Sure thing."

When she moves on, I place the tampons in the cart,
confident that if I buy them, I'll need them soon.

*But you're regular as clockwork, Kiera. You're not going
to be needing them for a long damn time.*

I squeeze my eyes shut and shake my head. "Nope.
No. Not happening."

Determined, I look around the small selection of
hygiene care and don't see what I need. I leave my cart
and move to the next aisle and immediately laser in on
the stock of pregnancy tests.

Feeling like a cinder block is on my chest, I grab one
and head to the self-checkout. There's a loud buzzing in
my ears as I scan the box and pay for it with my credit
card. From there I half run, half walk to the back of the
store to the restrooms.

Somehow I manage to get the cellophane wrapping
off, despite my hands trembling, and I read the instructions even though my mind is spinning. My bladder

must be holding all my nerves or it might want the answer sooner rather than later as I have no problem peeing on the stick.

When I'm done, I place the test on the sink vanity and wash my hands. I start the timer on my iPhone and pace nervously near the door. I don't dare look at it... afraid I'll see what I don't want to see. No one comes in to bother me and for that I'm grateful. I'm on the verge of a meltdown.

The timer goes off and I whirl around, staring at the little white piece of plastic that holds my future in a tiny digital readout. I've never been more terrified in my life.

Never, ever.

Legs feeling like they're trapped in mud, I move cautiously toward the sink, my heart about to jump out of my throat.

CHAPTER 19

Bain

CAMDEN HAS PEP in his step as we traverse down the airstair of the team plane. We have exactly twenty-four hours before we have to get back on to travel to Boston for an out-and-back game. He's going to go set things right with Danica... the woman he loves.

As we were in the away locker room changing after our game against the New York Phantoms, he stood up on one of the benches and announced to the entire team he'd been seeing her.

This was done after much poking and prodding by me because I knew something was wrong with him. Turns out, Camden felt like he might be stomping on Mitch's grave so he broke things off with Danica.

Said it was "the right thing to do."

I told him that was bullshit. If something makes you feel horrible, then it wasn't the right thing to do.

He was being a little hardheaded, so I had to give it to him straight and with no regard for his feelings. "Then what the actual fuck, dude? You have an amazing woman who, as far as I can tell over the last several weeks, has brought you out of your funk. You care for her and her kid. She's ready to give her all to you, and you break it off? Are you stupid or something?"

Yeah… I was rough on the guy, but he was in danger of talking himself out of righting his wrong. After a little back-and-forth, he asked Hendrix, who knew Mitch well, "Are you sure I'm not doing anything wrong?"

"Does it feel wrong when you're with her?" Hendrix replied.

"Nothing has ever felt more right."

Then, I had to give my two cents. "I don't care if anyone has a problem with it. If she's that good for you and you for her, fuck anyone in this locker room and fuck any fan who has an issue with it."

Hendrix and I told him to go for it and he did. By standing on the bench and proclaiming his feelings to the entire team.

It was pretty awesome.

I tried to imagine myself doing the same thing for a woman. Would I ever feel that way about someone?

Kiera?

One thing I have in common with Camden— nothing has felt more right. It's a powerful statement to admit.

We hit the tarmac, duffels held over our shoulders as we head to the private terminal. "You going to Danica's house?"

"Travis has a scrimmage right after school. I'm going to go watch him and then talk to her."

Clapping Camden on the back, I give him assurances because I hear the nerves in his voice. "It's going to be fine, man. Danica will forgive your slight bout of cold feet."

"Yeah… I think she will. Still scared as fuck she won't."

I squeeze his shoulder. "You'll be fine."

Camden stops walking and turns to me. "What about you and Kiera?"

"What about us?" I ask. He hasn't said a word to me about her since he busted us kissing at the gala.

He stares at me, a pointed look that says he's not in the mood for my bullshit, especially since I harassed him into action about Danica.

I give him a wink. "Sorry, man… I don't kiss and tell."

Camden rolls his eyes.

"But I will tell you that everything's perfect between us. I'm on my way to see her right now."

Friends with benefits. Great sex. Just as good a friendship. Nothing less and nothing more.

"I'm glad," he says with a bright smile. A man in love who's happy his buddy might be experiencing the same thing. I don't disabuse him of that. What works for me and Kiera wouldn't work for him and Danica.

We say our farewells after walking through the terminal and cut in different directions in the parking lot.

I'm in a great mood when I pull into Kiera's driveway. We came off a successful road trip where yours truly played very well, Camden's got his love life under control and I'm getting ready to get lost in pleasure with an amazing woman.

Twirling keys on my finger, I trot up the porch steps. Kiera opens the door before I can even push the doorbell.

"There better be a damn good reason you're not naked already," I say as I step over the threshold and toss my keys on a nearby table. I pull her into my arms and proceed to devour her mouth. I manage to kick the door shut and start walking us toward her bedroom, but I come to the realization that she's not exactly kissing me back.

Her fingers are curled tight into my shirt and her hold seems almost desperate, but her mouth is a passive participant.

There's no return passion and it's like being doused with a bucket of ice water.

"What's wrong?" I ask, taking her by the upper arms and holding her back from me so I can get a good look at her face. How did I not see it when she opened the door? Was I just so dazzled by her that I didn't see the red-rimmed eyes or the dull expression? "Did someone die?"

She shakes her head as she steps back from me. My hands fall away and my stomach pitches when she says, "We need to talk."

My first thought is she's ending things and after I get over the initial gut punch, I shore up the resolve I know I'll need. I'm not ready to end things. No way.

Kiera turns on me, walks into the kitchen and I follow. My heart hammers, crashing against my breastbone, and then it seems to stop when she faces me.

Her expression is so bleak I start to reach for her, but she shakes her head, holds a hand up to stave me off. She squeezes her eyes shut for just a moment and takes a deep, stuttering breath. "I'm pregnant," she says on the exhale, eyes opening and locking onto me.

I feel like I've been zapped by electricity, the shock of her words jolting every fiber of my being. My world tilts, my entire body feeling so off-balance, I reach out to grab the back of a kitchen chair.

Kiera rubs at her temple, gaze dropping from mine.

"Are you sure?" I manage to croak.

"Pretty sure," she whispers as she stares at the floor. "I'm a week late and I took a home test yesterday. It was positive."

"Is it accurate?"

Her head snaps up and she glares at me. "Well, I don't know, Bain. I didn't manufacture the fucking test."

I don't even think to defend myself as I can tell she's

on the verge of flipping out. But before I can try to offer comfort, she holds out her hands, palms facing me. "I'm sorry. I didn't mean that."

I'm scared shitless, but I'm more worried about Kiera. I straighten my spine and take two large strides to her. I wrap my arms around her body, pulling her in for a hug. Her head turns to the side, her arms tucked into her chest as I just hold her. I want to offer all kinds of assurances, but I can't offer a damn thing. I have no clue what to say because this never crossed my mind as a possibility.

I'm not fool enough to question her birth control pills because I know they're not one hundred percent effective. I'll just assume we've run into a bit of shitty luck.

I loosen my hold to look down at her. She tips her head back and I study those blue eyes that aren't sparkling the way they normally do. It's clear she's been doing a lot of crying and I'm guessing by the way she was rubbing at her temple, she's got a gargantuan headache.

"I'm so sorry," she says, her eyes pleading for forgiveness. "I know this isn't what either of us wanted."

"Don't apologize." My tone is harsh, but I don't want her bearing any guilt for this. "This was an accident."

She nods, head bobbing quickly. "I know. Sorry. I'm just... I don't know what in the hell to do. I'm not ready to have a baby. I'm not ready to be a mom."

I sigh and bend to press my lips to her forehead. "I'm with you. It's not something I wanted either. Not for a long time, at least."

Kiera's voice sounds slightly hysterical. "So we should definitely... um... we should get... since neither of us is ready for a kid, the best thing we could do is..." She wrenches out of my arms and scrubs her hands over her face, letting out a sob. She looks at me helplessly. "I can't even say the words, Bain. I can't even make myself say the option we need to consider."

Her anxiety causes mine to flare again, and my heart pounds. I keep my tone gentle. "We have to consider it, though."

Kiera's eyes are wild and she looks as if I just slapped her, but she nods in agreement. I've never seen a human being more torn in two before and my heart breaks for her.

"What do you want to do?" she asks.

I shake my head. "Kiera... it doesn't matter what I want to do. This is your body involved, not mine. If you want to end the pregnancy, I'll hold your hand. If you want to keep the baby, I'll support your decision."

A harsh, barking laugh erupts from her chest. "Of course you'd say that because you're a good guy. I know you'll do the right thing, but I want to know what *you* want."

I rub at the back of my neck, now aching with tension. "I don't know. Do I want kids one day? Sure. Am I ready to be a parent now? Fuck no. No way am I ready. But I'm also a capable person. I can do it. Having a baby is going to change everything about our lives. Nothing will be the same again and trust me when I say I'm as scared as you. But it's your choice."

"So if I say I want to end it, but you want to keep it, you'll support my choice?"

"If that's what you want." My eyes lock onto hers, an unwavering, silent promise to have her back.

Tears well in her eyes and spill over like waterfalls. Her expression pleads with me to understand. "It's not what I want. I can't terminate. I'm not ready to be a mom, but I guess I'll learn how."

Near-crippling fear weakens my legs, but I force myself to give a supportive smile. I brush her tears away with my fingers. "You already know how. You're a second mom to Jake, Colby and Tanner. You're a natural."

She laughs, nodding her head. "Yeah... I can take care of kids. But my plans... my dreams to go back to school. I'll have to give it up. I can't do both, but I can't give up the baby. That I know for sure."

I pull her into me, understanding that the best way I can show support is with physical affection. Her arms go around my back and she rests her cheek on my chest. I want to tell her she can have it all… school and mother-hood, but I don't know any such thing. I only know that everything has changed and we're immediately in over our heads.

"I don't need anything from you," Kiera says. "I can do this on my own. This isn't anything you ever bargained for."

I see what she's doing and I adore her for it. She's giving me an exit. The door is open and I can walk out and she won't even hold it against me. Kiera is aware I'll support her, but she doesn't expect it.

"I'm not going anywhere. That's half of me in your belly, so it's half my responsibility." And if I'm honest… I've already got a connection to it. The idea of Kiera terminating was nauseating at best, despite the fact I'm scared as fuck that we're keeping it.

Her entire body goes lax, I think from relief, and I have to hold up her weight. "What does this mean for us? What we've had going on?"

"I don't know," I answer truthfully. "We have a lot to talk about. A lot of micro decisions to make."

The front door to Kiera's house opens and both of us jerk apart, turning that way. Drake walks in, palming a set of keys, but he hasn't seen us standing in the kitchen yet. "Kiera," he calls out and then his gaze slides over us.

It stops, freezes on me and I can almost read on his face exactly what he's thinking as he takes in his sister's red eyes.

"What the fuck did you do to her?" Drake growls as he advances on us.

"He didn't do anything," Kiera snaps, stepping in front of me.

"Why are you crying? And why in the hell is he in my house?"

"It's my house," Kiera retorts. "Not yours. And why are you walking in without knocking?"

That seems to stump Drake. I'm sure he meant no offense and I'm quite confident he never once considered I'd be here with her. He lived here not that long ago and he probably never once considered she'd need privacy.

I can see Drake putting it all together, though. I'm in Kiera's home, we were embracing and she's crying. He knows for sure we're intimate with each other and his jaw tightens in anger as he points a finger at me. "I told you and all the guys that no one touches my sister. I forbade it."

Truly, I'm not making light of his concerns, but I can't help digging at him. "Sorry, man. But last I checked, Kiera's an adult who can do what she wants."

"I'm so going to kick your ass," Drake snarls and then whips toward Kiera. "And I told you to stay away from my teammates."

One look at Kiera and I know she doesn't need this level of stress, considering what's going on. I step in front of her so Drake's eyes are forced on me. "You don't talk to her like that. It's with respect or you'll get a taste of why I'm one of the best enforcers in the league."

"Don't," Kiera murmurs, lacing her fingers with mine. It's a deliberate move to show her brother that he's got no say in what goes on between us. Of course, neither of us knows what in the hell we're doing at this point, but for the moment, we're a united front.

Kiera tugs on my hand and I look down at her. "Why don't you head out and I'll give you a call later?"

I don't want to go. There are way too many things left unsaid. Too many decisions to make. And honestly... I want to fuck my girl. Nothing about her being pregnant has lessened my desire for her and it might even make her a little hotter.

I don't have time to break down that thought and psychoanalyze myself, but probably the real reason I don't want to leave is that I'm afraid her brother will talk her into something contrary to my best interests. I know he won't ever insert his will into her decision to keep the baby, but he might just give her an earful as to why she shouldn't be with me.

"I'll be fine," Kiera says, pulling me out of my uncertain thoughts.

As I stare at her, taking in the steel in her spine as she readies to talk to her brother but the red eyes and nose from crying, I realize there's no way I'm leaving her alone.

"I'm staying," I say, tightening my grip on her hand and leveling a look at Drake that dares him to make me leave.

Kiera turns to me, puts her hand on my chest. I don't look at her right away, instead keeping my glare focused on her brother. But then she pats me above my heart, which is still galloping over the turn of events, and I finally drop my gaze to her.

"I need to talk to Drake alone," she murmurs low enough so only I can hear. "I need to straighten things out with him so that's one less thing we have to worry about. Mind giving us some time? Maybe you can come back in a few hours with food. We can talk some more."

I don't want to leave her, but I also respect that she should have privacy to heal this rift with Drake. And she is inviting me back and asking for food, so it's not like she doesn't want to see me.

Plus, I should probably step away from her for a hot second and think about the future for myself. I'll call my parents... either one will do as I'm equally close to both. I could call my brother. I only know I'll need their support and they'll give it to me without question.

I don't care if it burns her brother up or not, but I put my hand on the back of her neck so I can show Drake that I'm involved with his sister. With just a bit of pressure, I force her up to her tiptoes. I don't kiss her because that would be too easy and instead press my forehead to hers. "I'll be back in two hours. Text me what you want to eat. Also, be waiting naked, okay?"

She nods her head against mine and then pulls back, a genuine smile aimed at me. "Okay."

CHAPTER 20

Kiera

"WHAT IN THE hell is going on?" Drake says as soon as I close the door behind Bain and I actually feel sorry for him. He sounds like a child who has lost his parents in a huge store and can't find them. "I feel like I'm going crazy."

I lean against the door and face my brother. "I've been seeing Bain for a while now."

"I specifically forbade every teammate from even looking at you. And that fucker Hillridge went behind my back."

"You don't own me, Drake. You can't tell me who I can and can't see."

"I didn't tell *you*. I told *Bain* and he betrayed—"

"I came on to him."

That stops the tirade and Drake blinks at me. "What?"

"I came on to him. At the Christmas party and then again on New Year's Eve. He didn't stand a chance."

"You're making that up," he says with exasperation.

205

"So what if I am?" I exhale, already exhausted by the distressing upheaval with Bain. So I just cut his legs out from under him. "I'm pregnant."

Drake's jaw drops, but he doesn't say anything.

Part of me feels bad for dropping that bomb so I gentle my tone. "I found out last night. I just told Bain about fifteen minutes before you walked in the door, so you kind of caught us in the middle of an emotional conversation."

"Jesus," Drake mutters and takes two steps to the right so he can flop down in an armchair. "How did I not know you were seeing each other?"

"No one knew," I reply as I walk onto the couch. "Well... Brienne knows. And Danica."

"Brienne knows?" Drake explodes but immediately drops it down ten notches. "And she didn't tell me?"

I sit on the end of the couch, curling my legs under me. "I asked her not to."

"Why not?" Drake demands.

Kiera sweeps out her arm dramatically. "This is why... your attitude is crappy."

Drake's face flushes and he deflects. "He's not long-term material, Kiera. That's why I don't want you to mess with my mates. They're not the settling-down type."

"I wasn't looking for a settling-down type, Drake." My brother frowns at me. "Bain gave me exactly what I needed, which was a casual fling with no commitment."

"You don't want monogamy?" he asks, brows knitting even tighter.

"We have monogamy, but that's it. It's fun, it's casual and up until today, it was most likely temporary."

Drake sits forward, rests his elbows on his knees. "What's Bain going to do?"

I smile at my brother. "I note you don't ask what I'm going to do."

Drake waves his hand. "You'll keep the baby. Never a doubt about that." I don't disabuse him of that sweet idea, but I had serious doubts. It wasn't until I saw that Bain wasn't overly freaked out and was supportive of whatever I wanted that it became clear to me what I'd do. "So I ask again, what's Bain going to do?"

I shrug. "We haven't discussed details, but he's going to support me, the pregnancy. He'll co-parent. That's about as far as we got before you interrupted us."

"Sorry about that," he mutters. "I'll knock from now on."

I smile. It's wan, but it's the best I've got right now. "I didn't want to hide this thing with Bain from you. I knew you'd be mad and I didn't want to argue. And really… it's none of your business."

"Your life is always my business," Drake growls. "And that includes your love life."

"Hypocrite much?"

Drake's eyebrows shoot up. "Pardon?"

"Pardon?" I mimic sarcastically and point at the kitchen table. "It wasn't but five months ago we sat over there and I tried to ask about your love life and you told me it was none of my business."

"That's because I'm a man and can take care of myself—"

I whip a pillow at him and it smacks him in the face.

Drake grins at me and tosses the pillow back to the couch. "Fine. I understand your reasoning. But Bain? Why him?"

"Can you explain your attraction to Brienne?"

"Got about ten hours?" he quips.

"Exactly," I say with an emphatic nod. "It's more than what you see as a teammate."

"So, you're serious about him?" he queries.

"No," I say, way too fast. I've been programmed to deny my feelings for Bain. But this is Drake, the one person I can be fully honest with. I take in a breath and let it out. "Actually... I'm not sure what it is. It was supposed to be casual, no strings. But little by little, we've committed to each other in small ways."

"Monogamy," Drake points out.

"That... and we're spending time together outside the bedroom." Drake grimaces, but I push on. "I like him as a person. He's funny and smart. He's a good guy. I like being around him. He's just... easy and solid."

"Are you going to get married?" he asks.

I'm faster in this denial and it's accurate beyond measure. "No way. Neither of us is interested in that."

"Good," Drake says. "You get married if there's love and I'm not hearing that's what this is."

If you had asked me ten seconds ago, I would have laughed at the notion of loving Bain, but the minute Drake dismisses it as plausible, there's an ache in my heart.

I shove it away, not willing to be worried about those things.

"Are we good?" I ask him.

"Yeah… we're good. But Brienne's not. She's going to get a piece of my mind for not telling me."

"Oh, no you don't," I snap at him. "You leave her alone. I asked her to keep a confidence and she agreed. You don't get to interfere with that."

Drake glares at me, but he knows I'm right. I also know he'll probably still give her shit about it, but I know Brienne will put him in his place.

Finally, he sighs and settles back in his chair, propping one ankle on the opposite knee. His fingers pick at the piping that runs along the armrest. When his gaze rises to meet mine, he asks, "Your life is about to change in a big way. I don't need to tell you how hard parenting is because you've helped me with the boys. You've been more of a mom to them than their own mom."

"I think I'm pretty qualified on what to do once it comes out, but I'm a little freaked about pregnancy."

Drake grins. "I don't envy you that." But then his expression sobers. "However, I'm worried about what this means for your future."

I scowl in confusion. "What do you mean?"

"You had big plans," he says softly, and I note a bit of guilt in his tone. "You put your dreams to go back to school on hold to help me with the boys. Don't think I don't appreciate that sacrifice because I have guilt about it every day." I start to protest, but he holds up a hand to shut me down. "Brienne and I had been working on a solid plan to alleviate you of that. She'll stay back with the boys when the team travels, and we can use a sitter for other times we need coverage. I honestly thought you might go back to Minnesota."

"You don't have to do that. I never mind staying with the kiddos when you travel. And as owner, Brienne needs to travel with the team."

"No, she doesn't," Drake says and I blink in surprise. "She travels because she wants to... so we can spend time together. But that was back when we were trying to carve time out of all the responsibilities we have. Now that we're living together and now that we're going to get engaged—"

I grin. "She has to say yes first."

"She'll say yes." My brother's confidence and ego

know no bounds. "The point is, we don't need to rely on you. You'll have the chance to go back to school and I think you should aim to start this upcoming fall."

"I can't do that while pregnant," I exclaim.

"The hell you can't. Plenty of women go through graduate school while pregnant. Hell… Molly did her second year of law school while she was pregnant."

Molly's our cousin and a complete overachiever, but I understand what he's saying.

"And Brienne and I are going to pay for your degree," Drake adds.

"No way. No fucking way. I don't need a handout. I can get loans and grants."

Drake again holds up his hand and waits for me to snap my mouth shut. "Brienne is a multibillionaire. I'm worth millions. You're a peasant compared to us."

I roll my eyes.

"We want to do this for you. You've done so much to support me and this is a gift I want to give to you. So please… just accept it."

And… I burst into tears, big fat drops pouring out and dripping down my face. I've been crying so much about being pregnant, I didn't think I had anything left. The tears obstruct my vision so I don't see Drake rise from his chair, but I feel his hands on my wrists, pulling me off the couch.

He tucks me into his safe embrace and kisses my

forehead. "I love you, sis. And I've got you. Even if that fucker Bain leaves you high and dry, you have me and you'll never have another worry in your life."

I sob harder but feel the need to proclaim, "This must be hormones."

Drake chuckles. "Yeah… I'm sure that's what it is."

♦

I'M NOT NAKED when Bain returns only because I'm starved. I'd been too stressed to eat this morning, then Drake stayed awhile to talk. With things good between me and my brother when he left and the solid decision to proceed with the pregnancy, my body now demands nourishment.

I tell Bain that very thing when he walks in carrying a pizza. He laughs but gladly leads me into the kitchen. I don't get any of the "you're eating for two" jokes, but instead, he says, "I've heard pregnancy hormones make you horny. You'll need to keep your strength up."

I have a slice of pizza halfway to my mouth and it's a good thing I hadn't taken a bite as I would've choked.

His expression is innocent as he picks mushrooms off. He knows I love them and suffers their presence, even though they gross him out. "What?" he asks as I laugh.

"I'm always horny for you," I say. "We didn't need to get pregnant for that."

Bain's smile is soft. "I like how you say 'we.' *We didn't get pregnant...* We're a team."

I can't describe the flush of warmth that lights me up from within. His proclamation that we're a team is more romantic than any declaration of love. At least to someone like me who is afraid that loving someone can be very dangerous.

"You seem awful Zen about this whole thing," I say conversationally, trying to dig down to what seems to be his complete acceptance.

Bain flicks a mushroom off his finger, grimacing as he wipes his hand on a napkin. His gaze comes to me. "I called my mom. It was a good conversation. There were a lot of reassurances that I can do this and having their faith in me makes all the difference. While she had no thought she'd be a grandma this soon, she's pretty psyched about it."

"Really?" I ask, insanely curious about Sheila Hillridge. Bain's told me some things about his parents and I know he's close to them both. He models himself after them in that they were both free spirits when they met. They didn't want to settle down and start a family until they'd had all the time to do things for themselves. That included solidifying careers—he's a research biologist and she's a college English professor—as well as having children. Bain was following their same life journey... live wild and free while you're young and don't settle down too soon.

"They want to make a trip here soon to get to know you," Bain says before taking a bite of his pizza and my jaw drops.

"But… why?"

Bain stares at me as if he can't believe I'd ask such a question. "Because you're carrying their grandchild."

"Well, yeah… but it's not like you and I are a couple. I'm more like an oven for her grandkid."

Setting his slice on the plate, he locks eyes with mine. "Maybe we should be a couple."

I set my pizza down only because my hands shake slightly and I'm afraid it will drop. "What would that even mean?"

Bain shrugs. "We make it what we want. I imagine it's not much different from what we're doing now. We're already monogamous. The last few weeks we've spent all our free time together, so it's not like we felt our freedom was being impinged. We'd be open and public about our relationship."

"That seems… logical." And why am I so sad that there's no warmth to his words or a declaration that he cares for me? I'm a very logical person, so why does that seem wrong?

Bain shakes his head and looks a little exasperated. "I probably didn't say that right." He leans over, takes my hand. "We're in a place we never wanted to be or thought we'd be. I never thought I'd want to settle down with one woman, but here I am, completely happy to be in your bed and no others. And if I'm honest, I felt that way before we found out you were pregnant. I guess it's time to put it all on the table. I care about you, Kiera. When I saw how upset you were earlier today, it fucking broke my heart and I wanted to fix it. I've never felt that before nor have I wanted to be responsible for another's happiness, but I found myself wanting to soothe you. I wanted to see you smile, not cry. I don't know what you call that, but I can tell you, I've surpassed our friends-with-benefits deal we had going. There's nothing casual about the way I'm feeling now."

Maybe it's the hormones, but I have to blink against the prick of tears. Gripping his hand tight, I push out of my chair and drape myself across his lap. My arms loop around his neck and I brush a soft kiss over his mouth.

I press my forehead to his. "I care about you too. There's nothing casual about my feelings either." I think about all my fears around falling for someone and the walls I've built up so that I'd never fall prey to a man like Peter again, and they all come tumbling down. "You make me so happy and I feel so secure and safe with you. I never thought I'd be able to say that about a man, and yet I know, to the depths of my soul, that you would never hurt me. You're kind of it for me."

Bain's arms come around me and he squeezes, then

tilts his head to kiss my neck. "Think you can handle cold pizza?"

Leaning back, I frown at him. "Cold pizza. Why?"

"Because I'd really like to fuck you now. Apparently, sweet words make me horny."

As if to punctuate his sentiment, he rotates his hips and I feel the growing length of him under my butt.

Grinning, I wiggle against him. "Yeah… cold pizza is just fine."

CHAPTER 21

Bain

MOST OF THE team has boarded the plane that will take us back to Pittsburgh. It's quiet as we load due solely to the fact the Cold Fury kicked our asses big-time. I'm pissed about the game and my nasty feelings following a defeat usually plague me all night. But while I'm still angry about the loss, I can't deny the pleasure within me that I'll be heading back to Pittsburgh.

To Kiera.

I decline the attendant's offer of a drink before take-off, instead pulling my phone out and texting Kiera. I know she was up as of an hour ago as she texted me after the game. *I'm sorry about the loss. I think you played amazing.*

Christ, that felt good to hear, even if I'm not happy with my performance.

It was so energizing to know that I had someone watching the game just for me, cheering me on. Well, someone who wasn't my family.

I got more of the same encouragement at our away

game in Boston day before yesterday. Pregame texts of support and a call after when we talked for almost an hour once I got to the hotel.

Hell, ever since Kiera and I committed to each other—not just because of the pregnancy, but to pursue the growing feelings we've both acknowledged—I can't seem to get enough of her.

I shoot her a quick text. *On the plane. Be home soon.*

Funny... how it doesn't even feel the tiniest bit weird that I think of Kiera and home synonymously.

I'm naked, she texts back.

I groan, imagining her splayed out on her bed. Hand between her legs, back arched in pleasure... a private show just for me. I don't know what it is about her being pregnant, but it somehow makes her sexier. There's not a single, discernible change to her body yet, but somehow... I want her more and that's about near to impossible.

Oh, the filthy things I'm going to do to you tonight. Send me a picture. I barely hit send before someone drops down into the seat next to me.

I immediately turn my phone over in case said picture I requested comes through. I twist my neck to see Drake sitting there.

Fuck.

We've avoided each other on this road trip, unless it was to talk about the game. While Kiera assured me

Drake was okay with everything, the fact he's been aloof with me says otherwise.

I want to drop my head and pretend to be interested in my phone, but if I turn it over, I'm afraid there will be a naked picture of his sister. Can't risk that.

I can tell by the scowl on his face that he's not as cool about things as Kiera seems to think.

He doesn't say anything and I'm not sure if I should start a conversation. I mean… what do I say? *Sorry I knocked up your sister?*

Hell no. I'm not apologizing. But he clearly needs to get something off his chest, so I'll poke him to get things moving. "I'm not going to say I'm sorry to you."

"Didn't think you would. I'd rather know how you feel about Kiera. She told me that the two of you were going to try to make a go of a relationship. I don't know what in the hell that even means, but it appears you're here to stay. So I want to know exactly how you feel about my sister."

"That's none of your business." Drake's eyes flash with ire and I decide to throw him a bone. "But you have to know I care about her. I'm going to stick by her side and support her through this. Help her raise our kid."

He seems slightly mollified by my response and sighs. "Do not hurt her. I will fucking kill you if you do."

It's not something I'm worried about as I have no intention of hurting Kiera. "Understood."

The attendant comes and asks Drake if he'd like anything. While he's ordering, I take a quick peek of my text exchange with Kiera.

And yup... hot, naked picture awaits.

I quickly shut off my screen as Drake turns my way again. "I need you to do me a favor."

"What's that?" I ask, trying not to sound suspicious.

"I want Kiera to go back to school. She wants to—"

"—be a nurse practitioner," I finish for him.

"She's going to balk at it now that she's pregnant. She doesn't think she can do school and be a mom."

"That's ridiculous."

"Agreed," Drake says as his eyes lock on mine. "So I want you harassing her to go for it. You're the one who says you're going to support her, so you do that. You do whatever she needs to feel comfortable in being able to handle both."

"Of course I will," I say, slightly offended he thinks I need this talking-to.

"You better or else—"

"Yeah, yeah, yeah... you'll fucking kill me."

"We're understood, then," he says with an evil smile. The attendant returns and hands him what looks like a club soda with lime. Drake takes a sip and rests it on his thigh. "You tell anyone yet?"

Kiera and I discussed this before I left on the road trip. How we were going to drop these bombs on the team. It's two bombs, actually. The first, that we're seeing each other, and the second, that Kiera's pregnant. We decided to tell those closest to us and others as it comes up in conversation. Mostly, we'll let the information filter through the team organically.

"I told Baden, Hendrix, Boone and Camden so far. Also, Coach West."

Drake smiles. "Yeah… Baden texted me congrats on being an 'uncle to be.'"

I try to hide my smirk. As affronted as Drake wants to pretend to be about me being with his sister, he's excited about the pregnancy.

Word will filter quickly enough, though.

"Kiera said your mom took the news pretty well," I say. She called her after we had our cold pizza the other day and I listened to one side of the conversation. It did things to me to see Kiera exhibit some excitement as I know she'd been wallowing in fear and uncertainty.

Drake nods. "She was surprised, but she's also excited about being a grandma again."

Kiera and Drake's mom is going to visit soon and I'm not sure if I'll be introduced as Kiera's boyfriend, her future baby daddy or the guy who knocked her up. Doesn't matter… I'm happy with the way things are.

A mere five days ago, I was just a guy who had a hot-as-hell hookup who had somehow become my girlfriend. I had no worries in the world. Now I'm going to be a dad before the year is over, I've tentatively admitted to feelings for Kiera, and our parents are salivating over a grandchild.

Talk about a fucking whirlwind and yeah… sometimes my head still spins. There have been plenty of moments where I'll get struck with an overwhelming sense of panic or dread. I won't let those insecurities drive me away, but they are very real and causing some sleeplessness. Maybe a bit of mourning for my life of freedom and lack of responsibilities.

Still, I do get Kiera in exchange and as terrified as I am at times, I'm more than placated by having her as a prize.

Yeah… I said it. I'm falling for her and this pregnancy has forced us to face those feelings.

"Earth to Bain, come in, Bain."

I blink and turn to Drake who's smirking at me. "Did you say something?"

"Based on the look on your face, I don't even want to know what you were thinking. But I was asking if you could help me out this weekend."

"Doing what?" I ask suspiciously.

"Kiera tell you I'm proposing to Brienne?"

"Yeah."

"Well, it's going to be on Valentine's Day and I want Kiera and my kids to be present. I'm taking Brienne out to a romantic dinner and Kiera will pretend to be babysitting the boys. When I pop the question, they'll come out. Since you're sort of with her, that means you're invited too."

"I'm touched," I say sarcastically, banging my fist over my heart.

Drake rolls his eyes. "Don't be. I need to put you to work. I need help to pick up the ring. It's being held at the jeweler and it would be great if you could pick it up that morning. Brienne has got me hopping this weekend, so I can't sneak away to get it. Think you can handle it?"

"Sure," I say easily, and I'm kind of touched he's asked me to pick up the ring instead of Kiera.

"If you lose it, I will have to kill you."

"Expensive?"

"Hundred and thirty-two thousand."

I wheeze in shock. "Jesus Christ… who spends that much money for a ring?"

"A man who is crazy in love, but you wouldn't know anything about that."

If he's trying to make me feel bad that Kiera and I are taking a very nontraditional route, it's not working. "I'll be glad to pick up the ring for you."

"Thanks," he says and then pushes up out of the chair, taking his club soda and walking farther back into the plane.

I know the dude is now going to be in my life forever because he's related to my kid, but I'm not sure we'll ever get along all that well because he'll always see it as a betrayal that I went after his sister after he warned us all off.

CHAPTER 22

Kiera

I T'S FRIGID OUTSIDE as we walk from the car to the restaurant. Bain and I walk hand in hand and that's such a new and unsettling experience, my tummy flutters with every step we take. We've always been affectionate toward each other, but that usually came in the form of touches and cuddles post-sex. We've never been public before tonight and I wonder if he feels as weird as I do about it.

We enter the restaurant with him holding the door open for me. It's a gesture that before tonight I wouldn't have thought twice about—just a kindness extended. But tonight it seems romantic and protective.

I'm not sure who chose this steakhouse—Camden or Bain—but it was their mutual idea for a double date tonight. The atmosphere as soon as we step in is warm and inviting. Soft clinking of glasses, murmured conversations and candlelight. The décor exudes sophistication and elegance with crisp linen-covered tables set with fine china. The aroma of wood-fired steaks and spices waft through the air, mingling with the subtle fragrance of freshly cut flowers placed on each table. The restaurant hums with a subdued activity as the waitstaff glide among tables and speak in hushed tones. Lovers hold hands as they converse.

It's the perfect place for a romantic meal and I suppose it works well for a double date. Camden and Danica are here already and we're led back to their table. As we maneuver through, I'm hyperaware of the people who gawk. Women drooling over Bain, men looking in awe. Tonight he's dressed in a pair of dark jeans with a fitted black sweater and a black leather jacket, giving him an effortlessly cool vibe. He's beyond hot and it's not lost on me that women want him and men want to be like him. It makes me squeeze his hand tighter and he looks over his shoulder at me curiously. I just shake my head and smile in return.

Camden and Danica stand as we get nearer. Both are in winter casual—jeans and sweaters—and we all engage in hugs for the girls and fist bumps for the guys. I went with skinny jeans and ankle boots tonight, topped off with an oversized cream-colored sweater. Bain helps me out of my cranberry-red wool coat with big black buttons and I shiver when one of his fingers caresses my neck as he slides it off. He folds and places it over the back of my chair before holding it out for me to sit down.

I had no clue he was so well mannered, even though

he's never personally done anything to make me think he was a barbarian. It's just a completely new journey tonight and I'm digging it.

A waitress dressed in black slacks and a starched white shirt approaches with a smile, handing us the menus. She expertly describes the chef's specials, recommends their signature steak dishes and takes our drink orders.

Camden and Bain both go with bourbon while Danica orders a red wine. It's water for me and I'm astonished when Bain says, "On second thought... I'll just have water."

"No," I exclaim as I touch his arm. "You get a drink. You don't have to go without just because I do." The waitress smiles knowingly and Bain looks unsure. It's beyond sweet that when he said he's going through this with me that he's taking it to the extreme. I pat his arm. "I promise. Get your drink. It won't bother me in the slightest."

He still looks unsure but nods to the waitress his assent, adding, "And water too."

Danica and Camden duck their heads in amusement and then we all take a moment to peruse the menus. My eyes rove over the mouthwatering descriptions of perfectly cooked cuts of meat and exquisite side dishes. I've had a little nausea the last few days, but I can't say it's necessarily morning sickness. In my research, it's possible to start feeling some effects if I'm indeed going to be plagued with them, but it could also be just nerves because my world has been upended. Regardless, tonight I'm hungry and ready to chow down.

"Looks like we're in for a treat," I say, my voice filled with anticipation. "I think I'm going to get the filet topped with crab."

"I was looking at that too," Danica says.

Bain leans over and points to his menu. "Want to get this tomahawk rib eye for two? We can add the crab on top."

"Oh yeah," I say, mouth watering. I do love me a good rib eye.

"Jesus," Camden groans with faux disgust. "You two are fucking adorable."

Danica laughs and Bain smirks. I don't know how to react to that because somehow... despite this being new and a little disconcerting, it also feels right. So much so that it doesn't feel *cute* or *adorable*, two words that imply it's not deep.

A sudden realization washes over me, flooding my senses with a profound understanding. The emotions I harbor for Bain are pretty intense and I think layers are being peeled back, revealing a more intense connection than either of us understood.

All exposed because we're going to share a dish.

Camden puts his menu down and leans back, a cocky

smile on his face. "I knew when Danica and I busted you in the hallway at the gala there was something more than what we saw."

My eyes flare with surprise. He saw *more*? I don't know how because, at that time, I'm pretty sure Bain and I were only thinking about fucking each other. But maybe there was more and we were just too afraid to give it any credence.

Regardless, things are progressing fast since I found out I was pregnant and it feels a little like being caught in a turbulent storm. Dangerous and exciting all at once.

The waitress comes back and we give our orders. For a while, we discuss hockey, a given when you date someone who plays the sport. I grew up listening to Drake prattle on and on. The result is that I can hold my own with any person who thinks they know the sport on a professional level. Danica is the same, so both of us are active participants.

"You two should come watch Travis play," Camden says. "It's amazing the talent that kid has. Just like his dad."

It's a statement one would think might cause sad reflection, given that Mitch died in the crash, but Danica smiles with pride at Camden's words and then her expression softens to match that of the gooiest cookie straight out of the oven. "Camden's been working with Travis and his confidence has skyrocketed this past month."

None of us need to say it, but it's the value of consistent, positive influence in a kid's life. I know Bain and I both had it, but I'm not sure about Camden. So I flat out ask him. "You have that growing up?"

Camden nods. "Yeah... my dad always supported my hockey."

A statement of affirmation, but so much is left unsaid. I don't push, though, as Bain surprises me by stepping into the conversation in a very personal way. "While I'm ninety percent terrified of parenting, the one thing I feel confident in is helping my kid succeed in a sport."

"Want a boy who plays hockey?" Danica teases.

"Girls can play hockey too," he points out, and she inclines her head as if to say *Touché*. "But any sport, really. It's such a mix of encouragement and positive critique to keep the motivation up. My parents were so good at it and I can't wait to pass that on."

Those words punch deep and I blink furiously at tears that threaten to spill. Luckily, no one notices as Camden and Bain pivot to a discussion of sports psychology.

But I glance at Danica and she winks, which means she may not have seen the moisture in my eyes but she recognizes how incredibly sweet this conversation is.

The food arrives and Bain takes it upon himself to

cut up the massive rib eye and move portions to the extra plate the waitress brought, all while continuing to talk as if he's giving no thought to serving me. One more thing tonight that's not only endearing but hot as hell. It's quite possible he'll get lucky in the car before we leave the restaurant parking lot.

"Excuse me." We all turn to see a man standing there looking rather uncomfortable. His gaze cuts back and forth between Bain and Camden. "I was wondering if I could get an autograph from both of you. Maybe a picture."

Neither Camden nor Bain is put out, or at least they don't act like it. Danica and I share a knowing smile. It's part of the job, availing yourself of fans. It doesn't happen all the time, but when it does, it can be inopportune. Tonight we're just four friends having a meal together, so the interruption isn't bothersome. At least not to me.

It might be different if it were just me and Bain sharing a romantic meal and having intimate, private conversation, but in this case, the guys stand up with good nature and pose for pictures. It's always a risk that more people will come forward, but no one does and we continue on with our meal.

We all share a laugh, the interruption a lighthearted moment in our evening. It reminds us that even amid the fame and attention, we're just two couples enjoying a double date, trying to navigate the complexities of new relationships and impending parenthood.

For two hours, we eat, talk and laugh. Bain and I share a slice of cheesecake and by the time the men are signing the credit card receipts, I'm struggling not to undo the top button of my jeans. I wonder if I'm gaining weight already, but I'm sure if I am, it's nearly imperceptible at this point. I just feel completely bloated from too much food.

I've got a million questions on how things will progress. I've been researching like crazy, but that's just generated more curiosity and even some fear. I've made an appointment for next week with the OB-GYN I established with when I moved to Pittsburgh. Bain asked if he could go with me, so I set it for a non-game day. To say I was touched by his desire to attend is an understatement of epic proportions, but I'm still not sure how involved he wants to be. It's hard with his schedule, but if he wants to go to all the appointments, I'll figure out a way to make it work.

As the night draws to a close, we say our goodbyes outside the restaurant. Bain once again has my hand in his while Camden has his arm over Danica's shoulders. There are hugs, back slaps and promises to do this again, but then we're headed in opposite directions.

"This was nice," I say as he opens the door to his car for me to slide in. "It feels good to be out in the open, to have you by my side."

I tense, waiting for his reply. Bain has been slightly more open in his feelings than I have, but I still have hesitancy. It's hard for me to believe how things have changed sometimes and it stirs up a lot of wary emotions based on how my prior relationship soured. I'll admit… while I'm letting myself fall, I'm still scared to get fully invested for fear of being duped or hurt. My heart tells me that's silly with a man such as him, but my brain tells me to never forget that we may not know the real person behind the facade.

Bain leans in and kisses me softly. "This was very nice. New experience and all, but I rate it a ten out of ten and would definitely go out on a single date with you now that I've dipped my toe in the water."

He's serious and teasing at the same time and it makes me laugh with abandon. Not sure what it is about my amusement that has Bain's eyes darkening, but he kisses me again and this time, it's not so soft and sweet. His tongue invades my mouth, pleasure searing through me. Just that quickly, things heat up and when I pull back, I want to crawl into the back seat with him and have him fuck my brains out.

Bain ends the kiss with a groan, proof that he's as turned on as me, and just as quickly. His lips move to my jaw and he whispers, "Although… I'm just as happy never going on a date again and keeping you tied to the bed."

"I'm probably as happy with that too."

Bain chuckles and steps back, motioning for me to get into the car. "Let's go test out how much we like the concept of tying you to the bed."

My eyebrows shoot upward with interest. "Really?"

"I would never joke about something like that. You... tied up and spread-eagle... ready for me to do whatever I want to you."

"Let's go," I say, trying to pull the door closed, even though he's still in the way.

Bain laughs and leans down to kiss me once more. His eyes lock onto mine before he straightens, concern swirling within. "Is there, um... any way we can hurt the baby? We get a little rough sometimes."

"I don't know," I admit, the details I learned about pregnancy and obstetrics in nursing school long forgotten since I don't use that knowledge in my current field. "And you tend to rattle me with multiple orgasms. I wonder if that's harmful."

"Looks like I'll be adding those questions for the doctor next week."

"We're going to traumatize him." I laugh and then make a shooing motion with my hand. "But let's worry about it next week. Let's limit the rough stuff and we'll stop at just two orgasms per day for me."

Bain snorts and just before he closes the door, I hear him say, "I'm googling that shit first before I commit to an agreement."

CHAPTER 23

Bain

THE FEBRUARY CHILL stings my cheeks as I step out of the downtown Pittsburgh jeweler. The weight of the $132,000 engagement ring for Drake feels heavier than I anticipated. I'm in a safe area, but on the walk through the parking garage to my car, I'm alert to my surroundings. I have the small bag with the ring in an inside coat pocket for added safety.

Once inside my car, though, I can't help the grin that splits my face. I open up my glove box and pull out a black velvet box containing the gaudiest faux diamond ring I could find on short notice. Thank God for Amazon Prime delivery.

I snicker as I examine my purchase. It's like someone slapped a huge, ribboned bow on the top of the ring with fake diamonds crusted over it and the knot is a round gemstone that's not all that big. It's the oversized bow that takes up a lot of real estate on the band and it's tacky as shit.

Without hesitation or thought for my personal safety, I close the box and trade it out, putting the fake ring in the jeweler's bag and sliding the real one back into my coat pocket.

Drake directed me to meet him at a gas station not far from his house. The proposal is set for tonight.

He's waiting parked off to the side, away from the pumps. He doesn't bother getting out of his car so I do, patting my pocket for about the tenth time since I put the real ring in there, and head to the driver's door.

Drake rolls down the window, a gush of warm air from the interior bathing my face.

"Got your rock." I hand him the jeweler's bag. It's made of thick card stock, black with gold-foil lettering with the store's logo. I tuck my hands into my pockets to ward off the cold.

"Thanks," he says, and as I'd imagined he'd do, he pulls the box out to inspect his merchandise. I mean... you drop six figures on a ring, you should make sure it's what you bought.

My hands are admittedly sweating as Drake opens the box and my eyes nearly water as I try to hold a straight face.

The ring looks even gaudier now that it's an integral part of what's probably a very bad prank. But fuck... the guy has given me far too much shit about his sister and it's time for a little payback.

Drake explodes as he takes in the huge bow with a

dinky little diamond at the knot. Sheer horror coats his expression. "What in the actual fuck is this?"

"I don't know. That's what they handed me," I say, afraid a laugh will scrape its way out of my throat. "You paid $132,000 for that?"

"This isn't... this can't be..." he splutters, holding up the ostentatious knockoff that glints almost maliciously in the winter sunlight. "They fucking gave me someone else's ring."

Who would ever buy a ring like that for that type of money?

Drake's eyes meet mine, brimming with raw panic.

I can't help it. I double over with laughter, clutching my stomach as I start to wheeze.

"You fucking asshole," Drake growls as he tosses the ring at me. It bounces off my shoulder and tumbles under his car.

I straighten up, still laughing. "Hey... that ring cost me forty-nine bucks. How dare you treat it so callously."

Drake merely holds his arm out the window, palm up in silent demand to hand over the real goods.

I reach into my coat pocket and pull out the box. I open it and show it to him with a flourish of my hand. The jeweler showed it to me in the store and it's admittedly stunning. Drake's shoulders relax and one corner of his mouth curves in pride over such a beauty.

"You should see your face!"

Drake throws me a sour glance as he takes the ring, though he looks ready to throttle me. I expect him to rail at me or at the very least call me an asshole again. Instead, he blows out a huff of air and scrubs his hand through his hair. He sets the box on the passenger seat and reaches for the gearshift. "I've got to get going."

My hand lands on the car door before he can roll up the window. "Are you okay?"

"Yeah... fine."

Guilt pricks at me that I did a switcheroo on the ring, but I'm not sure that's the cause of his angst. "What's up?"

"I'm fine," he growls, but he looks completely rattled.

"You sure look it," I point out sarcastically. "Should make for a very romantic proposal tonight."

His neck twists and he glares at me. "I'm nervous, okay?"

"That she'll say no?"

"She's fucking out of my league. She *should* say no."

"Okay," I say dramatically, shaking my head. "Just stop that right now. Watching Drake McGinn lose his confidence is wigging me out."

"Just wait until you're in this position one day," he mutters, but that's beyond my imagination. No desire to do this proposal thing anytime soon. Maybe never. That level of commitment is not my cup of tea and I've given about all I can to the situation with Kiera.

"Look," I say, making sure his eyes are trained on me. "Brienne loves you and loves your boys. She's going to jump at the chance to be your wife."

"Yeah?"

"Yeah," I say and then give him a clap on the shoulder. "Now, get your head in the game. You have a job to do."

Drake huffs out an exasperated breath and offers me a sheepish smile. "You're right. It will be fine. All this will go off without a hitch and she'll say yes."

"You're starting off right," I encourage. "You got the right ring, at least."

That earns me a brief glare but then he asks, "You're good to get everyone to the restaurant?"

"Got it covered."

"Can I trust you after this ring debacle?"

I laugh and take a step back from his Tahoe. "That was a prank, man. I wouldn't do that to you. I'll have Kiera and the boys there well before you pop the question."

"And you know to come out as soon as she gives me her answer," Drake prods. We've been over the game plan more times than I care to remember.

"Unless she says no," I say with a grin. "If that's the case, I'm running."

"Asshole," he mutters and shifts the Tahoe into reverse. "Just have them there on time and I'll refrain from beating your ass for the ring prank."

"Deal." I chuckle as I turn away to head for my car, but Drake calls out to me. I look over my shoulder. "Thank you for getting the ring and helping Kiera get the boys there tonight. I appreciate you having my back."

"No problem."

"I've got your back too," Drake says, and that causes me to frown, but he clarifies. "When you become a dad... I've got your back. It's a wild ride, scary as shit and you never feel as if you're doing the right thing. Any doubts, you pick up that phone and you call me, okay?"

Well, fuck... Drake McGinn actually does have a heart. "I appreciate it."

I don't dare tell him just how freaked I am on any given occasion. Since the emotions inside me range from deliriously happy to terror-induced nausea, I'll take all the help I can get.

He gives me a rare, genuine smile. "Now get out of here and remember, no screwing around. This is important."

I give him a mock salute. "Got it. No screwing around."

Not that I need to give him assurances. I know when pranks are appropriate and when they're not. I have no intention of ruining his evening with Brienne.

♦

THE SWANKY FRENCH restaurant, Le Papillon Doré, shimmers in the evening light as I pull into the parking lot. It's almost empty since Drake rented the entire place for his romantic dinner and I assume the cars that are here are for the waitstaff and chefs.

Jake, Colby and Tanner are all dressed in little suits and ties, and they look fucking adorable. I put on a suit myself, even though our part in tonight's festivities is minimal. Still, it's an opportunity to dress up and I wouldn't deny Kiera, who's beyond giddy with excitement.

I glance at Kiera, her long blond hair elegantly cascading over one shoulder. She's wearing a gorgeous ruby red dress, which is most definitely her color. This dress isn't the sexpot number she wore to the gala but rather a formfitting, long-sleeve wool outfit she's paired with black high-heeled boots. Her stomach is as flat as ever, which is to be expected at this stage in the pregnancy, but I do wonder what she'll look like with a baby bump. I've seen pregnant women throughout my life, including the beautiful wives of teammates. I never really gave a second thought to any of them, but for some reason, I can't wait to watch Kiera's belly grow over the coming months. I don't know if it's a special kind of kink or what, but it's a turn-on.

Kiera smiles at me after I park behind the restaurant. The glow of the dashboard accentuates the twinkling in her blue eyes… a mixture of excitement and romance. Everyone piles out of my car, our exhilaration infectious as the boys giggle and Kiera squeezes my hand hard.

At the back door, the owner meets us as Drake had planned. He introduces himself as Maurice Aubert in a lilting French accent and motions us in and out of the cold. "Come in, come in."

We enter the kitchen area and not much is going on. There are two chefs—one uses a handheld torch over crème brûlée and the other surfs his phone.

"Monsieur McGinn and Mademoiselle Norcross are just finishing up their entrees," Maurice advises us. "And I must say, it's a very romantic atmosphere. You see it in the eyes… such a deep well of love. Very exciting this proposal, *non*?"

My hand rests at Kiera's back and I can feel her practically vibrating.

Maurice tells us that he served a classic coq au vin paired with a 2010 Château Latour. I must have had a blank look on my face because he adds, "It goes for fifteen hundred dollars a bottle."

Jesus fuck. Drake is not holding anything back, although I doubt expensive things mean much to Brienne. She could buy a country if she wanted to. I suspect just the act of renting out the restaurant will get him a solid *yes* tonight.

Maurice leads the boys over to where the chef is

working on the dessert. He explains how the sugar is being caramelized and we all watch as he writes "Will You Marry Me?" in chocolate before carefully placing the open ring box on the plate.

Oddly, that's something I probably would have called cheesy, but for some reason, I think it's a nice touch.

A waiter comes in from the dining area carrying the empty plates. He looks at Maurice. "They're ready for dessert."

Maurice claps his hands lightly and motions to the plate with the ring. He snaps at another who pulls out a bottle of champagne and a bottle of sparkling grape juice—presumably for the boys, although Kiera will be drinking it too. It's set on a tray with multiple flutes, which I assume will be carried out after the proposal.

The waiter picks up the plate.

"I should switch the ring again, right?" I tease, nudging Kiera.

"Don't you dare, Bain," she says, a playful glare in her eyes as I throw up my hands in surrender.

Maurice motions us to follow the waiter to the swinging kitchen door. "You'll all be able to peek out from here and watch. Mademoiselle Norcross's back is to us."

That's a nice touch.

The waiter walks out and before the door swings

SAWYER BENNETT

back, we poke our heads through. We're like a totem pole with the boys at the bottom, their eyes wide with anticipation. Kiera's in front of me and I'm tall enough to see over her head. I can't resist resting a hand on her hip as we watch.

Drake sees the waiter approaching Brienne from the rear and this was all evidently choreographed. As soon as the waiter starts to set the plate down, Drake takes Brienne's hand from across the table. She doesn't even dip her head to look at the dessert and Drake has his eyes locked on hers.

His voice is loud enough, it carries to us. "Brienne, I don't know how I did life before you. Maybe it was all a test to see if I was worthy of you and you've honored me with your trust, love and loyalty. You're my partner, my very best friend and the woman I will love until the last breath leaves my body. But it's not enough. I need more. Will you make me the happiest man alive and marry me?"

Drake nods down at the plate and we can see Brienne's head drop and assume she reads the question… sees the ring.

Then she squeals and I've never heard a sound like it before. Brienne Norcross is the epitome of elegance, sophistication and grace, and yet she lets out a bleat of pure joy as she jumps up from the table and flings her arms around Drake's neck. He stands from his chair and they kiss passionately.

"Can we go?" Jake whispers.

"Go for it," Kiera says and the boys burst out of the swinging door while Kiera and I follow at a more reserved pace, our fingers laced together.

The boys call out to their dad, breaking the kiss. Brienne whirls to see them and tears well in her eyes. Her hand flutters at her mouth and it's Tanner who slams into her, his little arms going around her legs as he tips his head to look at her. "Can I call you Mommy when you and Daddy get married?"

Brienne hugs him to her. "You can call me whatever you want whenever you want. But I'm going to take care of you for the rest of your life, okay?"

Kiera's fingers reflexively grip hard onto mine and I look down to see her crying. My arm goes around her shoulders and I pull her in close as we watch Drake shoo the boys away so he can put the ring on Brienne's finger. She admires it and then the boys ooh and aah.

Finally, Brienne's eyes pin on Kiera and she pulls away from me to hug her future sister-in-law. The waiter comes out with the champagne and sparkling grape juice. Flutes are filled and toasts are made. There are more hugs and kisses and Drake even tells the story of how I switched out the ring and gave him a heart attack. Brienne laughs so hard, her face turns red.

Eventually, I gather Kiera and the boys. I'm taking

them back to Drake and Brienne's house where Kiera will stay the night with the kids. Drake booked a suite at the Omni William Penn and while I'll stay for a bit with Kiera, it won't be an overnight thing.

While the boys chatter on the ride home in the back seat, I notice that Kiera is quiet. She stares out the passenger window as the downtown lights fade behind us.

"You okay?" I ask.

She turns her head my way. "Yeah... just reliving that. I'm so happy for Drake."

"It was a pretty cool proposal, I'll admit."

"He's always been a family man. The settling-down type. When things didn't work out with Crystal, my heart broke for him. As much as he tries to act all gruff and standoffish, he's a teddy bear on the inside. His circle is definitely complete now."

I don't reply because I can't tell if that's wistfulness in Kiera's tone. Is she wondering if she'll have that one day? I've come to know the woman well the last several weeks and I know marriage has never been an immediate goal. But admittedly, I have no clue how she really feels about settling down now that we have a kid in the picture. I know we're giving the relationship a go, but should we consider something more permanent?

The word *marriage* makes me feel off balance, but the answer is elusive and nothing feels right.

But then again, my life is incredibly tumultuous right now. Other than committing my support for the baby, all other decisions will have to be made when they do feel right.

CHAPTER 24

Kiera

IT'S GIRLS' NIGHT.

Not at the club, but in the Pittsburgh Titans' owner's suite.

Normally, Brienne uses this space to entertain business guests and sometimes conduct meetings, all while watching her team play. Tonight, though, it's closed off to all business acquaintances and more importantly, open to her closest friends.

Over the last year since the crash, Brienne's circle has grown. Once she stepped into the shoes of her late brother as the sole owner of the Titans, she became more personally invested. That included bringing all the significant others under her wing.

It was hard for her at first because she's never really had time to cultivate personal relationships and she works in such a ball-busting career, it's awkward sometimes for her to let her hair down.

But tonight we're all carefree laughs as we cheer on our men.

The suite is beyond luxurious. It's located at a premium vantage point, offering unobstructed views of the ice. At the front is a balcony with three rows of leather seats so plush you sink into them. That spreads backward into a living area with sofas and chairs to relax in as well as round dining tables and high tops. Large screen TVs dot the walls so you can watch the action while getting a drink from the open bar.

The walls are covered with personalized memorabilia and other Titans decorative elements, including the logo recessed into the ceiling and outlined in neon tubing.

The food is the best and tonight we've got a buffet of sliders with a build-your-own taco station, warming trays of loaded potato skins and hot wings. For the more health conscious there's a massive veggie platter and a Caesar salad. And if that's not enough, an array of chocolate brownies, cheesecake bites and fruit tarts for dessert.

I don't know if it's my imagination, but ever since finding out I'm pregnant, I'm hungrier than ever. I think about food a lot.

I think about sex a lot, too, but that's just because it seems to have gotten better and better with Bain. Which I'm not even sure how since it was the best I'd ever had. Maybe it's hormones. Maybe it's an increased intimacy based on sharing something so personally deep.

Regardless, I can be bought with food or sex with

Bain at this point in my life.

I'm sitting in the front row of seats with Danica, Tillie, Harlow and Stevie. Behind us sit Brienne, Sophie, Jenna and Ava.

It's pure coincidence that we're sorted with us in the first row dating players and the second row coaches. Of course, Brienne is unique, given she sits above everyone on the food chain.

She is, however, my friend and secondly, she's going to be a sister to me when she and Drake tie the knot.

The first period is winding down and neither team has scored. We're playing the LA Vipers and they've been having a rough season with injuries. Their goalie, however, is hot this year and it's hard to get anything by him.

The players converge on the defensive zone face-off circle after a TV timeout. Drake rolls his shoulders and crouches, ready to stop a quick shot.

I fix my gaze on Bain, positioning himself nearer to the net. The deafening cheers of the crowd reverberate through the arena, fueling my excitement. Twenty-five thousand cheering people coalesce and that massive buzz of excitement is how I feel every time Bain is on the ice.

The ref drops the puck and Stone reaches it first, but there's a scrabble for control. It squirts free and Bain gives chase, managing to collect it off the boards and shovel it to Kirill just before he's slammed into the glass.

I wince but he's fine, pushing off and giving chase as the Titans race down the ice toward the Vipers' net.

We're quick to capitalize on the transition. Coen charges forward with lightning speed, accepting a quick pass from Kirill. Stone matches Coen's strides along the near side with Boone just opposite him, their movements synchronized beauty. Bain and Kirill hover back to defend if we lose the puck. Coen jukes, fakes a pass to Stone, but sweeps it cross ice to Boone with pinpoint accuracy as he makes a beeline for the net. The cheers intensify with each passing second and all of us women stand up in a giant wave of frenzied support.

"Go, go, go!" Harlow screams. She's so fashionable in her gray blazer over a white blouse, paired with black pants and ankle boots. She's wearing a purple beanie with the Titans' logo on it, her crimson hair in a fishtail braid down her back.

Boone Rivers has really stepped into his position. Last season, he took Coen's spot after Coen's suspension, and Boone did so well, they kept him on the first line after Coen returned, moving Boone to a winger position.

His agility is off the charts and his stick handling is among the best on the team. He weaves through the Vipers' defenders with the strength of a bulldozer and the grace of a dancer. Boone rips a fast shot that catches the goalie in the chest. It bounces off... right at Boone who connects his stick perfectly to do a little scoop shot over the goalie's left shoulder.

The red light comes on behind the net and the arena explodes into a deafening roar.

"Yes," Tillie screams, hopping up and down with her arms around Harlow. While she normally wears Coen's jersey, tonight she's sporting a black-and-purple plaid shirt that I think might be Coen's it's so baggy on her. She's adorable in her tattered jeans and black combat boots, her golden curls bouncing with her exuberance.

I turn to Danica and give her a stinging high five and then lean across her to do the same to Stevie. They're both wearing their men's jerseys and while that's not ordinarily significant, it is tonight for Danica. She's got on Camden's jersey rather than Mitch's, which is a solid statement that she's living in the present and not the past. I'm sure she'll wear Mitch's jersey again and she told me that Camden never minds that she keeps his memory alive, but I think it's sweet she's embracing her new relationship.

We watch as the final minute and a half winds down and when the buzzer goes off signifying the end of the first period, we all scoot out of the rows and hit the buffet.

I'm first in line and load my plate up. I grab some vegetables, but I mostly have a mountain of tacos to consume. Parking at a high-top table, I'm soon joined by Jenna and Ava.

"Where did you get that jacket?" Ava asks, eyeballing the purple puffer vest with the Titans logo. "I love it."

I look down, happy with my wardrobe choice tonight. Unlike some of the other women here who have their men's jerseys, I don't have a Hillridge sweater. I have my brother's, of course, but I didn't want to wear it tonight. Instead I went with a white turtleneck sweater paired with gray jeans and white Chucks. I've got a gray knit infinity scarf, which looks great with the puffer vest.

"It's Brienne's," I say, picking up a taco and pushing stuff back in that's falling out. "One of the benefits of her dating my brother is I raid her closet all the time."

"Lucky," Ava says, nibbling on a chocolate chip cookie. I admire her going straight for dessert.

Ava's dating Coach West and she's probably the one I know the least out of the women. We have a massive group text thread going and most of my interaction with her has been there, although we've met up for coffee a few times.

"Who's lucky?" Brienne asks as she nudges in beside me. The wink of her massive diamond makes me smile. Drake's proposal was perfect and Brienne's been walking around on cloud nine.

"Your future sister-in-law," Ava quips, shooting me a wink. "She said she gets to raid your closet."

Brienne shrugs. "Any of you can raid my closet."

Ava's eyes widen. "I'm so there."

Tillie pouts. "I'm too short and curvy, but I appreciate the generosity."

"I've totally got stuff that would fit you," Brienne scoffs. "Maybe not the length of my pants but tops for sure."

"Party at Brienne's house to steal all her designer clothes," Tillie yells to the other women and we all laugh.

Once everyone has a plate and we're all huddled around two side-by-side high tops, Harlow demands to hear more about Drake's proposal. I listen with a smile on my face, not just from the romanticism of how my brother pulled that off, but also because Bain was involved. It was hilarious he switched out the ring and almost gave Drake a heart attack, but just standing in that kitchen doorway, hand on my hip while we watched my brother seal his destiny, was special. Bain probably had a million other things he could have been doing that would have been to his liking, but he chose to be there with me and my family.

"Okay... enough about Brienne," Jenna says, her eyes landing on me and sticking. "The more interesting story is that somehow Bain and Kiera have been canoodling behind everyone's back and she got knocked up."

Yeah... the secret is fully out of the bag. Bain pretty much ensured the players knew and I sent a text to my girls on our group thread. There was no easy way to say it, but I gave a fairly lengthy explanation of casual hookup to an oopsie to trying for a relationship. Of course, the thread blew up and there were lots of questions, but this is the first time we've all been face to face.

"Do you even know how far along you are?" Sophie asks.

"Not sure. My guess is we got pregnant the very first time, so around seven weeks. We see the OB-GYN tomorrow."

"It's so exciting," Tillie chirps. She's the cheerleader of our group. "What does it feel like? Do you have any symptoms?"

"Yeah," I reply with a wink. "I'm hornier than normal."

Stevie was unfortunately taking a sip of her beer at that point and she chokes. Danica pounds her on the back while asking a follow-up question. "Any weird cravings?"

"Sex," I reply with a grin. "But also food. I'm so hungry, but that's probably psychosomatic."

"Hopefully you won't get morning sickness too bad," Danica says. "It's the pits."

"My tummy feels off at times, but I can't tell if that's morning sickness or just the mix of excitement and all-consuming terror."

The women cast me sympathetic smiles and Brienne hooks her arm around my shoulders to squeeze me. "You got this. You are one badass woman and we're all here to support you."

There's a chorus of affirmations from the others and more questions thrown at me.

"Will you find out the gender of the baby tomorrow?" Jenna asks.

"What do you want... a boy or a girl?" This from Stevie.

Sophie nudges me with her elbow. "How excited is Bain?"

I go around the table nodding at each woman who asked the question. "I'm not sure. I'm not sure. I'm not sure."

Brienne laughs. "You'll figure it out."

"They did say when I made the appointment that we'd be able to see the little niblet. The nurse said they'll most likely use a transvaginal ultrasound wand since I'm pretty early."

Stevie winces.

"Just think of it like a sex toy," Tillie says.

Laughing, I hold my taco in front of my mouth, indicating I want to eat. But not before I say, "I'm sure Bain's going to have loads of jokes for the doctor tomorrow when he uses it on me."

"You better have Bain start minding his tongue,"

Danica warns with a grin. "Babies start hearing sounds from the outside world at eighteen weeks."

I roll my eyes. "Trying to get him to stop dirty talk would be like trying to stop the flow of water over the edge of a cliff."

Jenna sighs. "I love it when Gage talks dirty."

All of us go silent, our gazes snapping to her with mouths open. Gage is like the nicest, most upstanding man in the world. He's the epitome of a cinnamon roll guy. I'm not sure any of us have even heard him cuss before.

"He dirty talks?" Stevie asks with wide eyes.

Jenna blushes and ducks her head. "Forget I said that."

"Oh, no you don't." Brienne wags her finger. "Spill the details."

While we eat delicious food, we share laughs, give unsolicited advice and poke fun at one another. I'm not sure how I got to be so lucky to land in the midst of these women, but they're my tribe.

"Oh, I forgot," Jenna exclaims and then moves over to a large black bag sitting by the wall. "I got something for all of us."

We all crane our necks as she pulls out individual clear bags that hold some type of white material inside. Our names are written on the front with Sharpie and she hands them out.

No one waits, opening the gifts and extracting what appears to be a long-sleeve T-shirt. Harlow is the first to get hers fully opened, followed by Ava, and they start howling.

I pull mine out and see a logo in purple and gray on the front breast pocket. It reads, "Titan Queens."

"Turn it around," one of the ladies says, and I do, not able to control the laugh that pops out of my mouth.

Across the back, it reads, "The real power behind the Titans."

"I fucking love it," Brienne says.

I cut my eyes to her before rolling them. "Yeah, well, everyone knows you are really the power behind all the Titans, so technically you don't need this T-shirt. But I love it."

Without waiting, I undo my puffer vest and pull my turtleneck off, hoping we're far enough back from the edge of the suite balcony that no one can see us.

It fits perfectly and I twirl for everyone to admire.

"Let's all wear them to Mario's after the game," Sophie says.

We'd all decided to make it a full night out and we're going to meet the guys there—provided we win.

I hope we do, not just for the good of the team, but this is the first opportunity for Bain and me to be out as a couple. I'm not sure how it's going to go and it'll be a little awkward, but I'm looking forward to being in the group and having someone rather than being the odd one out. That's silly, I know, but since Bain and I agreed to give this whole relationship thing a go, I find myself willing to trust in a man again.

I always hoped there'd be a day when I could get past my bad experience and be willing to take a chance. Bain made it easy when he committed to staying by my side and helping me raise our child.

CHAPTER 25

Bain

KIERA'S OB-GYN'S OFFICE is not what I expected. It's not clinical or sterile like other doctors' offices I've been in but rather warm and inviting. It's a space that's deliberately designed to be calming. Walls painted in soothing blues and greens, nature-themed art on the walls, the space lit with only natural sunlight through big windows and small table lamps scattered about. If I didn't know it was a doctors' office, I would have thought it was a spa.

The receptionist is efficient but warm as she has Kiera fill out some basic forms. Her fingers fly over the keyboard as she takes information down. I stand beside Kiera and glance out over the lobby, filled with couples like us and several women who are alone. I wonder if they're pregnant and their partner isn't here or maybe they're just here for the regular yearly checkup.

Honest to God, I didn't know what that entailed, but as Kiera and I were researching the upcoming appointment and what would occur, she sort of educated me on Pap smears and I was horrified. I mean, I knew women had them, but I didn't know about tables and stirrups and what sounds like a torture device Kiera called a speculum.

After she's checked in, Kiera and I sit together on a small sofa. There's a coffee table and I'm a bit cramped, but it's all good as Kiera leans her weight into me. I glance around, observing the other couples. Some are fidgeting while others chat quietly. The married couple adjacent to us are discussing baby names, which is something they need to decide soon as she's very, very pregnant. They're called by the nurse and the husband stands first and has to help his wife up from her chair. I bite back my grin, knowing I'll relish doing that for Kiera one day because she'll hate needing the help.

I get a few looks from some of the men here, likely trying to determine if they recognize me. I wore a khaki baseball cap with an Audi logo on it. No clue where I got it from because I've never had an Audi, but it was in my closet with about a hundred other caps I've collected. I steered clear of anything with a Titans or Vengeance logo, though, as I prefer not to get recognized here.

Kiera flips through a magazine, the picture of serene contentment. She hasn't seemed anxious about this appointment, but I'm not sure she'd admit it if she was. She likes to showcase her resilience and independence. I, on the other hand, am a buzzing mixture of nerves and anticipation. My heel rhythmically taps on the carpet as I wait to see the miracle of life I helped create.

Twisting her neck to look at me, she nods down to my bouncing leg. "Nervous?"

"No," I lie.

Her grin tells me she doesn't buy it for one second, but she doesn't call me on my bullshit, instead going back to her magazine. I resist the urge to brush a lock of hair behind her ear, just like I resist the urge to pull her in closer. Every day that goes by, I seem to want more of her.

Last night after we put the Vipers away, the team went to Mario's. There were wild cheers and applause when we walked in, but I tuned it all out. Despite riding the thrill of the win, all I really wanted was to see Kiera.

She was already there with the other women waiting for us. They all stood around a few tables laughing. Kiera's so fucking beautiful when she laughs and I stopped just to stare at her until Camden plowed into me.

It was hilarious to find all the women wearing matching T-shirts. Jenna had them made and they've officially proclaimed themselves as the "Titan Queens," their new title emblazoned on the front breast pocket. The back reads "The real power behind the Titans" and I roared with laughter when I saw it.

But I also paid attention to the weird sensation of

possession flowing through me. I slipped my hand behind Kiera's neck and pulled her closer so I could whisper, "I'm going to take that shirt and have my name and number put on the back."

I'll never forget the look she gave me. I've watched a myriad of expressions cross over Kiera's face since we first met. I've seen lust, humor, fear, passion, sadness and utter calm. But last night when I told her I wanted my name on her shirt, there was a blaze of joy within a breathtaking smile laced with hopefulness.

It was a silent message that she was looking forward to a future with me the way I was with her. I made her happy and I was struck by a realization that I wanted to make her feel like that, always.

At Mario's, we were an unmistakable couple and it was an absolute new experience for me. Kiera, with her warm smile and sparkling eyes, had been a part of the team, but as my friend, not my girlfriend. For me, a player who had never taken relationships seriously, to have her beside me, to have my arm draped around her, it just felt right.

I took ribbing from some of the guys. Kirill was gleeful in giving me good-natured shit. "Bain, always scoring on and off the ice."

I laughed along with them and accepted bro hugs. Hendrix clapped me on the shoulder and squeezed. "I didn't think you had it in you, man. But I think you'll make a hell of a dad."

And the guys... they were good with Kiera. They congratulated her, pulled her into bear hugs, already referring to our unborn child as the newest little member of the team. I loved seeing that, watching her blush, the way she'd laugh, the happiness radiating from her.

The whole night was surreal. I'd transitioned from a playboy to a man deeply connected to a woman. It was a full one hundred and eighty degree change from who I used to be and I have no self-recrimination from straying so far from my hard-core single values. Kiera makes me want to embrace the change.

"Ms. McGinn." I blink out of my reverie as Kiera stands. I scramble up after her and she reaches out her hand for me to take.

A nurse with a friendly smile leads us down a hallway. It's decorated with the same calming colors and along the walls are pictures of the babies the doctors here have delivered. Each step I take makes my heart pound with a little more anticipation.

The first stop is a small alcove with a built-in desk where a laptop sits. The nurse records Kiera's blood pressure and weight, then hands her a cup for a urine sample. I lean against the wall to wait.

The nurse ignores me and types into her laptop. When Kiera returns, we're led into the exam room and my eyes are immediately drawn to the table with the stirrups that Kiera had described to me.

Handing Kiera a gown, the nurse says, "Only need to disrobe from the waist down."

"Because we'll be doing a transvaginal ultrasound?" Kiera asks.

"That's right. It will give us the best picture at this early stage."

When the nurse exits, Kiera moves to the corner where there's a small bench with hooks on the wall for her clothing. I move to the sleek exam table covered with crisp white paper and examine the stirrups.

"This is giving me all kinds of dirty ideas," I muse.

Kiera snorts and I glance over at her to see her shimmying out of her jeans. Ordinarily, that's all it would take to get my dick hard, but not here. Not in this environment. I'm all about the pregnancy experience.

I move to one of the guest chairs and prop an ankle on the opposite knee. We're silent as Kiera shrugs into a robe that ties on the side. She starts to move past toward the table, but I grab her hand, tugging her to me.

She doesn't fight me but allows me to drag her onto my lap where I hold her loosely. Placing my chin on her shoulder, I ask, "You nervous?"

"Little bit."

"Shit's getting real," I murmur.

"So real," she agrees quietly and tilts her head to rest against mine.

That's how Dr. Segal finds us when he knocks on the door and walks in. He's a short man, probably in his late fifties but incredibly fit looking. He's got dark curly hair with a bit of gray sparsely mixed throughout. A pair of black-framed glasses perch on the end of his nose and his smile is easygoing.

"Ms. McGinn… it's good to see you again."

"You too, Dr. Segal." Kiera stands from my lap and I stand along with her, holding my hand out.

As we shake, I introduce myself. "Bain Hillridge."

"Nice to meet—" Dr. Segal jolts and his eyes narrow at me, trying to see past the ball cap. "Well, I wasn't expecting to cross paths with a Titan today. Great game last night."

"Thanks," I say, and I expect him to want to talk about it or even get a picture. Instead, he turns and gives all his attention to Kiera.

"Go ahead and hop up on the table," he says, moving to the sink to wash his hands.

I move to Kiera's side as she lays back. Dr. Segal moves to the end and locks out the stirrups. "Slide down a bit more," he says as he sits on a stool and rolls right on up between my girl's legs.

I have a moment of distinct discomfort and my hands fist, but I take in Dr. Segal's clinical expression as he doesn't even look at her there yet. Instead, he pulls the ultrasound machine over and explains the test.

He shows Kiera the ultrasound wand and then covers it with a medical condom and lube. It's thin, the end a little bulbous, but it's quite long.

Way longer than my dick.

I take her hand and she squeezes as the doctor inserts it into her vagina. I wince but Kiera doesn't even flinch.

She's a stoic person, though, so I ask the doctor, "Does that hurt her?"

"It doesn't," Kiera said, her head tilted to look up at me. "Weird, but not painful."

Dr. Segal uses his free hand to press down on her lower belly a little and then makes an adjustment on the computer. He rotates the wand and the screen is filled with a gray, hazy static that looks exactly like nothing.

But then I see it. Just briefly… a large black circle, then it's gone.

Then it's back again, much clearer.

"That's the gestational sack," Dr. Segal says, and my heart hammers in my chest. "And that small gray area is the yolk sac."

It's so small, no bigger than a bean. "And that's our baby?" I ask incredulously.

"Sure is. Let's listen to the heartbeat." Dr. Segal taps a few keys and then the room is filled with a fast, rhythmic pattering.

I glance at Kiera. Her eyes are as round as saucers and I know mine look no different.

"Why's it so fast?" Kiera asks the doctor.

"The fetal heart rate at this stage can be between 100 and 180 beats per minute."

"It's like a hummingbird's wings," Kiera says in awe and emotion clogs my throat. That's the perfect way to describe it.

I lean over and brush my lips over her forehead. I've never felt closer to a human being in my life and it's all due to the miracle flickering on the computer screen. That's both me and Kiera, thriving against all odds.

It's pure magic.

"I'd say date of conception was around January 1, which means your due date will be September 24. Although it could be a few days before or a few days after."

"Holy shit," I wheeze. That's this year. Just months away.

Dr. Segal grins at me, then Kiera. "Congratulations."

We walk out of the doctors' office hand in hand with a picture of the ultrasound in Kiera's purse. I already snapped it with my phone as we were checking out and sent it to my parents and brother.

"What do you think about grabbing a few nights' worth of clothes and come stay at my place?" I ask.

Kiera's been to my place before and she's stayed the night, but we mostly have settled into a routine at her house.

"Sure," she says because she's easygoing that way.

"It's closer to the arena and we have a game tomorrow, then the memorial the day after, which will be there. Save us some driving."

"That it would."

We play the Denver Blue Devils tomorrow and then the day after that is the twentieth—the first anniversary of the crash. A remembrance celebration has been planned at the arena. It's a given that Kiera and I will go together after we talked about it earlier this week.

I push that out of my head, though. That's two days away and I don't want that dragging me down from my high of seeing my kid in Kiera's belly.

CHAPTER 26

Kiera

I HUM TO myself as I pour the eggs into the pan, swirling it to evenly coat the bottom and lower edges. I precut all the things that Bain likes in his omelet and add them in large clumps. I'm using his largest pan and six eggs, so it can handle a lot.

Crisp bacon, diced ham, cheddar cheese, onions, red peppers.

I want to add mushrooms, but we're going to share the omelet and he'll gag if he gets one in his mouth.

Smiling, I consider what the omelet says about our relationship. I enjoy cooking for him. We love to share food. I know the things he likes and doesn't. In fact, I got up early this morning and grabbed a quick shower just so I could do this for him and we could share a meal.

It's game day and he'll be heading to the arena around noon. He spends a lot of time getting into his headspace and derives energy hanging with his team-mates. They might play video games in the players' lounge or they might kick a hacky sack around in the parking garage. They'll eat together and do warm-up preparations.

But then Bain also takes alone time. He'll put on his game-day playlist filled with, oddly enough, Viking war music. It's guttural lyrics with a heavy metal flair, and it gets his adrenaline going. He has a ritual when lacing his skates that he recites the various skills he uses on the ice.

We're creating our own rituals and I like this morning game-day habit. Me slipping out of bed and making him breakfast.

My stomach grumbles as the smells intertwine and I have a brief curiosity as to how much weight I'll gain. Dr. Segal gave advice to eat healthily and continue exercising, so I imagine I'll be fine, but damn if I don't feel like I can eat this entire omelet myself. That I know is psychological because the little "bean" isn't big enough yet to pull on my resources.

I move to flip the edges of the omelet but jerk as I feel Bain's big body step into mine. His chest is bare and warm, and I can smell the lingering scent of toothpaste as he kisses my neck.

"I don't know what smells better… you or that omelet," he murmurs as he buries his nose in my hair. He loves my coconut-scented shampoo. I was touched to see he bought some and put it in his shower.

His hands move from my hips so that his arms circle around my stomach. His teeth graze my ear and I shiver.

Bain chuckles over my reaction and then takes the spatula from my hand.

"You going to cook now?" I ask, leaning my head back against his chest.

Tossing the spatula on the counter, he turns off the stove. "Not hungry for an omelet."

There's a tinge of disappointment that I misjudged what he might want to eat for his game-day breakfast, but then he has me in his arms and whirls me toward the kitchen island.

Bain deposits me on the granite and nudges his way between my legs. He's wearing a pair of low-hanging sweatpants and my mouth waters at his muscular perfection.

His palms lightly rest on my thighs and he leans in to kiss me... a mere whisper of his lips over mine.

"I only have eggs for breakfast. I can run out and get something else for you."

"I'm craving something different," he says.

"It's game day, so whatever you want. I can run to the grocery store." I place my hands on his shoulders and then immediately move one up to brush the hair threatening to fall into his eyes.

Bain leans into my palm, eyes closed like a cat getting rubbed just right.

When they open, they're burning with something I've come to recognize as gluttony of a different kind.

"You shouldn't have slipped out of bed so early," he says, placing a hand on my chest and pushing me back onto the counter.

I wiggle my body as his hands pull at my leggings, my panties sliding down my legs along with them. Bain's hands press against the insides of my knees, a command to spread my legs wider.

I don't fight him on it but instead rise onto my elbows so I can watch.

Bain is fascinated with my pussy and has spent countless hours touching me in all ways imaginable. My body tenses as his fingers glide along the outer lips of my sex and then bucks when he glides a finger inside me.

I groan as he curls it, then a harsh breath wheezes out of me when he pulls his finger free and licks it, his eyes holding me captive.

"You taste like fucking magic, baby."

My body is his slave but my heart swears fealty to him when he bends over and pushes my shirt up. He presses a kiss over my belly and whispers, "Hi, little bean. Better hold tight because I'm getting ready to rock your mama's world."

Bain's gaze rises and meets mine ever so briefly before his mouth descends on me. His fingers caress and his tongue tastes. The intimacy of oral with Bain has always made my heart flutter because he so obviously enjoys doing this to me. His groans of pleasure heighten my own and he barely sets up a mind-blowing sucking on my clit before I'm exploding so hard, a sob of pleasure bursts from my chest.

I'm delirious, barely understanding why Bain's pulling my body a little closer to the edge of the counter but then I realize it's the perfect height for him. His cock is out and sliding into me, stretching me in all the right ways.

"Goddamn," he mutters, a curse of appreciation over how great this feels.

Bain forces my legs around his hips, then places his hand behind my neck, pulling me up so he can kiss me. I taste my pleasure on his lips and feel his desire straight through to my bones.

It's a gentle fucking, just like he did last night. Before we left Dr. Segal, Bain asked a litany of questions, among which were concerns about sex.

"We have a very vigorous sex life," Bain proclaimed, not in a bragging manner. It sounded almost clinical. "Can I hurt the baby?"

Dr. Segal's been around the block. He didn't even bat an eye. "You can have sex as often as you want."

"But how gentle do I need to be?"

I placed my hand over my mouth to cover my smile, but Bain wasn't joking. He looked at Dr. Segal expectantly.

Dr. Segal smiled. "Hard thrusting is okay. The baby's in a fluid sac. But the cervix tissue can be sensitive, so if you see any spotting, maybe go a little gentler."

Despite Dr. Segal's assurances, last night Bain treated me like I was fine china. He made love to me slowly, even though I tried to urge him faster with my hands on his ass.

He refused and being much stronger than I am, I had to go along with it. It was so beautiful and for the first time in our relationship, we actually came together. That was all Bain as he knows my signs and he watched me carefully. He also knows exactly how to touch me between my legs to get me where he wants me. I've never had that experience before… simultaneous orgasms, but it was so beautiful that I want them all to be that way.

It appears that's what Bain's trying to do again. He moves inside me gently, his face all harsh angles of pleasure, and I can tell he wants to let loose.

I wrap my arms around his neck and tighten my legs around his hips. Bain's mouth is on mine, kissing me deeply while fucking me so sweetly. The angle I'm sitting only lets him thrust in shallow measures, but it's hitting my clit just right.

My head spins as I feel another orgasm brewing. I start to pant, my sure sign, and Bain kisses me harder. His hand slips between us and he strums my clit so it's getting pressure from all angles.

Letting my head fall back, I close my eyes and give in

to the pleasure. Just as my orgasm breaks, Bain slides in deep, actually lifting me from the counter with his hands under my ass, and groans deeply. His hips jerk as he unloads. "Fuck, Kiera… just… fuck, that's good."

I shudder uncontrollably from the shared experience, wishing it could go on and on forever.

When I lift my head and open my eyes, I find Bain staring at me. His face is flushed, his eyes turbulent. "Tell me it's better because of what we created."

There's a plea within his tone. He doesn't understand why we've grown so much closer in such a short period. The natural answer is the baby, and maybe that's it.

But maybe we're just two people who found a deep connection, regardless.

I press my palms to his cheeks and shake my head. "I don't know what it is. I just know it is."

He nods, accepting that I know no more than he does. Lifting me from the counter, he walks me into the master bathroom. Supporting me with just one arm under my ass and with me clinging to his body, he reaches into the shower and turns it on.

Only then does he let me slide down and remove the rest of our clothing.

Under the heat of the spray, Bain washes me, moving over my body leisurely. We talk about the game tonight and I promise to cook him another omelet when we get out.

After we're both dried off, dressed at the table eating—both of us with a fork but sharing the huge plate of food—Bain drops a casual question that somehow feels like a bomb. "What do you think of my place? Do you like staying here?"

"Your master bathroom is so much nicer than mine," I say. My house—or rather the one Drake bought when he moved here and lets me live in rent-free for helping with the boys—is a bit older. Bain lives in a condo, but it's spacious with tons of windows with amazing views and it's brand spanking new.

"We should consider moving in together," he says, and my fork freezes halfway to my mouth.

He grins at me. "What? It's not so unusual to be thinking of these things."

I lower my hand. "It is when you have two people who don't do relationships. You've never wanted one or even tried it, and I've had a horrible experience. It's a huge commitment."

Bain's knee nudges mine under the table. "So is having a baby together."

"Fair point," I concede.

"I'm just saying," he says as he picks up the fork I'd laid down, scoops up the bite I'd discarded and holds it out for me to eat. I lean over and accept being fed with no thought. "I've committed to helping you through this pregnancy. We already spend every night together. Why don't we just pick a place and stay there?"

"Move in together, you mean."

"Yes, that's what I mean. Pick a place."

"Where would you want to stay?" I ask curiously.

Bain shrugs, hands me my fork and picks up his own. "Your place is bigger and has a yard. Mine is newer and closer to the arena."

"We won't need a yard right away," I muse.

"Unless we get a dog," he says with a wink.

"Let's just start with a baby and see how it goes." I cut into another bite of omelet, chewing on the food and the idea. "This place is big enough. You have three bedrooms and the middle one could be the nursery."

Bain grins at me. "You said nursery."

I frown at him as he chuckles. "What about it?"

He shakes his head. "Nothing. It's just... sometimes a word comes up dealing with the baby and it's like a slap upside the head that this is so real. And I mean a slap in a good way. It just tickles me."

And there it is... another slide of my heart closer to the cliff's edge, ready to topple all the way over for this man.

"One other thing," Bain says as he stares at me, his expression hard. "My place is closer to Pitt. You're going back to school and this will make your commute easier."

"But I—"

Bain reaches across the table and claps his hand over

my mouth. "I don't want to hear a single negative thing about you going back to school. I promised Drake I'd work hand in hand with him to get you there. So accept it, okay?"

I stare at him, feeling that traitorous, blood-pumping organ in my chest take a flying leap off the edge of the relationship cliff. But I can't let him get away with covering my mouth and shutting off my words.

I give him a long lick on the palm of his hand and he jerks it away, just the way Drake did when he tried to silence me that way. "Gross."

Grinning, I watch as he wipes it with his napkin. "Okay… let's make your condo our place."

Bain's eyes shoot up to lock with mine. "Yeah?"

"Yeah."

CHAPTER 27

Bain

Y OU WOULD THINK that for an outdoor memorial to commemorate the tragic plane crash that killed forty people associated with the Pittsburgh Titans organization, occurring in February, there would be a gray cast to the sky with the threat of precipitation to set the mood. I equate sad occasions with dreary weather.

But today, February 20, it's mild, climbing into the mid-fifties with bright sun. The gathering is being held at the new monument Brienne had commissioned to be unveiled today and is open to the public. It sits on the outermost perimeter of the arena property, no more than fifty yards from the Allegheny River, and the design holds a ton of meaning. A roped-off area is provided with security for where the VIP guests will sit, such as the actual players, their families, executives in the organization and the widows and widowers who have chosen to attend. The rest of the crowd will spill into the arena parking lot, but there's a stage with a jumbo screen set behind it so everyone in attendance can hear and see what's going on.

When the large fabric covering is pulled off the monument, there's a collective gasp from the audience. I'd not seen the mockup of it, although Kiera had. She stands beside me, our hands clasped.

Brienne, on the stage, says into the microphone, "I present to you 'Titans' Valor.'" She goes on to explain the design, which is now being shown on the massive screen. "We commissioned local artisan Wayne Whitely who constructed this amazing piece from local Pennsylvania bluestone. The abstract sculpture swirls from the base over twenty feet high in fluid, graceful lines that represent the motion of our players on the ice. The inside planes are left with roughened edges to represent the trials and tribulations of the sport. At the base are forty individual plinths that represent our dear friends who died in the crash, along with their names and likenesses carved into the stone. And if the cameraman can show it... yes, there, thank you—it reads, 'In memory of our fallen Titans. Your spirit, your passion and your legacy will never be forgotten.'"

After a light smattering of applause, Brienne takes a deep breath. "I lost my brother on that plane and I grieve for him every day. I don't let myself get trapped in that grief of loss but choose to celebrate Adam's life. I use his memory to fuel my own passions and I think this city has done the same. For that, I honor every citizen of

Pittsburgh who has stood behind this new team."

There's a roar of approval from the crowd and Brienne steps away from the podium to be replaced by Callum Derringer. While the mood is somber, a palpable sense of community ripples all around us.

Callum clasps his hands on the podium and looks out over the players who circle the monument before lifting his face to stare out over the crowd. "This past year has been a testament to the strength and resilience of the human spirit. The task of rebuilding our beloved Pittsburgh Titans was not an easy one. Every decision made, every player signed, was done with a heavy heart and a sense of profound responsibility. We had to honor our past while looking toward our future."

I don't mean to tune Callum out, but I do because his words punch deep. He talks about rebuilding, which is exactly what I'm doing. I was traded to a team and I'm making new friends, have a girlfriend and we're having a baby. There's always that tiny part of me that wonders if I'm dazzled so much by Kiera that I forget the man I was before her, but Callum says to honor the past and look forward to the future. That's what I need to do.

As he talks about the family we've become... this new Titans team... I can't help but slip my arm around Kiera's waist and pull her in closer. She melts into me and it feels right.

Coen takes the stage next. As one of the three surviving members, he was chosen to read the names of those who died. As he does so, a small eternal flame flickers up from the center of the plinth around the base of the monument that corresponds with the person. It's incredible to watch. Once all the individual stones are burning, a large flame erupts out of the top center of the monument. There are murmured exclamations of surprise and delight at how beautiful it all is.

"Now we'd like to have a moment of silence to honor those who died," Coen says.

There are a few more speakers... the mayor of Pittsburgh and Cory Pearsall's widow who is working to establish a hockey scholarship fund. Closing remarks by Brienne are short but heartfelt, her last words setting the tone for the future. "Embrace tomorrow's dawn with a resilient heart. In every challenge, fill yourself with hope and let joy illuminate each step you tread. The best of our story is still unwritten, yet to be read."

♦

AFTER THE MEMORIAL and at their invitation, Kiera and I go to Drake and Brienne's home for dinner. Some of the players were going out to hoist beers in honor of those lost and I seriously considered going. Kiera urged me to, but really... I didn't want to.

Or rather, I just wanted to be with Kiera.

Call me whipped, matured or lazy, but I wanted a

quiet night after the heaviness of this morning. Of course, *quiet night* in the Norcross-McGinn household does include three rambunctious boys who never seem to slow down. I found myself playing with them, running through the mansion as we shot Nerf guns at each other. Kiera, Brienne and Drake all sat around the kitchen island, drinking wine (apple juice for Kiera) while nibbling from a charcuterie board.

Once, I chased Jake through the kitchen while he screamed in faux terror. I aimed my Nerf gun at his butt but at the last minute, I turned it and shot Drake in the chest. I didn't wait around to see what he'd do, continuing through a small butler's pantry that opened into the dining room, through the formal living room and back into the great room.

I careened around the corner looking for Jake when a Nerf dart struck me right in the forehead. It bounced off harmlessly, but I was shocked to see Drake there holding a gun he must have snatched off one of the boys. He blew on the end of it and walked back into the kitchen. After, we all eventually sat down for pizza. It was a great night.

Now we're at Kiera's house, her naked body wrapped with mine. We came here as it was closer to Brienne's.

"Want to start moving stuff to my condo tomorrow?" I ask.

She rolls in my arms to face me. "I don't know about

moving. I want to start packing some stuff up. I talked to Drake tonight while you were running around like a toddler with the kids." I chuckle and kiss her shoulder. "Told him I was going to move in with you and he's going to go ahead and sell the house."

"Makes sense, unless he wanted to rent it."

"He doesn't want to bother with it. So I told him I'd get it all staged nicely. Anyway, tomorrow I'll start packing. I'll have it done by the time you get back from the road trip this upcoming weekend and maybe you can get some of the guys to help move everything in one trip?"

"That will work. I'll ask Camden to help so we can use his truck."

Kiera brings her hand up and traces a pattern over my chest, her eyes focused on her fingers.

"Something wrong?"

"No," she says softly, her gaze lifting. "It's just… two weeks ago, you and I were fuck buddies. And now we're moving in together."

"It seems too fast," I say, assuming that's where she's going. But we don't have any choice. The pregnancy put everything on a different time line.

"It's just a little overwhelming," she admits. "But in a good, thrilling way."

Laughing, I squeeze her tight to me. "I know exactly what you mean."

CHAPTER 28

Kiera

'M NOT SURE if it's a good thing or a bad thing, but Bain is scrambling to get ready for the game. His duffel is packed and he's got most of his suit on—a beautiful light gray—but he's struggling with the tie. Over the course of our nearly two-month relationship, I've been with him on the mornings of game day and he's usually not this discombobulated.

But this morning, we didn't follow the normal rules of waking up, having a good breakfast and methodically getting him packed up to head to the arena for his personal preparations for the game. Instead, Bain rolled me under him and spent a long time playing between my legs. He was leisurely about it, using his fingers and tongue. He talked to me—filthy words—that had me begging. Just when I was about to come, he stopped and then did something he'd never done before and I'm telling you... it was hot.

He grabbed my hair. Fisted it tight and forced my mouth on his cock. It's not a hardship as I love giving him oral as much as he loves giving it to me. But this domineering, alpha play where he used my mouth for his own pleasure turned me on so much, I physically ached for him.

I tried to touch myself but he growled at me, "Don't fucking do it. You come when I let you come."

Ultimately, he did let me come by yanking me off his dick, flipping me on my stomach and hauling my ass up into the air. He drove into me and within three hard thrusts, I was breaking apart so violently, I had nothing left to give him in the participation department. I just lay there like a limp rag doll while he fucked me. Of course, Bain was so primed and ready after that amazing blow job, it didn't take him long either.

And after... he wanted to cuddle. We spooned, something we've made part of our sleeping ritual, except this morning we talked about nothing and everything. He leaves for a road trip day after tomorrow and I'll start packing my belongings for the next phase of our journey together. Bain's parents are coming in next weekend and oddly, I'm not nervous about hanging out with them. They'll stay with us at Bain's in the guest room. I've heard Bain talk about them enough to know they're cool. My mom is coming in next month for the twins' birthday and wants to help shop for the nursery.

That led to a long discussion about what we wanted to do. Do we find out the baby's sex? Do we do the room in pink or blue, or go with a unique color? Bain is partial to a hockey-themed room and I'd like a fairy-tale forest.

"Here," I murmur, stepping up to him. "Let me do your tie."

I often did this for Drake once I moved to Pittsburgh. He knew how to do it himself, but I always do it better.

I love the intimacy of it as Bain stares at me while I stare at the tie, looping, crossing over, again and pulling it through. I tighten the knot, straighten it and then pat him on the chest. When my face lifts, the intensity of his desire for me does funny things to my tummy.

"Why are you looking at me like that?" I ask coyly.

"Because something about you doing my tie for me makes me want to yank it off and tie you up with it," he growls, but he settles for taking my face in his large hands and giving me a soft kiss. "You're riding with Brienne to the arena?"

"Yeah. I'll be there around five p.m. She has a media interview scheduled so I'll hang out in the family lounge."

"I'll come by to see you," he says before pressing his lips to my forehead.

"Don't you dare," I say, giving him a playful push backward. "You do your regular prep and keep your head fully in the game."

"My head hasn't been fully in the game since I met you," he mutters as he turns toward the mirror on the inside of the closet door and checks out my handiwork.

I practically glow from the pleasure of those words. He doesn't mean it to the extent I'm messing with his game because Bain's playing phenomenally. He only means that I now occupy space in his thoughts.

"It's been the same for me," I admit, and our eyes lock through the reflection of the mirror.

"Do you want to go out tonight after the game?" he asks.

That was his habit when he was a single man, but he hasn't been doing that often, preferring to spend time in bed with me.

"Sure." I'm still a little uncertain how our relationship is going to work, so I add, "But if you want a guys' night out—"

Bain whirls on me. "I want you by my side, so whether it's here or out with the gang, you're the thing I want most."

I suck in a breath because he keeps hitting me with words that make me nearly swoon. I whisper a warning, "You better stop that."

He smiles, eyes dancing with amusement. "Why's that?"

I'm not willing to admit that I've fallen very hard for him, so I play it off. "Because it might make you late for the game."

Just to be sure, Bain checks his watch and grimaces. "I'm already a little late. I gotta go."

I put my hands on his ribs and turn him toward the door. I follow him out to the living room where he picks up his duffel and lays his suit jacket over the top of it. He won't put it on until he gets to the arena and he doesn't bother with a coat since he parks in the underground garage. One more kiss at the door that starts sweet but turns hot, causing us both to moan and then he's gone.

I watch his car pull out of the driveway and then realize I really need to pee. I've been trying to be diligent in upping my water intake and now that the man who has commanded all my focus is gone, my bladder is piping up.

In the bathroom, I shimmy my leggings down and sit on the toilet to do my business. My head is in the clouds thinking of Bain, but as I'm wiping, I glance down and see blood in the bowl. My heart skips a beat when I see the toilet paper has a large spot of bright red blood, about the size of a quarter.

I wipe again with new paper, and only a slight smear appears. It doesn't lessen the hammering of my heart or the fear constricting my chest.

My mind filters through all the stuff I've learned about pregnancy either through Dr. Segal or the voluminous reading I've been doing. Spotting can be normal and nothing to worry about.

But is this spotting?

It was a spot.

A large spot but it was so bright red.

Panic has me slinging my panties and leggings up, dashing through the house to the kitchen where I left my phone.

There's a moment where I consider calling Brienne but change my mind at the last second. Bain deserves to know what's going on.

He answers on the second ring, his tone playful. "Missed me that much?"

"I'm bleeding."

I'm not sure if it's the two words or the fear in my voice but all he says is, "I'm turning around."

And then he hangs up.

I run back to the bathroom, pull my pants down and terror clogs my throat as I see more blood in my panties. It's been mere seconds since I wiped.

Tears flood my eyes as I search through my cabinets, looking for pads I normally keep stashed away. I grab one and toss it on the vanity, pushing my panties and leggings all the way off. I turn toward the bedroom, intent on fresh clothes when the cramp hits me.

A sharp squeezing in my lower belly that knocks the breath out of me.

"No, no, no, no, no," I pant and then another cramp

hits, this one causing me to double over.

Tears stream and I hobble over to the toilet once again. Crossing my arms over my stomach, I lean forward as another cramp hits and this one has me seeing stars.

It goes on, and on, and on, and I've never felt anything like this in my life.

And then… it stops.

CHAPTER 29

Bain

I JUMP OUT of the car with my keys in hand because I know Kiera always keeps the door locked. I sprint across the lawn, up the front porch and somehow miraculously get the key to flip the latch with ease. The door slams into the wall as I throw it open and call out, "Kiera!"

I hear nothing so I head toward the bedroom, my steps slowing with dread.

I find her in the master bathroom, sitting hunched over on the toilet. Her long hair obscures her face. My eyes drop to the floor where I see discarded leggings and her panties, a bright red splotch shining like a beacon.

I ignore the wave of dizziness that hits me. Moving to Kiera, I squat before her, hands on her shoulders. "Hey… baby. I'm here."

Her head lifts and I brush her hair back. Tear-stained cheeks and tortured eyes. "Um… I had some really bad cramping, but now it's gone." Her lower lip quivers. "I'm afraid to look."

If there was ever a time in my life I needed to be strong, this is it. Kiera looks broken and although I'm terrified to look in the toilet, I take charge.

"Stay there a second," I say and head into the bedroom. I know exactly what drawers she keeps what I need. I grab panties and sweatpants and take a deep breath as I place them on the bed. I exhale slowly and despite my stomach churning, I return to the bathroom.

Grabbing a washcloth from the linen closet, I soak it with water, wring it out and then turn to her. "Let's get you up and into some clothes, okay?"

She nods and straightens. She doesn't appear to be in any physical pain, but I take hold of her arm to help her up. I keep her walking out of the bathroom, guiding her firmly so she doesn't dare turn around to see what might be left behind.

In the bedroom, she stands quietly while I wipe between her legs, the cloth coming away with a little blood. I help her slip into new panties, then the sweatpants, and guide her to the edge of the bed to sit for a moment. She doesn't say a word... doesn't even look at me.

Steeling myself, I kiss her on the top of her head and walk back into the bathroom. I look everywhere but the toilet, even bending over to pick up Kiera's stained clothes.

But my eyes go where they must, and I see enough to know it's not good. I flush the toilet and return to the bedroom.

Kiera's face lifts and she looks at me with bleak eyes. "Did I...?"

"I don't know," I answer truthfully. I'd never lie or sugarcoat it. I don't know exactly what I saw, but there was a lot of blood. I just know she won't have to look at it. "We're going to need to get you to the doctor."

She nods, her expression dulling by the second. Her tone is flat. "You have a game you need to get to. I can call Brienne."

I ignore the idiocy of that statement because she's in shock. I merely move back to the dressers and pull out socks. I hand them to her. "Put these on and some warm boots."

As she does that, I grab a sweatshirt for her.

When she takes it from my hand, I pull out my phone and call Drake.

"What's up?" he answers, and I can hear the chatter of the locker room. I knew he'd already be at the arena.

"Kiera's had some pretty significant bleeding and cramping. She seems okay now, but I'm going to take her to the doctor's office. I wanted to let you know."

"Did she miscarry?" he asks, and I wince. I can't even say the word.

"I don't know." Not a lie. "But I need you to get with Coach immediately and tell him I'm a scratch for the game."

"I'll do the same and meet you—"

"No," I say, eyes on Kiera as she puts her sweatshirt on like a robot and steps inside the closet to get her boots. I lower my voice and walk out of the room. "I'm not sure there's anything to worry about and if you show up, she'll think there is. Let her keep a little hope, okay?"

"You said *her*," Drake murmurs sadly. "That means you don't have any hope."

Sighing, I scrub my hand through my hair and watch as Kiera comes out of the room. "We're heading out the door now. I'll let you and Brienne know as soon as I can."

"Please take care of her." I've never heard a man beg for anything before, but that's as close as it gets.

"I promise."

◆

KIERA'S CONTINUED SILENCE is making my skin crawl. I try to talk to her, but her responses are in one- or two-word phrases that sound so brittle, I'm surprised her tongue isn't shredded. We're waiting on Dr. Segal to come into the exam room. It's not the same one we were in a mere four days ago. The table sits on a different wall but otherwise, it looks identical. I only notice because it's hard to look at Kiera as she sits on the edge of the exam table, staring at her clasped hands.

When the nurse explained about getting undressed,

she kindly held out a thick pad to her. "If you're still bleeding, just press this between your legs until Dr. Segal comes in."

I had expected we might be in for a bit of a wait, given that they worked us into his schedule, but we're in the room barely ten minutes before the door pushes open.

His expression is not grave, but it is worried. I rise from the chair and move to Kiera's side. I hadn't felt welcomed there when she got up on the table, awkwardly trying to hold that pad in place while she navigated it. I wanted to pick her up, cradle her, gently lie her down and help get her situated. Hell... I'd have held that fucking pad for her so she could just lie back and rest.

Her vibe told me she's closed off in a bubble that I won't be allowed near, but now that Dr. Segal is here, fuck keeping my distance. I place my hand on her lower back.

The doc comes to stand before Kiera, his hand grabbing hers for a comforting squeeze. "I understand you had some bleeding and cramping?"

She nods. "Bleeding first. Then some cramps that got worse, then they stopped."

He doesn't ask her how much blood. Doesn't ask her how long the cramps lasted. Doesn't ask me what I saw in the toilet.

Instead, he pats her shoulder. "I'm going to do the

same vaginal ultrasound we did the other day, okay?"

Kiera nods and Dr. Segal smiles at her. As she reclines, he cuts me a sympathetic smile before turning to wash his hands.

Gloves donned, he moves his stool to the end of the bed and repeats the same procedure as the other day.

There's no giddy feeling of anticipation.

Just oily dread.

It feels like it takes hours, but truly, it's only a minute or two. Kiera doesn't even look at the screen but I do. I stare at it hard, hoping to see that little bean I saw the other day.

Something appears on the screen, but it doesn't look like what we saw before. Dr. Segal taps a button on the laptop and holds his hand still.

Finally, he pulls the wand free and sets it aside on a metal tray, deftly covering it with a surgical towel. He snaps off his gloves and looks only at Kiera. "I'm sorry. You're in the process of miscarrying."

Kiera nods, her eyes dry and lifeless. I stumble back a foot and only hear bits and pieces as I try to comprehend that our lives just shifted a hundred and eighty degrees again.

Prolapsed gestational sac.
No heartbeat.
Incomplete miscarriage.
Dilation and curettage.

"I'm going to send you over to the hospital to get you checked in. You'll be sedated and—"

"Wait! What?" I exclaim, rejoining the conversation.

"She's going to need a surgical procedure to clean out the remaining tissue. Otherwise, it will cause an infection, which can be very dangerous."

"So, the baby's gone?" I ask, still not sure I understand what's happening.

"I'm very sorry."

Images of Kiera and I this morning flash through my brain and while they'd ordinarily be a turn-on, I think I might throw up. "Did I… this morning we… did the miscarriage happen because…"

I can't even get the words out, but Dr. Segal patiently waits. I scrub my hands over my face and laser my eyes onto the doctor so I can judge the truth of his answer. "Kiera and I had sex. It was a little fast. Did I…"

Dr. Segal shakes his head. "No," he exclaims. "Absolutely not. You did nothing to cause this. Miscarriages at this early stage are unfortunately not uncommon. Ten to twenty percent of women will miscarry for no good reason at all."

I trust his words, but they offer no relief.

I glance over at Kiera and she's sitting up again, staring at her hands. "I'm sorry, baby," I murmur and brush my lips over her temple.

That seems to jolt her out of her trance and her head

lifts. She looks at Dr. Segal. "Can I go home after the D&C?"

"Of course. You'll stay in the recovery room for a few hours, then Bain can take you home. I'll give you more detailed recovery instructions."

Kiera nods. "Okay."

"Any other questions?"

She shakes her head so he looks at me.

Yeah… a million fucking questions but only one that matters.

Where do we go from here?

CHAPTER 30

Kiera

THE MURMURED VOICES drifting from the kitchen to me in the living room are grating on my nerves. I've been camped out on the couch all day, doing a rewatch of *Sons of Anarchy*. I need something hard and brutal to take my mind off... well, things that are hard and brutal.

It's finally sinking in.

Yesterday was pretty much a blur. I try not to think about it, but flashes filter through. I knew I was miscarrying when the cramps hit. They were so painful that I immediately knew what was going on. I have vague recollections of Bain caring for me. He was strong and steady, knowing exactly what to do, and yet somehow, I can't seem to really appreciate it.

Maybe I will in time.

But for right now, the fact he's in the kitchen with Drake and Brienne, talking so low I can't hear makes me want to slap him.

I want to slap Drake and Brienne too.

I don't need to be treated as if I'm fragile. I'm tired

of Bain looking at me like a lost puppy and Drake looking confused and Brienne looking like she's going to burst into tears.

Reaching out, I nab the remote and turn up the volume to try to drown them out. All it does is pull attention to me and Bain is there. "Do you need something?"

"Yeah... I need to be able to hear the TV," I say glibly, tossing the remote back onto the coffee table. I curl my legs in, wrap my arms around the pillow and let my eyes drift back to Jax and the guys pulling out on their bikes.

The weight of Bain's stare is oppressive. I know if I were to look at him, I'd see confusion because I'm not acting at all like myself.

But how does one act in a situation like this?

He's hovered over me since we got home from the hospital yesterday. I had the D&C with no complications. Dr. Segal said I might have some spotting and cramps for a week or two and absolutely no tampons or sex until my follow-up appointment so he can make sure I'm fully healed.

I almost laughed at that because I'm pretty sure I'm never having sex again.

"Can I get you anything?" Bain asks hesitantly.

Yeah, you can quit fucking looking at me like that, I want to scream. Instead, I manage a small smile. "I'm good. Thanks."

His return smile is hesitant as he lifts the light blanket pulled up over my hips and tucks it around my shoulders. His lips brush over my head and he turns to head back into the kitchen where my brother and future sister-in-law do their own hovering from a distance.

Even as my heart squeezes in pleasure over his kind act, I shrug off the blanket, pushing it back down to my hips. It's a sullen, bratty move, which is so unlike me, but I can't help it. The emotions running through me are too much to process. I feel like I'm precariously perched on the edge of a jagged cliff and there's a terrifying drop before me, yet the safety of the solid ground behind me seems hollow… almost imaginary. There's a tight knot of anger deep in my chest, not only for losing the baby but for rushing so fast into this relationship with Bain because I got pregnant. I threw out every bit of protection I had enshrouded myself in so I wouldn't get hurt again. While I know it's not Bain who hurt me, I can't help but tie him to the irrationally terrible thoughts.

Bain and I only grew closer because I got pregnant. It was the catalyst that drove us forward. Without that baby to tie us together, there's nothing to keep the bond in place.

So yes, I'm fucking angry.

And so goddamn sad because it's not just that the baby is gone, it's that the foundation of what we've built has disappeared with it.

It's just not fair.

♦

IT'S DARK WHEN I wake up. The TV is off and there's a small table lamp across the living room that provides a soft glow that lets me see no one else is with me. I push up from the couch and stretch. I take stock of how I feel, expecting to be sore in my lower belly, but I don't feel anything. I see the kitchen is empty, only the light above the stove on.

I listen and am greeted with total silence, but I can feel Bain's presence in this house. Besides that, I know he'd never leave me alone without having some plan in place. He'd never leave without saying goodbye or letting me know where he was going.

After I fold the blanket and toss it on top of the pillow, I pad through the silent house to the master bedroom. I try to process my feelings as I see Bain asleep on the bed. The lamp on my side is still on. Bain is wearing a T-shirt and the covers are around his waist. I know without peeling them back he's got on a pair of pajama bottoms. Normally, we sleep naked and I know he slept naked before he met me. It says a lot that he dressed before sleep tonight, almost like it's armor.

I understand where he's coming from. I don't want to open myself up to any type of intimacy, and I'm not talking about the sexual type. Having clothes on provides a barrier. It sends a message.

Bain's duffel is on the bench at the end of the bed, opened and full of the clothes he's kept here. He leaves tomorrow for a four-day road trip. Then he's back for one day and off again for two more road games. He'll be gone seven days in total.

This wasn't the original plan. At least not for Bain. He announced to me when we got home from the hospital yesterday that he wasn't going on the road trips and that he'd already talked about it with Coach West.

He didn't discuss it with me.

Just told me that was what he was doing.

It resulted in an argument and I refused to let him stay home. "I don't need you here," I said. "I'm not dying or anything."

Bain's expression was a mixture of wariness and hurt, but he finally acquiesced because I gave him no choice. That's when Drake and Brienne showed up to make plans to babysit me while the team was away. They're all concerned to leave me alone for that much time. Ultimately, it's left to Brienne to stay behind and watch the boys as well as watch over me. It's a job she will gladly do, and it's not the first time she's had to take care of me when I was down.

I tiptoe into the bathroom and gently shut the door. I pee and change out my menstrual pad, feeling nothing at all at the slight brown spotting. It's expected. After I wash my hands, I brush my teeth and wash my face. After applying moisturizer, I stare at myself in the mirror.

My eyes are bloodshot. I've had crying bouts here and there. They crop up out of nowhere and nothing in particular sets them off. If Bain was around when it happened, he merely pulled me into his arms and held me. If I didn't want to be held, I'd go into the bathroom to cry in private. I'd bite down hard on a towel so I couldn't be heard.

My skin is pale, my eyes look sunken. Is that because I'm tired or does loss physically change how you look?

I press my hand to my lower belly. It's as flat as it was the day before when I was pregnant. It feels normal to me, as if the last week has been nothing but a dream unfulfilled. I lift my sweatshirt and stare at my stomach. I wonder what it would have looked like all rounded.

There's a soft tap against the door and I drop my sweatshirt. Taking in a breath, I open it to see Bain standing there. His hair is mussed, indicating he'd been sleeping for a bit. He rubs his palm across his stubbled jaw. "You okay?"

"Yeah… just getting ready for bed."

"Want me to make you something to eat?" he asks. I haven't had much all day. Some soup at lunch.

I shake my head. "I'm not hungry."

Bain takes my hand and tugs at my fingers. "You have to eat, Kiera."

I pull my hand away and try to move past him. "I'm not hungry."

He steps into my path, hands going to my shoulders. His face is an open book of concern, so painfully sincere that it feels like a punch to the gut. "I know how sad you are, but you need to take care of yourself."

He just doesn't get it.

Rage explodes within me and I slap his hands away. "I'm sorry I can't be as fucking strong as you, Bain. You're just going to have to give me a hot minute to process."

He reaches out to touch my arm, but I flinch away. He seems unperturbed, his expression patient, and it makes me feel lonelier than ever. "Why aren't you upset?" I lash out, suddenly bitter. "Why aren't you angry or sad or... anything?"

"I am," he says quietly. "I am upset. But right now, I need to be here for you."

"Like you could understand!" I snap, sidestepping him and moving to my side of the bed.

"You could try explaining it to me," he says, and when I glance back, he's standing in the same spot, his arms crossed over his chest. "Because I've tried to talk to you about it all day and you keep shutting me down."

I throw my arms out. "Well, I'm sorry, Bain. Sorry I

can't be there to comfort you just now."

Christ, I know how ridiculous and petulant I sound, but all the nasty feelings inside me are coming out in word vomit.

"I'm not asking for comfort," he says through gritted teeth, the first time his calm veneer has cracked all day. "Just for some conversation. You're not the only one who lost something."

A hysterical laugh bubbles up. "What exactly did you lose, Bain? In fact, what exactly did I lose? That baby was a mistake and you know it. We weren't a couple. We weren't trying to get pregnant. We weren't looking to build a future. We had shitty luck but then tried to put on a happy face and make the best of a situation neither of us wanted." My voice pitches higher, my words coming out over erratic breathing and I feel like I'm spiraling out of control. "In fact, now that I think about it, why aren't we both rejoicing? Now we can go back to just being fuck buddies. Except I'm going to have to insist we double up on the birth control because no way am I ever fucking going through this again."

Those last words are screamed at him and I'm pleased to see he recoils. I hope it hurt because I want to make sure he feels as bad as I do.

As ludicrous as that may sound, and despite the fact I've never wished pain on another person, I want Bain to suffer along with me.

Sadly, he probably is and I'm now doubling it, but I can't seem to find it within me to care.

"Do you even want me here?" he asks, his lips pressed into a flat line.

I suck in air, trying to expand the tightening in my chest. I feel smothered and out of control. Shaking my head, I turn my back on him as I pull the covers down on my side of the bed. "I think I'd like to be alone tonight."

Sliding under the sheet, I roll over on my side and give him my back. I curl into a protective ball and wait with tensed muscles for him to touch me. I fully expect him to slide in too, spoon his big body around mine and try to soothe me, despite the claws I keep raking down his heart.

Instead, I hear him zip up his duffel and his footsteps whisper across the carpet. He doesn't close the bedroom door behind him on the way out, but the minute he's gone, I can tell. His presence has always been tangible to me and now I feel like I'm in a void.

I hear the front door open and then close again. I know Bain will lock it behind him with his key, but I never hear the click of protection.

Frowning, I roll out of bed to see where he went. Maybe he didn't leave and the prospect of it makes me feel better. Or rather, lessens the shitty feeling for running him off.

I move through the silent house.

I can feel he's gone, no doubt.

When I reach the front door, I see the dead bolt isn't engaged.

Then my eyes land on the small demilune table that rests against the wall.

My house key sits there, stark against the dark cherry wood.

It's a clear indication that Bain isn't coming back.

CHAPTER 31

Bain

S TEPPING OFF THE bus, I hitch the strap of my duffel over my shoulder and turn for the lobby doors.

"Come on out with us," Hendrix says. "We're going to grab some food, maybe a beer."

I glance over my shoulder, see him standing with Boone and Camden. They invited me on the bus, but I declined. They're being persistent because as far as they know, I have no valid reason for declining. We're in Montreal, an amazing city, and we're riding high off defeating the Wizards tonight in a very close battle.

"Not tonight," I say with a wave of my hand.

I barely make it to the lobby doors when someone pulls on my duffel strap to stop my progress. I turn to see Camden, frowning at me. "What's wrong?"

"Nothing. Just tired."

"Bullshit," he says and glances back at Hendrix and Boone waiting on him. He waves them off. "You guys go on ahead and grab a table. I'll be there in a minute."

Hendrix and Boone walk off and Camden steps back

from the lobby doors, indicating for me to do the same since other players are heading into the hotel.

"What the fuck is going on? You've been nearly mute since you got on the plane for the trip here."

I rub the back of my neck, which has been in tight knots since Kiera miscarried. I'm clearly storing every bit of stress right there. "Kiera lost the baby day before yesterday."

"Oh, Jesus," Camden breathes out, and his hand comes to my shoulder where he grips it tightly. "I'm really sorry, man."

"Yeah… me too."

"How's Kiera?"

I shake my head. I have no fucking clue how she is. "She's dealing."

I can see a million questions in Camden's eyes, but I don't feel like answering any of them. I throw my thumb over my shoulder to the lobby doors. "I'm going to head up."

"If you want to talk…"

"Yeah… I appreciate it. Just processing, you know?"

Camden claps me on the back once, a sign of affection and solidarity. "I'll catch you later. Let me know if I can do anything."

I start to turn away but then something comes to mind. "Hey… actually, do you mind spreading the word? I don't feel like making a statement about it."

"I got you covered."

"And maybe tell the guys to give me space for a bit," I add. "I've got my head in the game, but away from the ice, I'm still…"

I don't know what I am, but I know I'm not ready to talk about it. I'm certainly not ready to make any type of bold statement about the status of my relationship with Kiera because I don't fucking know if anything exists between us anymore. I haven't talked to her since I left her place last night and I'm sure she saw the key I left. Not sure why I did it, but I know it was an emotional reaction to the way she kept rebuffing me.

I did text her this morning to ask how she was feeling. Her response was short and it didn't invite further follow-up.

Fine.

I'm glad she's fucking fine because I'm not. I feel like I'm on the verge of losing my shit, like I want to scream until my throat shreds and my lungs collapse. I want to pound someone into the ground just for looking at me wrong. I want to crawl under the covers and sleep for days.

I take the elevator up and I'm not all that surprised to see Drake waiting outside my room. He's leaned against the wall, hands tucked in his pockets. His duffel is on the ground, meaning he came straight here from the bus and by the look on his face, I know he wants to talk.

I don't say anything, merely pull my key card out and open the door. Drake bends to grab his bag and follows me in.

I'm shrugging out of my suit jacket by the time the door is closing. I loosen the knot on my tie and don't wait to find out why he's here. I take the opportunity to get a better update than what Kiera gave me this morning.

"How is she?"

Drake moves past the beds over to a corner chair and settles his large frame into it. "I tried to call her once and she didn't answer. Texted her to ask how she's doing and I got a 'thumbs-up' emoji back."

I blink in surprise that she's being terse with her brother. "I asked her the same question. She at least typed out the word *fine*. What has Brienne said?"

"Said physically, she's fine and she worked today. But she's not overly engaging. Have you talked to her?"

With a sigh, I pull my tie loose and toss it on the bed. "Things aren't good between us."

Drake's eyebrows draw in and his jaw tightens. He's gone into overprotective brother mode. "Why not?" he growls.

I hold my arms out. "Fuck if I know. She went off on me last night and told me to leave. So I did."

"You just left her?" he says, eyes wide.

"No, I didn't just leave her," I exclaim in exasperation. "I took care of her and you know I did. You saw us the night we came home from the hospital. You saw me yesterday. I was there for her, ready to do whatever she needed. I was willing to miss a week of games. Ready to do anything for her and she didn't want a fucking thing from me."

"Okay," Drake says, motioning his hands downward. "Chill out."

"No, I'm not fucking chilling out," I retort, that need to scream my lungs out creeping up on me. "I understand your sister is hurting and I want to make it all better for her. I can't do that unless she lets me, and she's not letting me. But you know what... I'm devastated too. No matter how she and I came to be pregnant, we'd committed and then we got excited about it and now neither of us has a damn thing. We don't even have each other because she pushed me out."

By the time I'm done, Drake is leaning back in his chair as if I just punched him. "I'm... well... I'm sorry, man. I can't imagine what you're feeling."

"Oh, I think you just got a tiny taste," I say with a maniacal laugh. I don't even bother to fill him in on the sense of guilt weighing me down that perhaps I caused the miscarriage. I know Dr. Segal said absolutely not, but it still feels like my fault because I got all domineering on her in bed that morning. It may have only been a handful of thrusts because her mouth on my cock had me on the edge, but they were hard and deep and it's killing me to think I might be responsible.

Drake surges out of the chair, but I hold my ground. Thank fuck he doesn't hug me but veers right to the mini bar and nabs two bottles of Jack Daniels. Not even bothering with glasses, he tosses a bottle at me. "You need this."

I twist the little plastic cap off and tip the bottle back. I don't take a sip but instead chug the entire thing, hissing after I swallow.

Drake doesn't say anything, merely returns to his chair, holding the other bottle. I toss my empty in the trash can and plop down on the end of the bed. Resting my elbows on my knees, I press my hands to my face. The smell of the liquor on my breath blows back as I breathe into my palms.

"You know that anything Kiera said or didn't say since the miscarriage probably isn't an accurate representation of how she feels about you, right?" Drake asks.

I lift my head. He has my attention.

"She's a tempest of emotions and clearly so are you. Just as she probably doesn't mean what she said to you, you probably aren't in a great place to be the one to help her out. You're hurting too."

My tone is dry. "What's your point?"

"My point is that you two care about each other. You're both going to figure things out and you'll heal from this loss. But you'll still have each other."

I can't help my snort of skepticism that pops free. "Didn't you hear me? She told me to leave. She didn't want my comfort or care. We're done."

"I don't believe it," Drake says dismissively. "You two just need to talk things out."

I rise off the bed, take a step toward him and yank the other bottle of Jack out of his hand. I twist the cap and while I don't chug the entire thing, I take a healthy sip. "You think we should talk things out?"

"Yeah," Drake says hesitantly.

"At the risk of getting punched, your sister and I aren't known for our long conversations. We were fuck buddies—"

"You better watch it," Drake growls.

"We were fuck buddies," I reiterate as I glare at him. "It was sex and that was it. It was amazing sex and we had good times and lots of laughs, but that's all it was."

"Bullshit," he says quietly. "You were more than that."

I nod, waving the bottle at him. "Yeah... we became more. But only because she was pregnant. Only because we had that tie binding us. Now that's gone and we're not anything."

"I call bullshit again."

I take another sip of the whiskey, waiting to hear his pearls of wisdom. "I saw the way you were with her after the miscarriage. You were a man who wanted to care for his woman. You were protective and tender. And that didn't stop after the baby was no more. You were still in it."

I sink back down on the edge of the bed, my head dropping to consider the bottle. "I was still in it, but she wasn't."

"She was drowning in grief. You've got to give her a pass on anything she said and did. You need to sit down and talk this out."

I don't reply because the truth is, as much as she pushed me away, that felt an awful lot like abandonment and I needed the support I was giving her reciprocated.

Still, he makes me curious. I lift my gaze to his. "Your sister had a bad experience with her last boyfriend."

Drake grimaces. "Fuckwad. He was an obsessive nut job."

"She was completely happy to remain single. It's why our relationship wasn't deep at first. She was fine just being a casual fling. She doesn't want a relationship. What could we possibly have?"

He lifts one shoulder. "I don't know. But let me turn it back on you. You were fine playing the field and fucking puck bunnies. Do you want to go back to that?"

"I want your sister," I say, and that's about the only thing that has felt right in this entire conversation. "I need her to want me back."

"Then you have to talk to her. You have to lay your feelings out there. My suggestion is to give her space for now. Maybe when we get back to Pittsburgh next weekend, you sit down and hash this stuff out."

"You think she'll be receptive to it?" I ask, afraid to hope there could be a chance.

"Yeah," he says, and I don't think he's sugarcoating things. "I think Kiera cares for you and once the clouds lift, she'll be able to focus on that again."

I nod, feeling a bit energized. Or maybe that's the Jack.

"And listen," Drake says, "I'm here for you. I get she wasn't able to support you emotionally, but I've got you. If you want to talk about the miscarriage or the swirl of emotions you have going on, I'll let you cry on my shoulder."

His tone is joking to lighten the mood, but I know he truly means it.

"Thanks," I say, holding up the bottle. "This talk has already helped a lot."

CHAPTER 32

Kiera

M Y DOORBELL RINGS and I put my phone on mute as I listen to the weekly nurses' meeting for the practice I work for. I've been working remotely for four months now, and these weekly meetings help keep me bridged with my coworkers.

I see Brienne on my front porch and sigh as I open the door to let her in. She's got a box of doughnuts in one hand and a cardboard tray with coffees in the other.

I nod toward the kitchen. "I'm just finishing up a meeting. I'll be done in about ten minutes."

Brienne wastes no time getting to work on cleaning my kitchen. I'm a neat freak by nature, but I haven't felt like doing much of anything the last few days. My motivation has been nearly nonexistent, and it's taking everything for me to even log in to my job this week. I called into the nurses' meeting rather than Zoom because I know I look like shit and I don't want anyone seeing me this way.

When I end the call, I say, "I was going to do that

this morning."

"Sure you were," Brienne says as she rinses plates and places them in the dishwasher. "Just like I'm sure you were going to brush your hair at some point today."

I rake my fingers through my long locks and try to remember when I last ran a brush through it. I washed it last night when I showered, but I went straight to bed and didn't even bother combing out the tangles.

I sullenly refuse to reply, instead leveling an attack. "Why are you here? I'm in the middle of my workday and really don't have time to chat."

"Tough shit," she says, rinsing her hands and drying them on a towel. "You can't shut everyone out and not expect me to show up. Your brother is beside himself because you're not responding to his texts and—"

"I'm responding."

"Thumbs-up and smiley-face emojis don't count," she says, rolling right over me. "And you won't return my calls, so how can you be surprised I'm here?"

"I've been busy with work," I mutter, pushing up out of my chair and moving to the fridge. I grab a bottle of water.

I expect her to call bullshit on me again, but she grabs the doughnuts and coffee and carries them to the table. I grit my teeth when she closes my laptop and nods at the chair. "Come eat some doughnuts."

I've been in such a crappy mood for going on five

days straight, I almost grumble that I don't want her doughnuts, but truthfully... I'm hungry. My appetite returned yesterday, but I haven't had any motivation to go to the grocery store.

With a huff, I plop into one of the chairs and pull out a chocolate-frosted pastry. Nibbling at it, I stare at her. I know she's here to talk, but I'm going to make her work for it.

Brienne ignores the doughnuts but takes the top off one of the coffees, blowing across the steaming java, which sends the delicious fragrance my way. I break immediately and take the other coffee.

"How are you doing physically?" she asks, her tone clinical... almost shrewd.

"Good, actually," I admit. "The spotting is almost gone and I haven't had any cramping at all since the D&C."

Brienne nods with a soft smile. Happy my body is feeling okay and I'm sure happy to see me be able to say *D&C* without crying.

Truth of the matter, the swirling emotions ranging from grief to anger to regret to confusion had a solid hold on me for the first three days, but that's mostly gone. Only anger was left behind. I came out of the fog and... my life was back the way it was before I ever met Bain. Except now, I know what it's like to have Bain, and I mean have *all* of him—heart, body, mind—and now I don't.

I'm mad at him and I'm mad at myself, but I'm not sure either of us is actually to blame. In addition to the anger, I feel lost. Like I don't even know who I am or what I want.

"Why are you hiding yourself away from everyone who loves you?" she asks.

That actually hurts. Because yes… I've been ignoring both Drake and Brienne and that's not fair to them. I know how worried they are.

But it hurts more because Bain hasn't reached out. Not that I would lump him in with people who "love" me, but I thought he would check in.

I mean… he did. Texted me the morning after he left to see how I was feeling. I told him I was fine and that was that.

He didn't text again.

Didn't call.

And God help me, I'm angry about it, even though I'm the one who told him to leave. I drop the doughnut onto the table and rub my aching temple. I've cried a lot this week, which has left me with a perpetual headache.

My gaze lifts to Brienne. "There's a good chance I'm very fucked up in the head."

I get a soft smile of understanding. "You've had a hard week, Kiera. It would fuck up anyone's head. Losing a baby… I can't even imagine so I'm not sure—"

"See," I blurt out, "I'm not sure that's really driving things for me. I mean, yes... it was awful having the miscarriage. I wouldn't wish that on my mortal enemy. It was one of the worst things that has ever happened to me... just watching that life fade out and I had no control over it. But..." My words trail off as I try to compose my thoughts. It's tough for me to admit this. "I don't know that I'm grieving the loss of the pregnancy anymore."

Brienne nods as if she understands. "You weren't trying to get pregnant. It wasn't something you wanted in your life at this time, so it makes sense the loss wouldn't be the same as if you were trying to get pregnant."

My head bobs. I pick at the doughnut, bringing a tiny piece to my mouth. "Once we decided to keep it and make a go of it together, I was invested. But Brienne... it was barely two weeks from the time I found out I was pregnant until I lost it. It was easy for me to be circumspect... to tell myself this wasn't meant to be, that this wasn't the right time. And as I sit here right now, I can tell you with a clear conscience that I accept that."

"Not a lot of time to wrap your head around it," she murmurs. "It all happened so fast."

"I think I was more invested in what I was building with Bain."

There. My dirty secret is out. I'm mourning the loss

of Bain more than anything.

"I can see that," Brienne says. "The pregnancy was a catalyst to get you two to take a chance on a relationship. I bet in that two weeks, you bonded in ways you hadn't ever imagined."

"And then the baby was gone, and now so is Bain." I duck my head sheepishly. "I fell for him, Brienne."

She doesn't say anything but taps a finger on the table. "Drake has been talking to him. He told me that you kicked him out and he left his key behind."

"I wouldn't say I kicked him out. I told him I wanted to be alone that night, but I understand why he left the key. I wasn't exactly nice to him."

"If it makes you feel better, I believe Bain understands why you did what you did."

"Really?" I ask, unable to contain the blatant and desperate hope in my tone.

"He's torn up about a lot of stuff. He's confused and upset about how you reacted to him and I don't think he had anyone to help him process the loss."

"Oh God," I say, my hand covering my mouth and my eyes immediately welling with tears. Yes, more tears. Apparently, I'm not cried out. My voice is watery. "He wanted to talk about it. He wanted to help me as I think that made him feel better, and I pushed him away. I was so blind with anger and sadness, he was the easiest one to lash out at. I did that to him and what he really needed was someone to take care of him too."

Brienne reaches across the table and grasps my hand. "Cut yourself a break. There's no playbook on how to handle this. You do the best you can and if your best wasn't good enough, you fix it."

"But how? What do I do? Is Bain even interested in fixing this? He hasn't tried to contact me since he left. It's been four days of silence."

"I don't know," she says. "I expect the first step would be to reach out to him. Tell him you want to talk."

I frown. "As simple as that?"

She grins at me and shakes her head. "No, I don't think it's going to be simple at all. You two are on shaky ground. You both suffered a loss and are still trying to cope with the aftermath. And both of you are trying to figure shit out on your own when you need to be supporting each other. You have to explore whether you have anything worth pursuing."

"I doubt he'll want to talk. He hasn't even tried to reach out to me."

"Did you give him any reason to believe you'd want that?" she queries.

"No, but, Brienne... our relationship was never supposed to be a relationship. It was only sex and fun times. If it weren't for the baby, we would still be having casual sex in secret."

She arches an eyebrow. "You really believe that? Because if there wasn't already some foundation there before you found out you were pregnant, no way in hell both of you would have so easily agreed to give it a go."

God, I hope she's right about that.

Brienne's phone rings and she pulls it out of her pocket. She glances at me, a smile of apology on her face. "I have to take this, but I won't be long."

I wave my hand at her.

"Hey, Callum," she says as she connects the line. "Is it a done deal?"

I watch as she listens, her expression serious for several long moments as he talks. Then I see a smile start to form and it grows bigger and bigger. "That's excellent. And he'll be able to start at the next home game?"

They must be talking about a trade. The deadline is tomorrow. As long as the contract is signed, doesn't matter when he starts. Playoffs are on the horizon and a lot of wheeling and dealing is being finalized today. While trades can still occur after the deadline, anyone acquired after that date cannot dress for the playoffs.

"I'll have Jenna coordinate a press conference," Brienne says, and I blink in surprise. They don't do that for just any player. "Do you know if Gray Brannon will issue any kind of statement?"

Gray Brannon? She's the GM for the Carolina Cold Fury. Are we getting a Cold Fury player?

"Okay. If she doesn't, that's fine. I'm sure she'll get pelted with questions by the press, so she'll come up with something."

Brienne listens for another minute and then says, "Great work, Callum. This is a huge feather in our cap."

She disconnects the call and places her phone on the table. "As I was saying, you and Bain clearly had something special. I'm sure you can work things out."

The possibility of a Cold Fury player coming to Pittsburgh is pushed straight out of my mind. "Do you sincerely believe that? Or are you just saying that to make me feel better right now?"

"I can only tell you what I saw with my own eyes. I recognize the look on Bain's face. It's the same look Drake has when he looks at me. He's got major feelings for you and I think you'd be a fool not to try to get back on track with that. I suppose you'll need to start with an apology."

She's not wrong about that.

I owe him a really big apology and hopefully, it's enough to start over.

CHAPTER 33

Bain

"**I** LOVE YOU." She kisses me on the forehead and pats my cheek.

Classic Mom.

My parents arrived last night before the team plane did and were already settled into the guest room at my condo and asleep when I arrived. We've been drinking coffee together this morning and talking. We planned their visit after we found out Kiera was pregnant. Although my parents met her briefly several weeks ago in the family lounge, they wanted to be able to spend time with her and get to know her. They wanted to be a part of this journey with us.

I told my parents there was no sense in coming when I called them the day Kiera miscarried, but my mom said, "That makes it even more important we come in to see you and Kiera."

They wanted to offer emotional support.

Of course, I had to fill them in this morning that things weren't great between me and Kiera, but that we

329

were going to talk today. My mom offered solid advice, which was mainly to listen, be open to her feelings and make sure I'm clear about what I want. My dad reminded me to tell Kiera how beautiful she is because all women liked to be told that.

Mom rolled her eyes and I laughed.

I keep repeating Mom's advice over and over in my head as I drive to Kiera's—Dad's advice isn't necessary since I will tell her that because I always do—but when I see her house in the distance, my mind blanks out with panic.

Christ, my hands are sweating as I pull into the driveway. Whatever is going to happen to us and our relationship will be decided very soon—and that reality is crashing down on me.

She texted me last Friday. It was a travel day and we were on the plane headed from Quebec City to Ottawa.

How are you?

I stared at that question for a good half hour before I could come up with a response. Should I go with honesty, which would require paragraphs? Should I give her a taste of her own medicine and answer tersely? Ultimately, I was moved that her first contact showed concern for me and I decided not to be a dick.

I'm hanging in there. How are you?

She wrote back immediately. *I'm better. And I'd like for us to talk. Can you give me some time on Sunday?*

I wanted to talk. I've had dreams where we talked

and we made everything better. But while I was encouraged she reached out, I was also well aware it could be to say a final goodbye. I wasn't ready for that. I'd only be in Pittsburgh for a day and then back on the road. If things went south, I didn't want my head fucked up for the upcoming games. The only reason I've stayed a bit sane is the prospect of us talking. And besides that, Drake told me he thought some space would be good for us.

For both of us to really think about things.

And now is the day of reckoning.

I turn off the ignition and wipe my hands on my jeans. My stomach is threatening to expel my breakfast and I only remember being this nervous once before in my life. It was right before I stepped onto the ice in my very first professional league game. I'd made it to the big time and my entire life was full of promise. Nothing but good things ahead if I played well—or nothing but terrible things if I failed.

It's exactly the precipice I stand on right now.

Despite the nerves and fear, I never back down from a challenge and Kiera has been one since the night I met her. It's among the top reasons I'm attracted to her and why intimacy is so fulfilling.

"You've got this," I whisper to myself as I exit the car.

I don't even make it up to the top step before the door opens. Emotions slam into me hard as I take Kiera in. Pure joy, lust, tenderness. There's a low-level wariness as her smile is thin, but everything else about her is as stunning as ever.

"You're beautiful," I say, the words falling out of my mouth before I can stop them. Mom will be disappointed I put Dad's advice over hers.

"You're a sight for sore eyes too," she replies.

I don't know if it's the right thing to do, but I move into her, wrapping her in a gentle but encompassing hug. Her arms go around my neck and her face buries there.

We stand that way for a few moments and I take note of how right she feels in my arms. I thought it might be weird or there would be a barrier, but even if I'm here for her to end things, this hug feels right. She and I have shared something many people don't.

Kiera's the first to pull away, but her hand slips into mine. "Come on in."

She leads me over the threshold and once I'm in and the door is closed, she releases me. I follow her into the kitchen and she moves to the Keurig. "Want a cup of coffee?"

"Sure." I say, mainly because I don't know what else to say.

While Kiera works the machine, I ask, "How are you doing physically? Are things okay?"

She twists her neck, gives me a smile over her shoulder. "Yeah. I've had no problem, really. Spotting for a few days, but that's stopped. I've got a follow-up with Dr. Segal on Monday."

I restrain myself from offering to go with her. I want to but not sure she wants it, and I don't want to pressure her about anything. I can't forget she pushed me away at the moment we should have stuck together if there had been a solid foundation between us.

Kiera turns and hands me the coffee cup. She motions to the table and I follow her. It's a square table with four chairs and I choose to take the one adjacent to her rather than opposite. I want to be close to her so I can touch her if the opportunity presents.

Placing her hands on her mug, she lifts it to her mouth to blow on the steam. My eyes laser focus on her lips and fuck... I miss them. I miss the way they curve when she's amused or the way they pout when she wants something. I long to see them wrapped around my cock again, but I'd settle for them on my mouth.

She sips and sets the coffee down. Her eyes meet mine and I'm surprised by the contrition I see. "I'm so sorry how I treated you last week. There was no excuse for it."

"You were hurting. I understand it."

"I know. But now that I'm feeling... more grounded, I'm actually ashamed of how I acted. You were doing everything right in supporting me and not only was I ungrateful for it, I deprived you of the right to have the same back from me. You were hurting too."

"I was hurting for you," I say because I want her to know that while the loss of the baby pinched, my biggest source of pain was seeing Kiera tormented.

Her eyes fall away and I want to take her by the chin and force her to look at me again, but I know she has more to say and she needs to get it out any way she can. If she can't meet my eyes, so be it. "I've been doing a lot of thinking. Everything we had was a house of cards. We started building it fast once we found out we were pregnant and once that fell, it all came tumbling down into a big, confusing mess."

I nod because that summarizes exactly the thoughts that have been plaguing me. "We moved fast."

Her gaze comes to mine and she smiles. "Super fast."

Despite her tone sounding amused, am I wrong in hearing regret? Is she focusing on a mistake we made because all her future decisions regarding us will revolve around that?

Moving too fast?

I latch onto that and roll with it. I want her to know I'm solidly with her... in whatever she's thinking because that's the best way for us to start over. "We're two people who weren't built for all that serious shit and then we floundered when shit got serious."

"Yes," she replies effusively. "We were both acting against our inherent natures. We committed to the baby and I don't regret that, but we went from casual to committed at the speed of light."

"And we crashed and burned," I conclude.

I see where she's going. It's clear we didn't have the fortitude to give it a solid go. It didn't work and we can't just pick it back up. Without the baby, we've got nothing.

But fuck if I'm willing to throw in the towel. "We could go back to friends with benefits."

Her eyes flare with surprise and for a moment, she looks terrified at the prospect. But her features smooth and she smiles. "We were very good at being fuck buddies."

"Yes, we were." I reach out and tuck a lock of hair behind her ear. "I'd say we even excelled at it." I slip my hand to the side of her neck and give a light squeeze. "So maybe we should just go back to that."

The words taste like ashes on my tongue. I don't want to be fuck buddies with her. I don't want to go backward. I want her to realize how deeply I cared for her when all that went down and that I want to be devoted to her no matter if she's carrying my child or not.

But Kiera is sealing the deal. Her hand curls around my wrist and she nods. "Okay... we go back to casual sex."

"But not until after you see Dr. Segal," I say with

faux admonishment.

"Of course," she replies with a nervous laugh.

I wait for her to say something else. Maybe to invite me to lunch, perhaps ask me to go to Dr. Segal's or even ask about the road trip.

Instead, she says, "I've got a meeting I've got to get ready for in a bit. But I'll call you after I see Dr. Segal."

My heart fucking bottoms out as my hand falls away from her neck. She really doesn't want anything from me other than sex. The fact she won't talk to me until after the day he'll supposedly give her the go-ahead to fuck me again tells me all I need to know.

But I manage to plaster on the biggest fucking smile as I stand from the table. "Sounds like a plan."

Kiera scrambles out of her chair and follows me to the door. She opens it and I lean down to give her a quick kiss on her forehead. Her arm starts to reach out for a side hug, but I pretend I don't see it and step onto the porch.

I risk a glance at her and her eyes are shuttered, revealing no secrets. She holds her hand up in a wave goodbye and I lift my chin before trotting down her steps.

My guts feel like they just got stomped by a giant with steel-toed boots. My heart feels shredded.

The woman I love doesn't love me back.

CHAPTER 34

Kiera

I WATCH THROUGH the window as Bain pulls out of the driveway. I stare at the street long after he's out of sight.

What the fuck just happened?

I had every intention of apologizing to Bain and then proposing that we pick up right where we left off. I had intended to focus on how close we'd gotten over the past few weeks and that we were good together.

And now he's gone and we're nothing to each other.

"Fucking idiot," I seethe at myself as I wring my hands.

I think it was the stupid "house of cards" comment I made. I was trying for a good analogy and I meant to point out something very witty about the cards being flimsy but the foundation they laid upon was solid, and next thing I knew, we were both talking about how fast things moved.

Then it got worse... both Bain and I reminisced about how we are inherently not relationship driven, how good we are at being fuck buddies and boom... we've decided to be casual again.

Spinning away from the window, I pinch the bridge of my nose. This is not what I wanted to happen. I wanted to let him know that I adore him and baby or not, I want to make a life with him.

I was ready to tell him that he has every piece of my heart.

Now he's expecting that I won't even bother to call him until after I meet with Dr. Segal, which is still five days away. He didn't seem put out by that either, which means I can't break down and call him any earlier. And truly... there's no other reason to call him since we just agreed to be fuck buddies again, and we can't actually fuck until I'm cleared by the doctor.

"Certifiable idiot, Kiera," I mutter as I sag onto the couch. I flop back, head resting on the cushion, and stare at the ceiling.

I replay every moment of our barely ten minutes together, analyzing every word and his tone of voice and the menagerie of expressions on his beautiful face, desperately seeking some clue that perhaps I missed.

A signal he was sending that might be contrary to the actual words he was giving me.

My breath freezes as I remember him walking out the door. He kissed me on the top of the head just before he stepped out onto the porch and there was a fraction of a second where I caught his expression and it looked… pained.

Like he didn't want to leave?

Like he wasn't happy with what we had so quickly and without much effort decided on?

Is there a chance Bain is feeling like I am? That we just made a colossal mistake.

Bolting off the couch, I pace the living room. I hem and haw, trying to rationalize what we said to each other versus what I might have seen on his face. I attempt to decode a mystery that might not even be a mystery. If I could get just an inkling… something more concrete, then I could go to him and let him know how I feel. That I want more from him than being his fuck buddy.

I just need…

"Fuck," I groan, slapping my palm to my head. "Idiot."

I'm worried about all these what-ifs when I should stop leaving shit up to chance. I simply need to tell Bain how I feel. I need to let him know that I want to be so much more than casual with him. I need to be truthful so I don't leave anything on the table.

♦

IT'S NEARLY THREE p.m. when I pull into the parking garage for Bain's condo on Oliver Avenue. I have the parking pass and key card to the private resident elevator

Bain gave me the night we went on the double date with Camden and Danica. It was our first real date and with our commitment to raise the baby together decided, he wanted me to be able to come and go from his place as desired. This was before we agreed to move in together and put Drake's house on the market, but I'm glad I held on to these things. It means I can walk right up to his door, bang on it and demand he talk to me.

I know that sounds dramatic, but it's really not. I'm on a mission.

After parking, I sling my purse over my shoulder and open the trunk. From within, I pull out the two large suitcases plus a duffel. They're stuffed full of my clothes, toiletries and shoes. I couldn't fit everything in here, but it's enough to get me firmly settled in Bain's home.

I should do two trips with the stuff, but I want to make a big statement when he opens the door. That I've got my entire life right here and I'm not leaving.

It's nearly impossible to roll the big suitcases together while carrying the duffel and my purse, but I manage to hook them over the telescoped arms and pull the wheeled bags behind me in each hand. Still it is slow-going, every little dip or crack in the concrete threatening to flip one out of my hand. I'm huffing and puffing by the time I enter the elevator.

I nudge the twelfth-floor button with my elbow and lean back against the wall. I'm sweating and I blow out a long breath. This is either really smart or really stupid.

The elevator stops on Bain's floor and the doors slide open. His unit is down the hall about thirty feet. I try to maneuver the suitcases out, but the largest case with my duffel starts to tip over. I have to release my hold on the other case to catch it.

"Shit," I mutter as the doors begin to close and I pop my butt back to stop them. They bounce off my hips and reopen, but I lose my hold on the cases, which fall over onto their sides. The largest one springs apart and my underwear and bras spill out, followed by a certain sex toy Bain likes using on me.

"Goddamn it," I mutter. I glance over my shoulder and note that his door isn't that far. Making a command decision, I pull the other case out that's still closed and shove it into the hall. I next grab the duffel and toss it. Pulling the last case forward by its telescope handle just far enough that the doors can't close all the way, I bolt into action.

I grab the two bags in the hall, sparing a glance as the elevator doors start to shut but catch the handle of the other bag. They slide back open as planned.

"Sweet."

I run as fast as I can, dragging the two items of luggage behind me. They bump and jostle, the larger one catching me on my heel and pulling off my tennis shoe.

"Fuck," I snarl as I reach Bain's unit, glancing back

at the elevator. The doors are now repetitively trying to close on the long handle and with each bang, it's pushing it back into the car. If it goes fully in, my case and underwear are going somewhere without me.

I drop the luggage at Bain's door and then immediately trip over it in my haste to get back to the elevator. The larger case tips over onto his door and scrapes down the beautiful dark wood, gouging it.

I curse and then the elevator alarm goes off. I see the suitcase handle is mere inches from being pushed back in. I bolt that way, hobbling with one shoe on and one shoe off. I reach the elevator just as it's getting ready to close and fling my arm and leg inside the gap. The doors knock into me good but then spring all the way open.

I sag in relief, sliding onto the floor near my suitcase as I try to catch my breath.

"Kiera?"

I turn toward the sound of Bain's voice as he leans out his door. He glances down at the luggage at his feet and then back to me.

"Hi," I say with a wave.

It's easy with his long legs to step over the suitcases and head my way. He stops and grabs my tennis shoe and when he reaches me, drops it in my hand. I look up at him sheepishly.

"What is all this?" he asks.

"Well," I say as I work my foot back into the Nike.

"I'm moving in."

Bain's eyebrows shoot sky high, his eyes almost bugging out of his head. I don't know how to take that reaction, but at least I don't see fear.

I quickly gather up my unmentionables and tuck them back in the bag before closing it. Bain's hand takes my upper arm and he helps me stand.

"Let's get this all inside and I'll explain." I stare at him expectantly, daring him to deny me entry.

He looks at me in shock so I push past him, hauling my suitcase along with me. I march right up to his condo door, which is still open, and manage to right all my luggage and push each one inside. I glance back at Bain who watches but doesn't stop my progress.

I follow the last bag in and can feel Bain right on my heels. I whip around as soon as he crosses his threshold, stopping just inside the doorway.

"I have something to say to you." I point at the door. "You might want to shut that as this could get heated."

One of Bain's eyebrows rises but he reaches back and shuts the door. Crossing his arms over his chest, he says, "Okay… what do you want to say? And I hope it involves an explanation about why you have suitcases with you."

"Not much to say. Like I said… I'm moving in."

"And why would you do that?" he asks.

I scrutinize his face, but I can't tell a damn thing

about what he might be feeling. His words are even and calm.

"Because," I say, but then my words falter. Fuck... I can't just come out and tell him I love him. I'm a coward, so I chicken out and lift my chin. "Because if we're going to go back to being fuck buddies and have wild monkey sex all the time, then I think we need to be in closer proximity."

Bain chokes as his eyes bug out, but it's the tiny gasp I hear from behind me that causes my face to flame hot. I turn ever so slowly and see Bain's parents sitting at the kitchen island.

"Oh my God," I mutter before clapping my hand over my mouth. Bain's dad is grinning and his mother is staring at me in shock. My head whips back to Bain who still has his arms crossed over his chest, but his head is lowered to hide the smirk I can still see well enough.

I can't think of a single intelligent thing to say and it's pure self-preservation that has me rushing past Bain. I manage to dodge my suitcases and whip open the door, flinging myself out into the hallway in a mad sprint for the elevator.

"Whoa, whoa, whoa," Bain says as I feel his hand latch onto my arm. He brings me to a complete stop and turns me his way. "You are not leaving after saying that to me."

I don't even give it a second thought, instead walking

right into Bain to press my red face into his chest. "I'm so humiliated. Why didn't you tell me your parents were here?"

To my surprise, Bain's arms come around me and I feel his lips on top of my head. "If it makes you feel any better, my parents are super cool and they won't think badly of you for divulging that we have wild monkey sex."

I groan and bang my head on his chest. "I'm such a dork."

Bain chuckles but then leans back, his fingers under my chin so I'm forced to look up at him. "As cute and utterly hilarious as that was, why are you really here? And don't give me that line about sex. We had sex just fine without living together."

I'm still so embarrassed, I'm not thinking straight. My fight-or-flight response still has me in defensive mode. "Truly... I just thought it would make things more convenient."

"Kiera," Bain says, his voice low and oddly dad-like. It says *you better tell me the truth because if I find out some other way, I'm not going to be happy.*

"I just..." I glance down the hall, fixated on the elevator. I should leave.

"Kiera," Bain says again, this time gently. My gaze comes back to him. "You can tell me anything."

I close my eyes, inhale slowly and then let it out.

When I open them again, I give it to him straight. "I love you. And I don't want to be fuck buddies. I want *you* to be in love with me too. If you can't do that, I'll take fuck buddies but my heart will be broken. So please, maybe be willing to take a risk and jump off the ledge with me into a real relationship where we love each other for eternity. I can't take a broken heart when it comes to you."

"Wow," Bain says... actually, more like wheezes. His expression is one of blindsided incredulity. "You love me?"

I nod. "But if it's too much or too weird, I'll gladly—"

Bain's mouth descends onto mine, one hand cupping my head and his other arm around my back. It's hot and ravenous and I'm immediately consumed by his touch again.

Fingers slipping into my hair, gripping hard, he pulls me back so he can stare down at me. "In case you didn't figure it out by that kiss, I love you too."

My heart thumps like a puppy's tail. "You do?"

"God, yes. I've been miserable this last week, holding that in... afraid to say it to you. I wanted to say it at your house, but I became really unsure of myself and then somehow we'd committed to go backward rather than forward."

"Right?" I exclaim. "That talk did not go how I

wanted it to."

"I'm guessing we were both too nervous. We're taking a big step."

"The biggest... two reformed fuck buddies."

Bain shakes his head. "No, we're still going to be fuck buddies. And we're going to have wild monkey sex all the time since you're moving in with me. But we're going to do it with a whole lot of love."

And... I melt. "Will you kiss me again?"

I get a playful smirk. "If you say you love me again."

"I love you, Bain Hillridge."

"I love you, Kiera McGinn."

He dips his head toward mine, but I jerk back slightly. "After we kiss can we go back in and immediately tell your parents we're in love so we can smooth over my jackassery?"

"It's old news to my parents that I love you. They knew that already, but I'm sure it will set things straight if you tell them you love me too."

"Phew," I exclaim. "I want to start this off on the right foot."

Bain laughs and takes my hand, pulling me toward the door.

"Where are we going?" I ask, putting on the brakes.

He looks back at me. "We can't stand in the hallway all day."

I try to tug free of his hold, managing a sheepish

smile. "It's preferable to confronting your parents after my obnoxious commentary."

Bain reels me in and wraps his arms around my body to pull me in tight. The familiar flare of lust hits me, and God, how I've missed having this man in my bed, in my body. He tips his head, feathers his lips over my cheek and to my ear where he whispers, "If you'd just told me how you felt this morning when I came to your house, this could've all been avoided. So now this is your penance."

I jerk back from him, but he doesn't loosen his hold. I can only tip my head to glare up at him. "You could have told me how you really felt," I accuse hotly.

Bain grins. "That is absolutely true, and it's my penance too. The only difference is I'm not embarrassed about the wild monkey sex comment and you are."

A tiny growl emits from my throat. He's throwing down a challenge. "We'll see about that." I push out of his embrace and march back to his door.

I open up and step inside, my eyes first going to Bain's dad, then to his mother. They both look at me with hesitant smiles but hope in their eyes. They want this to work out for their son.

No better way to get this over with, so I just rip off the Band-Aid. I hear Bain come in, shut the door behind him.

I move to his parents, clasping my hands before me.

"Sheila… Dave… I am so sorry you had to witness that overly emotional display. It's true, your son and I do have wild monkey sex, but I don't want to be his fuck buddy." I hear Bain snicker behind me. "And I'm also sorry for the crude language. Hanging out with hockey players has stripped away some of my gentility, but it is with the utmost respect that I implore you to forget that exchange. What I meant to say to your son"—I glance back at Bain to see he's trying hard not to laugh—"is that I love him very much." I return my attention to his parents. "I will work hard to make him happy and you can rest assured that I'll have his back in all things. Furthermore, I—"

"Oh, for fuck's sake," Bain groans, stepping into my backside and wrapping his arms around me. His chin rests on my head and I can tell by the expression on his parents' faces that he's grinning at them. They're clearly beyond amused and are grinning right back at him. "What Kiera is trying to say is that we've made amends, admitted our undying love for each other and are now, officially, a couple once more."

Sheila claps and yells, "Bravo!"

Dave nudges his wife with his elbow but addresses me. "If it makes you feel better, having wild monkey sex is the key to a long-lasting and happy relationship."

"Dave," his wife exclaims in horror.

He squeezes her knee. "You know it's true."

They start arguing about the appropriateness of such a statement and while they do that, Bain and I cart my luggage into his room. He shuts the door behind him and immediately pulls me in for a deep kiss.

When he lets me up for air, he says, "That went well."

"Wild monkey sex aside," I say with a laugh.

Bain kisses me again and when my tongue swipes against his, he groans. Lifting his mouth from mine, he grumbles, "It's unbearable not being able to have sex."

I press into him tighter, feel his hard length against my tummy. "I can't have sex," I purr, bringing my hand down to stroke him. "But I can make you feel good."

Bain smiles but gently removes my hand from his cock. "No way. If you have to abstain, I'm abstaining. And I'm going with you to see Dr. Segal on Monday and don't even try to tell me you don't need me there."

"Actually," I say softly, bringing my hand to his face, "I do need you there. I need you always."

Eyes melting into soft pools of love, Bain runs his cheek against my temple and wraps his arms around me tight. "This is it. The beginning of the rest of our lives."

I smile as I squeeze him back. "No one I'd rather do it with than you."

Go here to see other works by Sawyer Bennett:

https://sawyerbennett.com/bookshop

Don't miss another new release by Sawyer Bennett!!! Sign up for her newsletter and keep up to date on new releases, giveaways, book reviews and so much more.

https://sawyerbennett.com/signup

Connect with Sawyer online:

Website: sawyerbennett.com

Twitter: twitter.com/bennettbooks

Facebook: facebook.com/bennettbooks

Instagram: instagram.com/sawyerbennett123

Goodreads: goodreads.com/Sawyer_Bennett

Amazon: amazon.com/author/sawyerbennett

BookBub: bookbub.com/authors/sawyer-bennett

About the Author

New York Times, USA Today, and Wall Street Journal Bestselling author Sawyer Bennett uses real life experience to create relatable stories that appeal to a wide array of readers. From contemporary romance, fantasy romance, and both women's and general fiction, Sawyer writes something for just about everyone.

A former trial lawyer from North Carolina, when she is not bringing fiction to life, Sawyer is a chauffeur, stylist, chef, maid, and personal assistant to her very adorable daughter, as well as full-time servant to her wonderfully naughty dogs.

If you'd like to receive a notification when Sawyer releases a new book, sign up for her newsletter (sawyerbennett. com/signup).

Printed in the USA
CPSIA information can be obtained
at www.ICGtesting.com
LVHW021759091123
763531LV00010B/113